The Holiday Friend

PAMELA HANSFORD JOHNSON

The Holiday Friend

HODDER

First published in Great Britain by Macmillan in 1972

This paperback edition published in 2018 by Hodder & Stoughton
An Hachette UK company

1

A CIP catalogue record for this title is available from the British Library

Paperback ISBN 978 1 473 67987 0
eBook ISBN 978 1 473 67988 7

Typeset in Plantin Light by Hewer Text UK Ltd, Edinburgh
Printed and bound CPI Group (UK) Ltd, Croydon, CR0 4YY

Hodder & Stoughton policy is to use papers that are natural, renewable
and recyclable products and made from wood grown in sustainable
forests. The logging and manufacturing processes are expected to
conform to the environmental regulations of the country of origin.

Hodder & Stoughton Ltd
Carmelite House
50 Victoria Embankment
London EC4Y 0DZ

www.hodder.co.uk

I

Visitors to Belgium will know the tram that runs, with a few inland incursions, along the coast from Ostend to Knokke near the Dutch border. It clangs along, past resort after resort: it is very convenient, and always crowded. About a third of the way along the line is the small town of Les Roseaux (Het Riet), where the tracks run through the market place past a cluster of sandy, wooded hills for the children to play in some sort of shelter when the weather is inclement. There are four hotels in Les Roseaux itself and three ten minutes away, down a straight road past the miniature golf-course which leads to the beach and the dunes. The hotels here are greatly subject to the visiting season, for they are exposed to the weather and after the peak months trade drops off rapidly.

The Hotel Albert, in the town, is different. This is a modest place, but it is expanding. It has only a brief closed period in the year, since it is the chief haunt of the local people as well as the holiday-makers. There is a glassed-in terrace and an open one with infra-red heating, so it is possible to drink there, or in the bar, for many months. It is kept by Armand Croisset, a widower, and his elderly mother, who has by now found the cooking too much for her but nevertheless keeps a Napoleonic supervision over the kitchens. The food, Belgian, plentiful, very good, is inspired by her. She sits most of the day just inside the bar, where she can keep an eye on the two terraces. She is tall and stately, with beautiful grey hair elaborately coiled: she wears dark dresses and many beads. Armand is still quite young; she had him late in life.

He works very hard. He is always up by a quarter to six, and never goes to bed till midnight. He is a burly man, fair-haired, with round blue eyes and a heavy chin. Walloon by birth, his familiar language and his sympathies are French. He speaks good English, and some German.

To Les Roseaux, in the last week of July, came Gavin Eastwood with his wife and son, for a fortnight's holiday. They had been to the Albert for the previous two years, and liked it because it was comfortable and cheap enough not to be a strain on a lecturer's salary. It also pleased them to be near to the pictures in Bruges and Ghent, and to play golf on the miniature course. They had come by the tram, and the walk from it across the tracks and into the town was an arduous one. Hannah carried her big case and Giles's small one, and Gavin his own case and another of hers. They were panting a little as they walked up the steps of the hotel into the hall lined with mackintoshes, spades, pails, beach-balls. They were met with cries of delight.

'Welcome back again!' Armand cried, opening his arms as if to embrace them all. 'It is so good to see you.'

'It's good to see you, M. Croisset,' said Gavin, 'we're beginning to feel like old habitués. Have we got the same bedroom?' This was a fairly large one, painted a somewhat violent pink, with a balcony and a bathroom.

'The same, and the same one for the little gentleman, on the floor above. How are you, Giles?'

'I'm fine,' said the boy. 'Thank you.'

'Pierre! Carry the bags up. Did you have a good crossing? The weather is magnificent.'

'I didn't,' said Giles, 'I was sick. But I feel better now.'

The feeling of comfort, of familiarity, descended on them all. Soon they would creep, somewhat shamefacedly, to the

2

frame in the hall where the dinner menu was put up round about half-past five, and their mouths would water at delights to come. But now they wanted tea, to give them the energy to unpack. Giles was for going to a pastrycook's on the front, which sold chocolate éclairs with confectioner's custard inside which he much preferred to cream, but they were firm with him. There would be time for that. So they went towards the glassed terrace, meeting Madame on the way. Both Gavin and Hannah spoke to her in French, since she knew no English, and Giles said 'Bonjour,' looking pleased with himself afterwards as though he had had a triumph and need never exert himself again. Greeting Madame was always rather awe-inspiring, like greeting an empress of uncertain temper, though Madame had never been seen to be put out. Gavin was always rather in fear that one or the other of them would do something to offend her; he was in some ways a timid man, given to irrational unease.

They sat at a table in the window, watching the sunlit crowds barging along towards golf-course or beach, children on bicycles threading a precarious way along, seemingly with small concern for life or limb, middle-aged women in trousers or even bikinis, men in flowered beach-shirts. There was a light wind, which had been enough to make the Channel choppy, but the sky was starch-blue with a few bright clouds.

'Oh, it is nice to be here again!' said Hannah, putting out a hand to pat Giles. She was forty-two, tall and well-rounded, as yet not going grey, with a girlish face. She had a great capacity for enjoyment.

Gavin did not at once reply. He was looking about him with an air of content, the comfortably shabby bar, so much in contrast with the newness of the terrace, at Madame in her chair, at the new barmaid smoking as she dispensed beer. Gavin Eastwood was just forty-eight, but looked less. He was tall and graceful, a dressy man with an inclination to identify

3

with youth; but he went no further in this than to wear his hair rather long over his forehead, though short at back and sides, and to indulge in a broad orange tie, bought specially for this holiday. He was greyish-fair and distinctly good-looking; it had always been a miracle to Hannah that she had never lost him to another woman, for she was humble and thought little of herself.

Giles was not quite twelve, small for his age, dreamy and bad at school. He was dreading his report.

That was the worst of coming away the moment school broke up; the beastly thing would follow you, sent on by your aunt who was looking after the flat, and then there would be the usual sorrowing row. Taking another piece of cake, he strove to put the thought behind him.

'Can I go down to the beach while you unpack?'

'May you, not can you. You *can*, obviously. But do you want to go alone?'

'I'm old enough, if that's what you mean. And nobody could drown in that sea, it goes on for miles before it reaches your knees.'

'But you're not going to bathe, of course,' said Hannah. 'You just go down there and look around, and don't be too long. We'll expect you back by' – she consulted her watch – 'half-past six at the latest. Maybe Daddy'll stroll down soon and pick you up. And don't go beyond the wind-breaks right at the bottom of the steps.'

They watched him go off.

'Another milestone,' said Gavin. 'A year ago he wouldn't have gone off on his own. And I admit I hate to see him do it.'

'So do I. But he's growing up. We can't keep him tied to us.'

They were uneasy all the while they were emptying their cases, and hurried down to the plage, to the row of Disney-like shops and cafés, earlier than they had intended. They

4

spotted Giles at once. He had certainly strayed further than they had told him to, but was harmlessly paddling in one of the three narrow strips of water that preceded the sea.

'Oh good,' said Hannah, relieved. 'Let's not go and fetch him right away, or he'll think we don't trust him. Let's go to the Star Café and see M. Van Damm. We can keep an eye on him from there.'

They sat down on the terrace, and soon M. Van Damm was there, greeting them as Armand had greeted them, with arms flung wide. A small spruce man, in his high-necked, red-braided, white jacket, he was something of a polyglot, though he would only with reluctance speak French. He had been a prisoner-of-war God knew where, and had learned many languages, most of them well. He had a little Russian. He was a fervent Flemish Nationalist, though this he kept hidden from his foreign customers, most of whom would not have understood his principles.

Aimé Van Damm, in his blinding white jacket, with military upturned collar, with his black trousers tapered towards his small feet. With outstretched arms.

'Welcome back! May I say, welcome home?'

They were charmed.

'And the boy, where is he? Have you brought him with you?'

'He's playing down there,' said Hannah, 'he'll be up soon. As you see, he's old enough to play on his own.'

'Well, he'll be growing up now. Quite a big young gentleman, I expect?'

'Well, not so big,' said Gavin, 'but getting on in years.'

They ordered beer, Stella Artois. M. Van Damm sat down a moment to chat with them, but was soon called away again by a press of custom.

Yes, it was a beautiful evening, despite the wind. The breeze blew in the canvas wind-breaks against which the deck-chairs stood in their ordered lines, and the sun flushed the sand and glittered on the sea. To the left, the dunes were white as ivory, and the reeds, from which the town got its name, shivered and whistled.

Gavin put his hand out over the table. She took it in her own and pressed it strongly. They still retained a certain passion, and were looking forward to the night.

Hannah stood up. 'He's coming!' She started towards the door, but he pulled her back.

'No, don't. He'll only think we're over-anxious. Wait till he gets to the top, and then we'll emerge, all nonchalance.'

She sat down again. 'Yes, you're right. How difficult it is to *grow* him!'

'I wish he would actually grow a bit.' He was watching the small figure as it came, head lowered, scuffling slowly up the beach. 'But his feet are big, so I expect he'll make a sudden spurt.'

They had hopes of all kinds for their son, that he should become tall, handsome, and perhaps even be clever. They felt he was a late developer, but that sooner or later develop he would. They had sent him to a private day-school, which was a strain on Gavin's earnings, because they could not bear for him to be lost in a class of thirty or forty boys, unprodded, unguided. They had had experience of this when they had sent him, from political and social principles, to a state primary school: it had been a disaster. At eight, he had barely been able to read.

They hoped he was happy. Sometimes they felt that, in his dreaminess, he was; that he might dwell in a magical inner world of his own. They knew that at this moment the question of his report was on his mind; how were they to deal with it when it came? They always tried to talk it over with him calmly, but he grew more and more frantic till the matter had to be dropped. Would it be there tomorrow? At Les Roseaux

6

the post arrived about half-past eleven. They would come in to lunch to find the thing waiting for them.

Giles reached the top of the steps. They came out of the café without haste.

'Hullo! What have you been doing?'

'Oh, just mucking around.'

'We've seen M. Van Damm. He was asking about you.'

'Was he? I'm hungry.'

'Well,' said Hannah, 'if we stroll slowly back we shall just be in time for dinner. Darling, let me wipe those sandy feet.' She took out her handkerchief.

'Don't. It'll dry soon, and then it'll fall off.'

They went back to the hotel, Giles's hand in his mother's. Now and then he raised hers up and rubbed it against his cheek.

'Shall we play golf tomorrow?' The course was full, people queueing at each hole to play. They watched for a minute over the privet hedge, then went on. Giles had brightened.

The dinner menu, the main course at least, was something of a disappointment: *oiseaux sans têtes*, which none of them much liked. But after the soup were *fondus au parmesan*, which they did; Giles could have made a whole meal of them.

The dining-room was crowded with English, French and Germans, but their favourite table by the window had been kept for them. In the lower frame was a strip of emerald-coloured glass, beyond which a row of geraniums strained in the breeze. It was a pleasant, unpretentious room, with wheel-like wooden chandeliers and brass ornaments on the walls. 'We'll have a bottle of wine tonight,' Gavin said to Giles, 'and you shall have a glass.'

'I'd like a bit of water in it,' the boy said. He did not really like wine at all, but it made him feel important.

The soup, a great metal bowl of it, was left on the table. It was excellent soup, and Hannah always wondered how they

7

made it. Somehow her own soups were always rather thin and lacking in flavour. The steam arising from it whetted their appetites still further; Giles had two helpings. They ate hungrily, while watching the holiday crowds stream back from the beach.

'It's good to be here,' said Hannah, with a great, replete sigh.

Armand came over to them, resting his big hand on Giles's thin shoulder. He supervised every meal, and afterwards supervised the bar. He was Argus-eyed.

'Is everything all right? It is good, yes?'

'Splendid,' said Hannah, 'it always is. We're so glad to be here.'

'That was an excellent bottle of wine,' said Gavin. 'You keep a good cellar.'

Armand tapped the label. 'I've had a new consignment of that. I'm glad you like it. Well.' His gaze searched the table-cloth as if there might be something missing, something yet needed for their pleasure. 'Would the little boy like another pastry?'

Giles, whose brow had darkened for a moment at this description, cheered up. 'Yes, please.'

'Oh, darling, you haven't room for another bite!'

'Please, mummy.'

When dinner was over, they sat smoking and drinking beer (Giles had Coca-cola) on the terrace. It was still warm enough to sit outside and watch the sun go down in a lemon glow behind the trees opposite. These trees were weather-indicators; when they rose in the morning they always looked to see if they were rattling too much. In fact, the weather seen from their bedroom was otherwise deceptive, for there was yellow glass in the top panes that gave an impression of permanent sunlight.

A German boy, well-grown, about Giles's age, detached himself from his parents and came over to them. He said, in

8

careful, precise English, 'Would your son like to come and play?'

But Giles, full-up and feeling sophisticated after his wine, replied politely, 'Not just now, thank you. Perhaps tomorrow.'

'My name is Hans Fischer.'

'Mine's Giles Eastwood.'

'We have never been here before.'

'We have. We've been here for years and years. Everyone knows us.'

'So. Well, till tomorrow then.'

'Couldn't you have played for a little while -' Hannah began.

'Not now.'

'- just to be polite?'

'Oh, Mummy.'

'Leave him alone,' said Gavin, 'he's pretty tired after a long day.'

'Yes, and it's getting near his bedtime. Hurry up and finish that coke.'

But Giles would not budge until the sun had gone down, and the lights shot up all over the town.

2

In the Pension des Colombes, in Byronlaan, a sandy, poplared road running off the main route to the beach, Melissa Hirst sat on the edge of the bed, her heart heavy with love and guilt. All the way across the Channel she had hidden from him, and at Ostend had sat about in a café for an hour in order to take a later tram. She longed to see him, and dreaded the questions he might ask her.

She was a fairly tall girl of twenty-one, very thin, a little stooped. Her features were pretty and regular, but by no means striking, and she wore her thin, light-brown hair in a long tail down her back, fastened at the back of her head by a slide with a prong in it. She was reading English at the university, but for the past year had attended Gavin's lectures on the history of art, sitting at the back of the room, taking no notes, her large and mournful eyes raised to him.

She was poor. She had only the small sum left to her by her father, who had died last summer; three hundred pounds, that and her student grant was all she had. To take this holiday she had sold some Victorian jewellery left her by her mother; she had only twice been out of England before, once with a school party to Austria, once with her parents to Boulogne, and she felt very strange.

She had fallen deeply in love with Gavin the moment she saw him; his image obsessed her. She lived when she was near him, and at other times she merely existed. She had spoken only a few words with him on one or two occasions after his lectures, when she had found questions to ask him. She knew he had a wife and a son and hoped he did not love them.

She was still a virgin. She had once tried, fashionably, to lose her virginity after a student party, but, unused to drinking and having had far too much of a sour red wine that came in great bottles, had no sooner got on the bed than she had to get off it to be sick. It was a shameful memory, and though she could not remember it very well, it seemed to her that the man had stood and laughed at her.

Three months ago, she had overheard Gavin talking to a colleague on the main staircase. There were many people going up and down, and she had found herself just behind them. She remembered the smell of his tweed suit, heated by his body. They were discussing holidays. 'Oh, we always go to the same place,' Gavin was saying, 'the Hotel Albert at Les Roseaux on the Belgian coast, not far from Ostend. It's fairly cheap and it's very good. They know us there.' Asked when he was going, he replied that they were taking their holiday early, leaving the day after the school term had finished.

From then on she plotted and schemed. She was going to follow him, if only to look at him from afar (but it would not be from afar, not in a small place, which she had discovered that Les Roseaux was). She could not bear the weary months of the long vacation, in the small flat she shared with two other girls, without a sight of him. But, when he saw her, when he came to speak to her (which of course he would) how was she to explain her presence? She could say she had come to Belgium to study the art there, and had hit on Les Roseaux by the purest accident. After all, why should he not believe her? He had no idea that she loved him, could have the slightest motive for going deliberately where he was. She would cry, 'Oh, this is a coincidence! Fancy seeing you here!'

There were moments when certain intimations of common sense came over her, but she fought them down. She had no hopes whatsoever except of being allowed to love him, and after all, who could allow her save herself? She could not live with common sense; it would be like being enclosed in a box of yellow cardboard, with her head touching the lid.

She did not believe she had anything to give him. Never very successful with men, she had no great conceit of herself. When she was fourteen, she had been pleased by her romantic name, believing that when she was grown up she would only have to speak it for a man to love her. Sometimes she had other names, she was Undine, she was Isolde, thin frail names in keeping with her body, but she was better pleased to be really Melissa. Now, however, she knew that the charm did not work. She was not really neglected; she went out a good deal with other students, and occasionally a man would take her out for coffee or a drink. But nothing had ever come of it, and now she wished that nothing should. She was all Gavin's. She had no heart for anyone else. She wished desperately that at night she could dream of him, but she never did.

She had eaten a pleasant, unfamiliar meal, and now she was wondering what to do until bedtime. She was afraid to go along the plage in case she met him; she could not face that tonight. It was for tomorrow, this adventure, this peril. So she read a book on art that she had brought with her, hoping that it would please him to see her with it. The lamp in the bulb over the bed was a dim one, and soon her eyes began to ache. But one could not go to bed at nine!

She decided to take a risk and walk in the lane itself, perhaps to have coffee in a obscure-looking little place just on the corner, within sound of the sea. There could be no chance of meeting him there. But just in case, she took the art book with her.

Lonely, she went out into the afterglow. There were few people about, for this was off the beaten track. It was still warm and still windy; suppose the wind should drop and it rained tomorrow? She sat in the café for half an hour and then, restless, ventured on to the beach, for it was dark and quite deserted. The wind-breaks had been taken down, and she could barely make out the white fringe of the surf. Walking in the soft sand, she looked back at the plage, at the line of villas curving off to the right. Windows glowed softly in the night. Behind them, what unimaginable joys, what blisses? She fancied secure lovers everywhere, shut into each other's arms.

3

It did not rain. Next morning the yellow pane of glass told no more than the truth, as Gavin saw when he pulled the curtains. The sky was a hazy blue, promising heat, and the poplars were barely trembling.

On holiday he always awoke at a quarter to eight, bathed and shaved, took a short stroll, and came back to breakfast with Giles downstairs. Hannah had her coffee, rolls and cherry jam on a tray in her room, at nine o'clock; this was a great luxury for her, since the early morning hours were always the worst and she loved to sleep late when she got the chance. She slept heavily; the light did not disturb her. Gavin looked at her fondly, thinking last night had been very successful. In the act of sex, she was still ardent, still joyful. In braggart mood, he thought that he, like the Duke of Marlborough, could have pleasured her with his boots on.

Before he went downstairs he looked at himself in the wardrobe mirror. It must have had some slight convexity, for it tended to distort; but he could nevertheless see no sign of a paunch. He went first to call Giles, who awoke in his usual fashion, slowly and with puckered brows, as though not sure who his father was.

'Come on, get up. I'll be back in about twenty minutes.'

He strolled into the market square, past the stalls heaped with fruit, the shop selling souvenirs and photographic film, the big grocer's on the corner. It was busy even now, and they were raising the stalls for tomorrow. He paused to look at a garish poster stuck on a wall. Next Saturday, Captain Keppel's Mechanical Circus was coming to the town. God knew what that was, but they would all go and see it. He stepped back to let the tram go by on its way to Blankenberge and Knokke, and followed it with his gaze. Soon they would take it as far as Blankenberge, and go on by train to Bruges. He rather wished they had someone to look after Giles, who was bored there, trailing his feet round the museums and fretting all the time to go on the boat trip along the canals. If only he were older he might have been left on the beach, with plenty of money in his pocket for pastries; but twelve was too young. Gavin looked forward to the day of liberty; he loved the boy, but on occasions he was an encumbrance. He and Hannah sometimes had a selfish longing to be alone together, just the two of them, but they had always brushed this aside as unworthy. 'That snuffy old place,' Giles had said of Bruges, 'I don't know what you see in it. Just a lot of old buildings and pictures.' Though of course there was one picture that he liked, in the Musée Communale: of the unjust judge being skinned. Two years ago it had frightened him, but now he revelled in it. The stretched and anguished body, blood and muscles of a leg exposed as the devoted executioner stripped away skin like kid leather. 'He's grinning in agony,' Giles had said without emotion. 'Not a bit of it,' said Gavin, 'He's smiling because such a great master as David is painting him.' But this was not believed, nor was it meant to be.

A cloud came over his mind; for the moment he had forgotten all about it. The report. What was the matter with the boy? He was not stupid; he was just lazy and remote. Gavin remembered with distaste the painful interviews with his teachers, all of them so polite, so considerate, making allowances. But pitying him because he had a son who made little showing. He had been hot with embarrassment. It was always he who had to make these confrontations; Hannah, obdurate in this alone, refused to go. 'It's no good. I always get angry, with Giles, and for him. I don't know what to say to any of them.' Common Entrance was coming up in about six months' time, and there was some doubt whether he would scrape through that. Even now, thought Gavin, if he could make an effort – but can he? Is effort in him?

Suddenly it came to him that Hannah and he were cruel to Giles because they had come to care too much for his performance. Wasn't there a good deal of self-love in it? But they had to do their best for him, to stimulate him, do something to submerge his sense of failure.

He found the boy already in the dining-room, making a start on his rolls and drinking the hot milk he preferred to coffee. Gavin said, rather too heartily, 'Well, it's a lovely day. We'll go on the beach early, before too many people are about.'

'What about golf?'

'This afternoon.'

Giles loved the game and was remarkably good at it. Like an experienced player in the club-house mulling over eighteen holes, Giles knew every hazard and how best to deal with it. It was the only game he cared for; bad at football, only passable at cricket, unable to swim yet, he could show some prowess here.

Gavin sat a long time over breakfast, but Giles was eager to be gone. 'All right, then, you can keep three chairs for us, on the sunny side.' He gave him some money. 'Put a towel on one, and your shoes on the other so that people will know they're taken.' He watched him going off with spade and bucket and shrimping net down the straight road; Giles really felt he was rather too old for such things – except for the shrimping net – but he could not bear not to have them.

It was nearly ten before Hannah came down.

'Better get to the beach straight away,' Gavin said, 'Giles is there already. It shouldn't be too crowded by now.'

But it was; the fine weather had brought the people out early, eager to get what there was of Belgian summer. The Eastwoods found the chairs Giles had reserved for them, and disposed themselves with their books. They saw him at once; he was only a little way beyond the wind-breaks, where the sand was damp but firm, playing with another boy. It looked like Hans.

'So he's cornered,' Hannah said. 'I'm afraid he doesn't much like the company of his peers. I'll go and see what they're doing.'

As she approached the boys, Hans sprang smartly to his feet, but Giles barely looked at her.

'Good morning, Mrs Eastwood. It is a lovely day, is it not? We are building a great castle.'

She paused to watch the work. It looked as if Giles was having to do most of it, under instruction.

'No, no, Giles,' Hans was saying, 'that isn't the way to make a wardbridge. No, a drawbridge. And we are going to have a tower on that corner.'

Hannah said, 'Don't let him tire himself,' as if Hans were a much older boy. 'It's getting hot.'

'He's not tired, are you, Giles?'

'No.'

'No, I said a tower on *that* corner. Let me show you.' Hans filled a bucket with sand, patted it until the surface was hard and firm and neatly up-ended it. 'His towers come to pieces,' he said to Hannah.

She returned to her book; it was good to be at peace. Gavin said he would swim later. She never swam herself, as she found the water too cold.

'You look nice,' he said. Even after all these years, he would pay her compliments and she would be delighted. She was wearing a modest white sun-dress and white sandals, and had done her hair in a French pleat. 'That's a new frock. I like it.'

'The only one I bought this year. But one must have something extra for a holiday.'

'If I had any ships that possibly could come in, you should have lots of frocks.'

'Dear.'

He caught her hand, held it for a minute, then dropped it. He said lazily, 'We are happy, aren't we?'

'*Ça va sans dire.*'

'Yes, but it's useful to say it.'

'Useful?'

'Well, then, nice.'

They returned to their books. She was reading Ngaio Marsh, he *The Eustace Diamonds*.

Around them, fathers and mothers slumped in their chairs, some of the women displaying unbecoming amounts of reddening flesh. Hannah did not think that fat women should wear either sunsuits or bikinis, and indeed, considered herself too plump for them now. A little boy of three or four with nothing on at all was making a hole and pissing in it. His mother roared at him in Flemish, pulled him away and gave him a smack. He roared back, with tears.

It was eleven o'clock. They saw Hans returning from play, his parents behind him. 'We're going to have ices now,' he said, 'are you?'

'Not just yet,' Gavin answered, 'a little later.'

They watched the family up the steps, all with backs like ramrods.

Giles came running up to them, hot and sweaty. 'Mummy I don't like playing with Hans, he's too bossy. He makes me do all the work. I'm going to hide up in the dunes, where he can't find me again.'

'He won't be finding you for half an hour,' said Gavin, 'he'll be stuffing himself. And by that time, we can go up and you can stuff *yourself*.'

'I want to go on the dunes, I've never been there.'

'All right, but only half an hour. Promise?'

He went off, looking behind him, as if fearing to find Hans on his heels.

'We'll have to get him out of that,' said Hannah, 'he obviously hates playing with him.'

'Aren't we making him anti-social?'

'I'd be anti-social if I were made to slog away under an overseer, like a slave building the Pyramids.'

'But he doesn't much like playing with anyone.'

'Nor did I, at his age,' Hannah replied doggedly. 'I remember being made to build castles with a horrid child called Rosemary, who had very thin plaits. How I hated her! And my mother thought it would be so nice for me to have a little companion.'

At that moment a tall thin girl in a white bathing-suit went by, with a quick glance at them. Gavin thought for a moment that she looked familiar, but could not place her.

Of course Giles was not back in half-an-hour, so Gavin went up to look for him.

It was hot on the white and powdery dunes, where the sand slipped beneath the feet, and the reeds were spiny. There were plenty of people up there preparing to picnic, but they were mostly on the inland side as even a slight wind could make itself felt from the sea. More roasting bodies and bikinis. A litter of orange-peel and ice-cream papers. He did not see Giles at once, and mechanically, his heart misgave him. But what harm could he get to, among those people? He began to call. There was no reply, but he found him at last in a hollow, lying on his face, scraping up the dry powder and letting it trickle between his fingers. 'Come on, it's nearly twenty to twelve, and if you don't come and eat quickly you won't want your lunch.'

Giles rose. He said, 'It's lovely up here. I like it. Hans will never find me.'

'I almost didn't find you myself. Buck up.'

On their way to the Star Café they passed the German family returning to the beach. 'So you're still safe,' Gavin said to Giles, 'for quite half an hour.'

'And then I'll go back on the dunes.'

'You won't have much time. And anyway, you'll make us late for lunch.'

'I wouldn't if I could borrow your watch.'

'And get sand in it? No fear.'

In the café, M. Van Damm came to Giles and gave him a quick hug. He was almost run off his feet, between the tearoom and the terrace.

'Let's go inside,' said Hannah, 'it's quieter, and I've had enough sun for the moment.'

They went to survey the beautiful pastries, all made daily by Madame Van Damm. There were cherry tarts, like jewelled cartwheels, sparkling under a golden glaze of jam. There were apricot tarts, resting on beds of custard; rice tarts, brown and crumbling, chocolate cakes and éclairs, *millefeuilles* marbled pink and white, apple slices, scalloped, each pale green scallop with a delicate edging of brown.

'I'll have that and that,' said Giles.

'You won't. You'll have one only. Don't spoil your appetite.'

'I shouldn't think I ever could,' Giles answered, with a small glimmering smile. 'Well, all right then, I'll have a slice of the cherry. And a coke.'

'Do you want anything?' Gavin asked Hannah.

'God forbid! I'd be as fat as a pig. But I wish I could. Let's share a pot of tea; they make it well.'

Just as they were leaving the beach for lunch, they met the girl again. This time she was wearing a blue cotton jersey and jeans, carrying her bathing-suit wrapped in a towel under her arm. She came face to face with them, and this time Gavin knew her.

'Miss Hirst! What on earth are you doing here?'

She answered rapidly, 'I just saw an advertisement. I thought I'd be near Bruges and even Brussels. How are you, Mr Eastwood?'

'Well, this is a coincidence. May I introduce my wife and son? Darling, this is Miss Hirst, one of my students, or at least, one of my hearers. She doesn't belong to my department, but she supports my lectures faithfully.'

Hannah smiled at her, thought her pretty and gentle but rather colourless. 'It's nice to meet you. This is Giles.'

'How do you do, Giles?' The girl put out her hand, and he just touched it. He was again withdrawn.

They exchanged comments on the miracle of the weather, the charm of Les Roseaux – 'at least,' said Gavin, 'it has charm for us' – the wonder that they should have chosen to stay at the same place.

Giles fidgeted. 'Well,' Hannah said, 'I suppose we'd better be getting back to lunch. We like to eat early, so that it won't be crowded at the Golf when we go out in the afternoon. We shall see you on the beach, I expect.'

'Where are you staying?' said Gavin.

She told him. It was quite a small place, rather hidden away. 'But it seems quite good.'

'We'll meet again,' Gavin said heartily. They went off towards the Albert, and that was all.

In the letter-rack in the hall was a long yellow envelope: their hearts sank. Giles flushed deeply.

'Well, here it is,' Gavin said lightly, 'but we won't read it now.' When they went into the dining-room he laid it beside his plate. Hannah was looking at him anxiously.

Giles burst out,' It's not going to be very good.'

Hannah said, 'Never mind, darling.'

The waiter was standing over them, with a dish of endives wrapped in ham, in a cheese sauce.

'Wonderful,' said Gavin, 'my favourite.'

But when the waiter went to help Giles, the boy refused. 'I don't want any.'

'But darling, you know you love them!'

'I don't want anything. I'm not hungry.'

'Look here,' said Gavin, 'I knew you oughtn't to have had that cherry tart.'

'It's not that.' Giles had gone pale, and his eyes were luminous. They were afraid he was going to cry.

'Just a little,' Hannah coaxed him. He shook his head. She looked up to see Armand.

'Everything all right, Madame? Would the little boy like something else? Some soup, perhaps, or a little pâté?'

'Would you, Giles?'

'No.'

'No what?'

'No thank you.'

He sat in silence while they ate, crumbling his bread. None of them could find anything to say. The yellow envelope was staring against the whiteness of the cloth.

The German family came in, and Hans stood reproachfully by Giles's chair. 'I lost you! I couldn't find you anywhere!'

No answer.

'He's a little tired,' Hannah said feebly.

'He's not eating anything. Perhaps he is sick.'

'Now, you run away now,' Gavin said, in a strained voice, 'and perhaps you can play this evening.'

Hans almost clicked his heels, nodded his grave head and returned to his table.

22

The roast veal went untouched, and so did the apple fritters.

At last Gavin burst out, quietly but violently, 'Look here, I can't stand this. Giles, do you know what I'm going to do? I'm not going to read this beastly thing at all. I'm going to tear it up.'

The boy's head shot up. He was scarlet again, and his eyes were full of tears.

'But—' Hannah began.

'It's a shame for him, and he shan't put up with it. Cheer up, old boy, we're going to have a bonfire.'

He brought the big glass ashtray across the breadth of the table. He opened the envelope, made sure there was nothing in it but the report, and tore that into small pieces. He set a match to it and the paper flared up, drawing astonished glances from other diners.

'Daddy!' said Giles, and his eyes overflowed.

'Quiet now. It's nearly all gone. Watch.' White paper turned from white to brown, to black: flames crept along it, spurting, gradually dying down.

Gavin said, 'I'm sorry you've been worried by this and sorry I didn't think of doing it sooner. Mummy and I don't give a damn this time what your old report said. The next one will be better. And if it isn't, we'll burn that one too.'

Giles jumped up and fled from the room. They heard him running upstairs.

'He'll be all right in a minute,' said Hannah, but anxiously.

'Do you think I did the right thing? I couldn't bear to see him worrying like that.'

'I'm sure you did. I'm glad.'

'And now that I've done it,' said Gavin, wonderingly, 'it simply seems quite obvious. Why have we been so hard on him? I didn't want to be. It's enough that he's Giles, without being a lot of other things as well.'

23

Hannah asked if she should go up to the boy, but he said No, not for a while. He had had a shock, even though it was a pleasant one.

'He'll want more pastries for tea,' Hannah said, with a flicker of a smile, 'he'll be starving.'

But she, too, had lost colour. Gavin was afraid that his gesture might have been too dramatic to have its proper effect. Why could he never do anything quite right? Or had he done the right thing this time? He felt a twinge of indigestion. He had eaten too much, in his jovial pretence of being hungry. He wouldn't have minded betting that Hannah had indigestion too.

Hans was standing beside them, pertinacious. 'Where has Giles gone? Didn't he eat anything after all? Has he got sunstroke?'

They assured him that there was nothing the matter. He stared at them doubtfully, and it was not until his parents came up that he would go away.

Giles was not in his bedroom. He must have crept downstairs again, for he was sitting out on the terrace by himself. They approached him with apprehension, but his face was open and clear. 'I say, Mummy, can we get off to the Golf now?'

'Yes, right away,' said Gavin, 'and then we'll go and bathe. I was too lazy this morning.'

'But you won't teach me to swim.'

'Not if you don't feel like it. Listen, you're to do just what you like these holidays. Have a really good time. All right?'

'All right.'

4

When Melissa came out of the bathing-hut and saw them there, she felt her heart and stomach drop, as if she had come down a high building in an express lift. Should she pause, if only for a fraction of a second, or go right past them to the sea? She saw a white blur, which must have been his wife, but could not bear to look more closely. He was clear in her sight, his good-humoured face raised from a book, his orange tie blazing. He was in a shirt with short sleeves, his jacket draped neatly over the back of the deck-chair.

She went on, and she did, for that fraction, pause. She thought he looked at her with a puzzled air, but at once went back to his book. She went to bathe.

When it was getting on for one o'clock, when she had changed back into her jeans, she climbed up to the plage, and leaning over the rail, waited for them. At last they began to come up from the beach, a little boy with them. She ran as fast as she could, leftwards, along the dyke, down the short street to the motorway, and crossed into Byronlaan. Slowing down a little, so that she would not seem breathless, she went along it to the place where it joined the main road. She met them face to face. This time, if they did not stop, she would.

She was in a storm of love, out of life, out of time; she no longer cared whether her excuses would serve, whether he would believe her story.

This time he did recognise her, and he did stop. He spoke to her, and she replied as if in a dream. Her story seemed plausible, as she told it, and he appeared to accept it naturally enough. Now he was introducing her to his wife, and she had to look at her. She saw a woman a little taller than herself, holiday-neat, with what she thought was a smug face. Politenesses. Then to greet the surly little boy.

It was over; she meant to see them again. She would contrive it. It almost seemed to her that he had been glad of this meeting, that his glance had held more than a common intimacy; but she put the thought away from her. A casual acquaintance, met on holiday; wasn't this always somehow a little exciting? Someone seen every day in London was surely likely to seem more attractive in, say, Paris. Melissa wished she had been to Paris.

She went back to her lunch, but she could not eat much. When would she be likely to find them again? About tea-time, she supposed.

She lay for a while on her bed, watching the reflection of leaves on the ceiling. I am vile, she thought, I am mad. But then again: Well, it was a success so far, wasn't it? I mustn't let him see too much of me, in case he gets tired. She thought of her squalid flat and of the two untidy girls who shared it with her. They would never pick up anything, their clothes were all over the place, their powder and nail-varnish spilled on the dressing-table, the washing-up left to her. If I had a bit more character, they wouldn't leave it to me, I would tackle them. The flat was too small for the three of them, and yet she was lonely. But I have never let them know that, I have tried always to be pleasant, I have made them like me. Is that to be my life, though, a scruffy one of endless dissimulation? Her thoughts floated away into fantasy. He had come to love her, he had thrown up everything, wife and child, for her sake, and now, guilty but enchanted, they had set out for Italy. She dreamed of Rome, of Florence, of Venice, on which he had lectured so eloquently. Yes, and she was wearing a beautiful dress, a rose-pink one, paid for no matter how. He said to her again, Melissa, Melissa, to think that we should be together!

She must have slept, for now it was twenty to four and they might be on the beach. This time she found them without difficulty, and they called to her in a friendly manner. Wouldn't she come and sit down with them? – 'If I wouldn't be in the way—'

Gavin rose from his chair, but she would not take it. 'I like sitting on the sand.'

His wife smiled at her, and so did the little boy, who seemed different from that morning. She suddenly thought that he was rather a pretty child, despite his frailness much like his father. From the infantile cleft down the back of his neck the hair grew blond and feathery.

'Do you like it here?' she said to him, and he replied, 'Very much, thank you. We always come here.'

'I sometimes think we ought to make a change,' said the wife, whose name appeared to be Hannah (how ugly!) 'but somehow we're lazy. And this is fairly cheap. Do you go abroad often?'

'No,' Melissa answered, 'I can't really afford to, much. I feel clumsy here, as if I'm going to get the money wrong. And my French is bad.'

'That doesn't matter in a Flemish town,' said Gavin, 'they'd far rather speak English, and most of them do. I say, you don't look very comfortable there.'

'I am, really.'

'Can I go up to the dunes?' Giles asked.

Gavin forbore to correct him. 'Well, not just now. It's almost time for tea and you must be hungry after your bathe.'

'Are you going to see pictures, while you're here?' Melissa could not quite bear to look at Hannah, and sat a little sideways from her.

27

'Certainly. We're going to Bruges tomorrow.'

Desolation. The beach deserted without him.

'The trouble about that,' said Hannah, with a glance at her son who had wandered a little way off, 'is that it's a bit of a bore for Giles. We have to take him with us, but he's much happier down here.'

'Look here,' Gavin said, 'it's ten past four. Come up to the café and have tea with us, won't you?'

She flushed. This was more than she had expected, and she did not know how to answer him. At last she said, 'You're very kind, Mr Eastwood. But I don't think I could do that.'

'Why ever not? The pastries are splendid.'

'Do come,' said Hannah, She called Giles to her and they collected together the paraphernalia they had brought to the beach. Melissa got up, shook the sand off her clothes and helped her with them. She hated to do anything for the woman, but knew she must.

They went up the steps to the Star, where they sat outside under a pink umbrella with 'Stella Artois' painted across it. They had to wait some time to be served, since M. Van Damm and the two waiters were frenetically busy, carrying tray after tray. 'Gome inside and choose some pastries,' Gavin said to Melissa. 'My wife avoids them because she's weight-watching.'

She went with him shyly, and, after much urging, chose an apricot tart. Excusing herself, she went off to the lavatory.

She spent quite a long time there, scrubbing the last of the sand from between her fingernails. She could hardly believe her luck, had no idea as yet how she might sustain it. She fancied they were talking about her, feeling that she would adore Gavin for his part of it (but what could he know?) and detest Hannah for hers.

She came out into the sunlight, to find tea and cakes waiting. Giles was wolfing pastry after pastry with a beatific look upon his face, and she found to her surprise that she was almost as hungry as he was. *Here she sat*, crowded in by holiday-makers; she could have put out a hand to touch Gavin.

'I hear you're reading English,' said Hannah. 'I did, once. I was a teacher for a time.'

'Why, how did you know?' said Melissa to Gavin.

'Oh, I have my spies.'

'*Beowulf*, and *Sir Gawain and the Green Knight*,' Hannah continued, 'I know. Aren't they bores?'

'Well, it seems mad to say so, but I rather like Beowulf.' Melissa tried to smile at her, to look her directly in the face. But she was still sitting a little slantwise at the table.

As they went on chatting, her mind suddenly became busy. There was a way in which she might bind him to her, make him feel under an obligation to her – that is, if she dared to propose it.

She tried once or twice, but there never seemed to be a break in the conversation. It appeared to her, despite herself, that they were a very united family. But the marriage had been a long one, and she felt that there were times when he might be tired of it. But you are very cruel; even if you had the chance you couldn't take him from her. Why not? If he wanted to go? Don't be silly, this is all fancy, this is all the dream.

Yet here she was, at Les Roseaux, sitting beside him.

'More tea?' Hannah said.

'Thank you, half a cup. I was thinking—'

'Well?'

'It might sound like cheek.'

'I'm sure it wouldn't.'

'Well, you don't know me very well.'

'That can easily be remedied,' said Hannah, with a motherly glance.

'But I was wondering . . . You say Giles is bored by Bruges.'

He looked up, interested.

'I don't know if you'd like to trust him to me for the day. I'd take great care of him. Of course, he mightn't like to be left with me.'

Gavin and Hannah both spoke at once. 'Well, I don't know—' 'That's very kind of you—'

'I could call for him in the morning and take him on the beach, see he had his lunch and then take him out again.'

'It's a munificent offer,' said Gavin, 'but I don't know whether we could possibly accept it.'

'I'd be all right on my own,' Giles said, 'I'm not a baby. And you can't drown in this sea.'

'No, darling, no,' said Hannah absently, 'but other things could go wrong. We'll be gone till dinner-time.'

'Don't you feel you could let me?' Melissa pleaded.

They both looked at Giles. Gavin said, yielding, 'You'd like to go with Miss Hirst?'

'Melissa, please.'

'—to go with Melissa?'

He had spoken her name. Even now, she could hardly believe it.

'Oh, all right.' Giles paused. 'I wouldn't have minded seeing the man getting skinned.'

'But we're going to see lots more than that,' said Hannah. 'Lots and lots.'

She treats him like a baby, Melissa thought. I won't do that.

'I'll go with Melissa.'

'And we'll do just whatever you like,' she said eagerly. From then on, it was all arrangements. She would be at the Albert by ten o'clock, just before they set out. She would have lunch there with Giles – they would tell M. Croisset that they were expecting a guest – and they would give her money for pastries, golf, or whatever Giles wanted.

'No, not money,' she said.

'Then it's all off,' said Gavin, 'he's an expensive monster, aren't you, Giles?'

Though it would be a dreary day without Gavin, she would endure it. Afterwards, surely they could not just shrug her off. She would be careful not to come upon them too often, in case they got tired of her. Just once a day, no more.

'You're sure all this won't be too much for you? It seems an awful imposition.'

'I think it will be fun.'

'Do you play miniature golf?' asked Giles.

'No, but you shall teach me.'

'It's pretty difficult.'

And then the meal was over. At the corner of Byronlaan she left them, with renewed promises for the morrow. She did not dread the evening, nor the night. She would review every minute of that day, hold in her senses the warmth of his smile, the smell of his coat, heated by the sun. He did not shake hands, simply waved at her and walked on with his wife and son.

5

'Oh dear, I wonder if we did right?'

They were drinking beer on the terrace. Giles had gone upstairs with a fairly good grace to play draughts with Hans.

'Why not? She seems reliable.'

'But what do we know about her?'

'Well, as I said, I have my spies,' said Gavin. 'I was interested enough to make a few enquiries. She's lost both parents, and I gather she's pretty broke. They say she's bright. Wouldn't you say she was a bit waiflike?'

'Don't slop, darling. I don't know that I like to entrust Giles to waifs.'

'Come, he'll be all right. He'll like to be free of us, for once.'

'That's as may be.'

'What are you worrying about? She won't take him out and drown him. She seems a sensible girl to me. Anyway, it was very good of her.'

'I shall fret just a bit. We've never left him to a stranger before.'

'She hasn't been exactly a stranger to me, for over a year. She's always there in the back row, concentrating like mad. But she never takes a note. And if you fret, you'll spoil our day. Come, darling, it will be nice to be alone for once, won't it?'

She admitted it, but with a sense of guilt that she knew he shared.

She did not sleep too well that night.

But in the morning, things seemed different. By ten to ten

Melissa was waiting for them. She had an abnormally high colour, and Hannah thought she was rather a pretty girl after all; prettier than she had thought. But terribly thin. Probably she did not get enough to eat.

Giles greeted her composedly, not seeming sorry that his parents should leave him.

'You'll take great care of him?' Hannah could not forbear from saying.

'Of course I will. You need not worry in the least.'

'You know,' said Gavin, 'you'll have to go to Bruges soon. There's so much to see.'

A shadow seemed to pass across her face; he could not understand it.

She said quickly, 'Of course I will. But I don't know if I'll get there all right. I'm silly about trains and things.'

'We'll give you full instructions.'

'Beach first,' said Giles. He added confidentially, looking full in her face, 'There's a boy called Hans. If he wants to play with me, I'd rather not. He makes me dig all the time while he gives orders, and then I get hot.'

She assured him that she would somehow protect him from Hans.

'I might say that I don't want to leave you, either, because you don't know Les Roseaux very well.'

'That's cunning,' said Melissa, 'we'll try it on. Well, shall we go now?'

Hannah and Gavin said good-bye to them, kissed Giles heartily, and went off towards the tram-station.

The weather looked a little doubtful. There was no wind at all, but a fair amount of cloud hanging low over the rooftops. It was market day, and the crowds were pushing and shoving between the lines of the covered stalls. A man was selling balloons. 'If Giles sees those he'll want one,' said Hannah. 'They might come up here.'

'I've given her enough to cope with balloons or anything else.'

'We must go to the market next week. They sometimes sell those very thin sharp knives that I like for the kitchen. Do you think it will rain?'

He said he didn't think so. 'But if it does, they can always come back to the hotel and play halma, or something.'

They were in Bruges by half-past eleven, and as usual were at once sucked in by its domestic charm. In the Grand' Place, the red, yellow and black flags with their bold lions drooped against the masts, and the belfry leaned back against the sky. Coaches were parked by the square, and load after load of tourists made their ways to cafés or quays. 'There's one thing,' said Gavin, 'there are always quiet places that they don't know.'

They went to walk along the quays, under the lime-trees, dusty with August, past the hump-backed bridges, the willows, the billowing swans, and made their sure way to the paddock of Notre Dame, where they sat on the parapet listening to the bass and tenor voices of the bells.

'I wonder what they're doing now?' said Hannah, lightly.

But Gavin was not deceived by her tone. 'You're worrying. Don't. What could possibly happen to him?'

'I was only wondering.'

'We'll have an expensive treat today, we'll lunch at the Duc de Bourgogne.'

She exclaimed appropriately, protested they couldn't afford it, at last agreed; but she did not, though she didn't say so, think she would be at all hungry.

'What they'll be doing right at this minute,' said Gavin, humouring her, 'is fending off Hans. That boy will grow up to be a storm-trooper.'

They went into the museum, which was just across the grass, and saw their favourite paintings; the Van Eycks, the

34

Davids. There were two David panels of young girls in black, kneeling in a deeply forested landscape. They did not enjoy them quite so much as usual, since there were so many tourists ambling through the rooms, and especially through the four rooms of Primitives and painters of periods slightly later that Gavin particularly loved. When they came out, they found it had just begun to rain. The shower was short and light, but the sun did not come out again. It was very humid.

'If it's like this, they can still go to the Golf,' said Hannah.

He halted. 'Now, for God's sake—'

'I was only speculating.'

'Well, don't. This is our day. This is the only one we have had to ourselves in a year or more.'

She put her hand in his and they walked on, unselfconsciously linked. They did eat at the Duc de Bourgogne, where Hannah found she was hungrier than she had thought. Slowly her anxieties were shredding away. Giles and Melissa would be back in the dining-room by now, under the watchful eye of Armand. It was only a momentary temptation to ring up and find out whether they really were, and she thrust it out of her mind.

They were looking out over the waters of the Rozenkaai to the small Germanic square opposite, where there were geraniums in the window-boxes. It was exquisitely still. It was indeed a luxury to be alone, to dawdle over coffee and cigarettes without the presence of Giles always fretting to be off somewhere else. A boatload of tourists went by, and then another.

'I don't know that I enjoy that trip so much,' said Gavin, 'when they tell you to put your heads down, they really mean it. If you didn't, they'd be knocked off.'

In the afternoon they walked up to the Beguinhof and the willowed Minnewater.

'Do you know,' said Hannah, 'I once threw a coin in here – when you and Giles weren't looking – and had a wish. I wished we should always be as we were then.'

'You got your wish, didn't you? – Dear.'

'Yes, I got my wish.'

They were silent, watching a party of nuns, with their white coifs, making their way across the bridge into the Beguinhof.

'I wish we could have had another child,' Gavin said. 'One invests too much in the one.'

'So you haven't been altogether easy,' said Hannah, understanding him. He did not answer, but smiled as if ashamed. 'Anyway,' she went on, 'we did try. We were simply unlucky. Sometimes I think there's still time, but there isn't really. I'm getting old.'

'Not old at all.'

'But for that.'

'We might have another, even now.'

'I'm not sure,' said Hannah, 'whether I wouldn't really rather give up hope. I hate the anxious way you look at me as the month goes on, and how excited you get if I'm even a day late.'

'I didn't know I looked at you.'

'Well, you do.'

'We'll count our blessings, then,' said Gavin with an attempt at sturdiness, 'we've got each other and we've got Giles. That should be enough for anyone. And God knows he's hardly had a day's illness in his life, not since his asthma.'

'Oh, touch wood when you say that.' And indeed, she pressed her fingers strongly against the bark of a tree, whistling as she did so.

'Touch wood,' said Gavin, matching his actions to hers.

He looked at his watch. 'We'll have to be going.'

'Already?' But in her heart she was relieved. Sitting in the

36

train, she inwardly spurred it on. It would be all right now; nothing would have happened. The short journey in the tram seemed interminable, and when they arrived at Les Roseaux both unconsciously hurried their steps. It was twenty-five minutes to seven.

They could see the hotel now, but in a blur. Nearer, past the souvenir shop, nearer still.

Hannah could have cried out with relief.

Giles and Melissa were sitting on the terrace, Giles with a coke, Melissa with a lemonade. They were chatting together as if bound in some deep common interest.

'Here they are!' Giles cried, jumping up. And – 'I've brought him back safe and sound,' said Melissa.

As she thanked her warmly, Hannah felt that she had been ridiculous. But for her apprehensions, she could have had a wonderful day with Gavin; as it was, it had been just a little less than wonderful.

'Mummy, we've had a super time! Melissa swims ever so well, and I let her teach me. I can do three strokes. And we played golf, I won, but she's awfully good for a beginner. She holed in one at the third!'

'He's eaten an awful lot of pastries,' Melissa said apologetically, 'I didn't know when to say stop.'

'Look here,' said Gavin, 'we're both immensely grateful to you. It was more than kind, it was heroic.'

'I enjoyed it. And I think Giles did. We evaded Hans.'

'Poor Hans,' said Hannah, luxuriating in her relief, 'I almost feel sorry for him.'

They ordered Stellas. It was wonderful to be sitting here again, with everything all right. The sky had brightened a little, and there was a strip of yellow light above the trees.

'Did it rain here?'

'No, but we thought it was going to,' said Melissa. And then, 'I must be going.'

'You won't go,' said Gavin. 'After all that effort, you must have dinner with us.'

But she would not. She was, she said, going to Les Roseaux's one cinema. She would not yield, not even under Hannah's pressure. Gathering together her beach-bag and her camera, she said good-bye to them all. 'And good-bye, Giles, we'll be seeing each other, I expect.'

'What do you say?' Hannah prompted him.

'Thank you ever so much.'

There was no doubt that he had taken to her. And why not? She was young, much younger than they were.

She went off, along the beach road, her pale hair in that long tail down her back. They had made no arrangement to meet again, but in this small place it was not necessary. They would see her again, and next time they would ask her to dinner and have her acceptance.

'She's a nice girl,' said Gavin later, when they had dined. 'But one wants to fatten her up, like a Christmas goose.'

'She's got one queer trick, though,' said Hannah, 'she sits sideways from me.'

'I'm sure she doesn't. It's only that trick some people have of curling one leg round the other.'

'She doesn't like me,' said Hannah, thereby spoiling the tenor of their evening.

6

Mindful of the gathering clouds, Melissa suggested that they should bathe the moment they got to the beach. It did not seem to her now that a day spent with Giles would be as tedious as she had thought, for as he ran a little ahead of her, he seemed to her more like Gavin with every moment that passed, and she felt that she might love him. She caught up with him. 'Don't be disappointed if it rains later. We'll find something to do.'

She took a chair for herself; he did not want one. She sent him to the bathing-hut first, saying that when he had changed she would use it herself. She wondered about him; he appeared as yet to have struck none of the usual problems of early adolescence. There was a certain babyishness about him, a ready seeking of affection; she had seen him walking with his hand in Hannah's.

They went down to the water's edge, across the powdery sand first, then across the sand that was firm and damp, then across the wet sand where the sea seeping through it at once filled up their footsteps. 'Br-r-r-r,' said Giles, 'it's cold!' He waded in.

She told him to wet himself all over first, then dip down; he would feel warmer then. He did not seem much afraid of the water, but he walked out to her side until it was on a level with his nipples. The plage seemed a very long way away, and the people were mere smudges of colour, 'hundreds and thousands' on a yellow cake. 'Shall I teach you to swim?'

He hesitated. 'I don't let Daddy.'

'But will you try with me? I'll make it quite easy.'

A long silence. Then, 'Well, if you promise not to make me put my head under.'

'I won't. But you've got to be prepared to get your face wet, you know. Come on, and trust me; I'll keep my hand under your chin.'

There was only a slight swell upon the sea. She taught him patiently for half an hour, how to keep up by kicking his legs, then to use his arms. She was touched by the confidence he seemed to have in her and in the instructions she delivered in a clear, bracing, schoolmistress's voice. 'That's enough for now.'

'Let me try it by myself,' Giles said. He threw himself upon the water, made two gasping breast strokes and then touched down. 'Look what I did!'

She told him it was splendid, that he had made an excellent start. 'We'll tell Daddy, shall we?' He nodded. He waited, occasionally attempting to do his two strokes again, while she swam for a few minutes alone. She was a strong swimmer; it was the only sport at which she was any good. The wet hair, released from the slide, floated out on the gentle waves.

'You look just like a mermaid,' said Giles, as she rejoined him.

'I feel even wetter. Come on, let's run up the beach to get ourselves warm.'

'I'm not a bit cold, I promise.'

But she towelled him vigorously and ordered him to do some digging while she went to dress herself. 'Make a deep pit, see how deep you can make it.'

When she came back, she found a tall boy standing over him.

'This is Hans,' Giles said perfunctorily. He went on digging as if his life depended upon it.

'How do you do?'

'How do you do? I'm Melissa.'

'I'm telling Giles it's no fun to dig a hole. We could make a Norman castle, with tunnels and everything.'

'No, thank you. I have to stay with Melissa today because she doesn't know Les Roseaux very well.'

' I'll come and help you up here, then.'

'No,' said Giles, 'the sand here is no good for castles. You have to go where it's wet. Thank you, though.'

As Hans wandered away, downcast, Melissa said that she was sorry for him, she thought he would be lonely.

'Mummy thinks so too, but she doesn't know him. Do you know, when I went to bed last night he sprang out of my wardrobe and jumped on me? He must have been hiding for hours.'

'How horrid. I shouldn't have liked that. I hate being startled. But I expect it was all in fun.'

'I don't like his sort of fun.'

She saw the German boy make his way to another group of children and introduce himself. It was not ten minutes before he was directing operations.

When Giles had finished making his pit, he sat himself in it and covered himself to the neck with sand. 'You do look rather frightening,' said Melissa, 'just a head lying by itself.'

'I felt lovely and warm. Do I look decapitated?' He was obviously proud of the word.

'You certainly do.'

He said in a few moments, 'Oh dear, I can't get out.' The sand cracked around him as he heaved, but he could not struggle up. She came to him, got her hands beneath his armpits and told him to push upwards as hard as he could. It was no easy job extricating him, but at last, with a great suck of sand, he fought free, and for a minute panted in her arms.

41

The feel of his small bones under the white, satiny skin disturbed her; it seemed to her that she was taking some strange liberty with Gavin himself. He was a part of Gavin. Never mind that he was also a part of Hannah.

'Now I'll have to go in the sea again and wash that off,' he said, seeking an excuse.

'No, you won't. It's quite dry and powdery, and it will simply drop away. Here, put on your shirt and we'll go up to the café. You needn't bother to put on your shorts if we're going to bathe again before lunch.'

Melissa had never taken care of a child before, and she thought she was doing quite well. She had not the heart to deny him a third pastry, though she wondered how he would manage to eat anything later on. Perhaps she was spending too much of the money Gavin had given her? She fretted a little. She did want everything to be right.

When they came back to the beach, Giles went off with his shrimping-net to a shallow pool, and she lay back in her chair, abandoning herself to day-dreams. Three days ago she had hardly known Gavin, except as a remote figure on the platform of the lecture-room, someone to exchange a word with occasionally, when she could think of some question to ask, and now she was in charge of his son. There would be a night when Hannah had a headache, when she didn't want to go out again and Giles was asleep in bed. Gavin went for a stroll before bedtime, and came upon Melissa on the plage, looking out to sea. In the lights pouring from the café she was looking beautiful, and he saw her properly for the first time. He asked her whether she would like to walk on the dark sands. Here he was very silent, but suddenly he took her in his arms and kissed her. I didn't mean to do that, he said, but I couldn't help it. She replied, Nor could I. Gavin, I love you. And he said, I love you; what are we going to do?

42

It was as though he had kissed her indeed. When she opened her eyes, sun and sea dazzled, and she felt giddy. Her body was on fire. There was heat in her groin.

Giles came back with an empty pail. There had been no shrimps. When he saw her he exclaimed. 'Melissa, you've gone all red!'

'It's the sun, I expect,' she said, coming back from a million miles away.

'The sun's gone in.'

'Then I don't know what it could have been. Shall we bathe now, or have you had enough for the morning?'

When they went in to lunch, Armand was there to welcome them. 'Have you had a good time, Miss Hirst?' He never forgot a name.

'Splendid, but it's going to rain.'

'No, no,' he said with a kind of civic pride, 'it won't rain. It is nearly always fine here. We have a very low rainfall.'

Madame passed through the dining room, nodding to all the tables like an empress. Hans and his parents were already at their meal.

'Oh,' said Giles, 'we never looked at the menu!'

'I'll tell you what it said,' Armand laughed, 'we begin with prawn crevettes, and then there is *bœuf bourguignonne*.'

'With *frites*?'

'Certainly with *frites*, if you like. As many as you please.'

'After all those pastries, too!' said Melissa.

'Daddy says I've got a great *capacity*.' But he could not eat more than half of his beef.

Afterwards they went to what Giles called the Golf, and from the small hot wooden hut where Michel had presided for over twenty years, got clubs, balls and scoreboard. 'But I don't think we'll need the scoreboard, not at first. We'll just play hole by hole till you're used to the game.'

43

The course was bright with flowers, salvia, calceolaria and lobelia in tubs of cement. The first hazard was simply a board with a hole in it. 'If you get it straight,' said Giles, 'you may do it in one.' He had an authoritative air now, somewhat reminiscent of Hans's.

Melissa did her best, but her ball struck the wood and rolled back again.

'I'll give you that one free,' he said magnanimously. 'Here, hold your club like *this*, and it will be better. You'll see.'

She tried again, this time surmounted the difficulty but missed her putt. 'Three,' she said ruefully.

'You'll get the hang of it in time. Two. One up to me.'

The second obstacle was a long tunnel at the summit of a slope: it frustrated both of them. She was lucky with the third, as there was no obstruction between tee and green other than a gentle hump a few yards from the latter. 'Two,' said Melissa, 'now you do better!' He did do better; he sunk the ball in one stroke.

The game began to absorb her, and for a while she stopped thinking of Gavin. She concentrated her thoughts, eager to do well in Giles's eyes. Making fantasies, she began to pretend that she was a real golfer, on a real course. But at the eighth, where the ground ran up smoothly to two feet of the hole and then rose sharply to it, her luck failed and she took seven shots.

'Bad luck, said Giles, 'but everyone does that the first time. Look.' He trickled the ball gently to the foot of the rise, then with a gentle upward shot, put it into the hole. She admired him. 'Oh, it took me ages to learn that trick,' he remarked casually.

The skies were dark now, but no rain had fallen. The game took a long time, since they had to wait their turn with other players.

The eighteenth hole she won; but she had lost the game. He had beaten her easily.

'Never mind,' he said,' you were fine.'

She felt sleepy. The effort of concentration had tired her.

They went down to the beach again. The sea was leaden; many visitors had deserted the sand and the dunes. Giles ran off to play; well, now she could rest, since she could keep an eye on him, could see his red shirt a quarter of a mile away.

That afternoon she lost him.

He had been pottering again with his shrimping net in one of the shallow strips of water parallel with the sea. His shirt made it easy for her to follow him. She saw him bending and trawling, making his slow way, his head bent. He seemed absorbed in what he was doing.

So, closing her eyes, she went back into the dream, this time with even greater intensity. They were in a high bright secret room; she did not know where they were, or how they had come there. They were sitting on a low divan, and his arm was about her shoulders. There was another room within, where they would soon go, but this was in darkness. At last he brought her to her feet, and he kissed her. Do you want me? she said. Of course I do. She said, I am all yours.

The dream became sleep. Perhaps she only slept for twenty minutes, but when she came with a start to herself, she could not see Giles's shirt anywhere. There were a few children in the pool but he was not among them.

Heart thudding, she left her chair and ran towards the sea. Yes, there he was! No. It was a girl with short yellow hair. She raced along the margin of the foam, calling to him, but though there was no wind to carry her voice away, it sounded to her as small as a voice in a nightmare. ' Giles! Giles!' She was terrified. They had put so much trust in her, and she had failed them. Her thoughts flew to horrors; the lost child, the police, the homecoming. She began to cry, tears of anticipation falling down her cheeks. 'Giles! Giles!'

'If you want him,' said Hans, coming from nowhere, 'he went up to the dunes about ten minutes ago. Shall I help look for him?'

But she pushed him aside and ran leftwards to where the dunes began, slipping and stumbling up the slopes. They were deserted, except for a party of picnickers making their way back to the plage. The sand was grey, and the sky was grey over it.

She skidded from hollow to hollow, each reedy fold concealing another. She screamed, 'Giles! Where are you, Giles?' She thought she would go mad.

And then she saw the orange-red shirt, some way away from her. He stood up and seemed to wave; not to her, though, but to someone on his far side.

'Giles! Giles!' She was crying afresh now, but with relief.

He did not hear her until she was almost upon him. Then he turned, and smiled. 'You are in a state. What's the matter?'

'I lost you. I couldn't think where you'd been.'

'Only up here. You do make a fuss.'

She wiped her eyes. She was panting, and her fright had not yet subsided.

'What a fuss!' he said, wondering.

She sat down. 'Wait, I must get my breath. Giles, who were you waving to?'

'Waving? Why, to nobody. I was just pretending. I often do.'

'What have you been doing all this time?'

'Oh, I don't know. It wasn't such a long time, was it?'

She saw that he was flushed, and that his eyes were shining.

'It seemed long.'

He was about to speak, then hesitated.

'What is it?'

46

At last he said, 'Better not tell Mummy and Daddy you thought you'd lost me. They'd only make such a thing of it, and of course you hadn't really.'

'All right,' she said, relieved, but wondering how far she could trust him. 'We won't say anything. Come and have tea now.'

'There's a place in the town, just across the tramlines. They've got the kind of meringues I like.'

He seemed eager for the treat, yet as they walked back down the dunes, appeared reluctant to go with her, lagging his steps, now and then looking behind.

'What's so charming?' she said curiously.

'Nothing.'

'Where's your shrimping net?'

'Damn, I must have left it in the pool.'

They found Hans waiting for them. 'I've got your net,' he said, 'you are silly to leave it there. Someone might have stolen it. We're going up to the Star Café now. Are you coming?'

'No, thanks,' said Giles, 'we're having tea somewhere else. Thanks for the net.'

'Melissa was in a terrible state about you. *I* told her where you were.'

'I don't know why everyone makes such a mountain out of a molehill,' said Giles, in his occasional grown-up manner.

'Of a sand-hill,' said Hans, as if this were a very good joke. 'Do you play chess? I'll teach you after dinner, if you like.'

'Oh, all right, though I expect I shan't be any good.' This was a kindness in return for the net.

'That is not the right way you should think,' said Hans severely.

They had their tea, and afterwards Melissa let Giles hire one of the long tricycles used by children to pedal round the foot of the wooded hills behind the town. It was six o'clock before she called to him to go back to the hotel; she had not once let him out of her sight.

So they sat on the terrace and waited for Hannah and Gavin. Melissa's heart had quietened. There they were, coming by the souvenir shop. And all was as it was meant to be. Safe.

7

Next morning the rain drenched down, striking the roadway in a million crystal cats' heads, swirling and bubbling along the gutters. The poplars rattled and creaked in the wind. It had turned cold.

Hannah, having seen all this, returned to bed and poured herself another cup of coffee. She could see a bleak day ahead, staying indoors for hours with Giles to be amused. She wished he were fonder of reading. They had tempted him with C. S. Lewis and Tolkien, but he much preferred the Bunter books, and returned again and again to a fantasy called *The Tale of Lal*, written at the turn of the century about a lion from Trafalgar Square who walked along the tramlines to Brixton, which Hannah had picked up from a junk stall in memory of her own childish pleasure in it. Poor boy, he would be unable to escape the attentions of Hans.

She wondered what Melissa would do with herself, cooped up in the small boarding house, and regretted what she had said to Gavin about her yesterday. Because if Hannah had suspected a dislike, he would expect that dislike to be returned; and there was nothing he loved so much as to have things calm and pleasant about him. Indeed, she had devoted her married life to ensuring this as much as humanly possible; it was understood that whoever suffered from any domestic mishaps, he should not be the one.

After breakfast, he came up to her. 'The Vennings are here. They got in from Brussels this morning.'

'Oh, dear.' This was a couple they had met the previous year, and did not much care for. They were interior decorators in a small way of business.

'Oh, dear, indeed,' he said, 'but at least they're only here for three days. They've got their daughter with them this time, rather a pretty child. She must be about thirteen. Hans introduced himself instantly; it was a sight to watch.'

'If it goes on raining like this, which it will, we'll have to be matey in the bar all day. Is there any hope of the children amusing each other?'

'Well, the three of them were talking about playing Monopoly. I hope they do. It lasts a long time.' He sat down on the edge of the bed and kissed her. 'How you can bear to sit in all those crumbs, I don't know.'

'Crumbs are part of the pleasure. Has Giles got something warm on?'

'He has now,' said Gavin, 'I had to send him upstairs to change. He came down in a cotton shirt and his bathing trunks; sometimes, I think he's an incurable optimist.'

She put aside the tray and slowly got up. Familiarity had not staled his pleasure in these uprisings. First she would sit on the edge of the bed, her pretty legs dangling beneath the short nightgown. Then she would press down with her hands and stand erect, with a long sigh. Her hair down, she looked more girlish. 'What's the time?' she asked.

'Ten to ten. You've taken your time this morning.'

'There didn't seem much to get up for.'

They stood side by side looking out of the window. The poplars were lashing their tops in the rain. People were hurrying along under umbrellas; cyclists in their perverse kit of yellow mackintosh sped by, throwing up water as they went.

'It looks as though the weather's broken,' he said.

'A fatuous understatement. But let's pray it mends itself again.'

He smiled. 'Let's. Well, you get dressed and come down as soon as you can. I'll see how the Monopoly school is getting on, if it is.'

She found the Vennings sitting by a window on the glassed terrace. Even at that hour, they were drinking Stellas. She fancied they were both in need of oral satisfaction; there had scarcely seemed a moment in the day when they had not been smoking, or eating, or drinking. They greeted her with enthusiasm. 'Hannah, dear!'

John and Verna Venning were both small, chubby and active. They were in their early forties. Both wore eccentric clothes which looked as though they had been gathered together from the secondhand shops of Kensington and Chelsea, which they probably had been. John wore rust-red corduroys and a green polo-necked sweater. Verna was wearing a gypsy-like skirt, which came to her ankles, and a shirt of a different pattern. 'Do come and sit with us,' she said. 'Isn't this weather horrible?'

Silver runnels streamed down the panes. The children were sitting in the small parlour at the back of the bar, where there was a table large enough for them to spread out their game.

'What'll you have?' John asked.' Beer? Coffee?'

'I've only just had my breakfast,' said Hannah, 'I don't think I want anything just now.'

'I'll have some more coffee,' said Gavin.

'Sure you won't have some beer? Or perhaps that's only for sots like us.'

'Mind whom you're calling a sot,' said Verna. 'You're drinking it too.'

'Only because you were,' said her husband.

'I like that! You've never got your nose out of a glass.'

'Well, coming from you—'

51

Hannah remembered why she had disliked them. They snacked at each other in a facetious manner that had something of ill-intention underlying it.

She peered round the door; she could see into the parlour. 'Is that your daughter? She's a beauty!'

'Handsome is as handsome does,' said Verna, 'but you can see she's already attracting the young men. I have hopes of her.'

How, Hannah thought, had she and Gavin ever got on Christian names terms with that pair? Somehow they must have forced it on them, like a forced card.

The Fischers were sitting at the next table. On impulse she turned to them, and praised Hans.

'His English is wonderful.'

'He is at the top of his class,' said Frau Fischer. 'And besides, he spent three months in England with us last year.'

'It is good for him,' Herr Fischer said, 'to be among young people. What terrible weather! And it was so fine yesterday.'

Armand came through onto the terrace. 'Don't worry!' he said.'It will clear up by two o'clock, you will see. It never rains for long here. Well, Mr Venning, Mrs Venning, it is good to have you back with us again.'

'Oh,' said Verna, with some flirtatiousness, 'we couldn't come to this part of Belgium without seeing you and the Albert.'

'I don't know why we had to take such a damned early train,' said John, 'it was a crass idea.'

'Your idea.'

'It wasn't!' She gave his hand a playful smack, and he glared at her.

Verna turned to Armand again. 'Your little bar,' she said,' I was just thinking.'

'Please?'

'If it looked quite different and I had the re-decoration of it, I should make it look just like this.'

But that was rather too much for him, so he bowed, not knowing whether a compliment had been intended or not, and went inside.

'What a fool thing to say to the man,' said John.

'How was it a fool thing, Hannah? I love it in the bar, it's so nice and old-fashioned. It's nicer than that glassed-in place.'

'I see what you mean,' said Hannah, and Gavin hastily agreed.

'A fool thing, all the same.' John Venning downed his beer, and went to the bar for another.

'He got out of bed the wrong side this morning,' Verna explained.

Hannah was wondering how and when, without too much of impoliteness, she could withdraw to the parlour and go on with Ngaio Marsh.

She was somewhat surprised when Gavin, having finished his coffee, rose without haste and said he was going to do some reading. 'I have to catch up on some stuff while I'm here. I go stale easily.'

'I'll come with you,' said Hannah. To the Vennings – 'We'll see you later.'

The light filtered so dimly through the lace curtains and through the pot plants in the parlour that reading was not easy; still, it was quiet.

The children were intent on their game. 'I will take Liverpool Station,' Hans was saying earnestly, 'then I have three stations altogether.'

Giles saw his parents in their corner. He raised a hand, and smiled at them.

'All right, old boy?' asked Gavin.

'All right. M. Croisset says it's going to be fine later. We can go to the Golf.'

'*Sancta simplicitas*,' said Gavin to Hannah.

At half-past eleven, the game was finished. Hans suggested that they play again, but both Giles and the girl were tired of it.

Hannah ordered Cokes for them all. 'Do you like Coke?' she asked the girl.

'Very much thank you.'

'What's your name?'

'Chloe.'

'That's very pretty.'

Giles went out into the hall, and soon came back again. He was looking pleased. 'It's *vol-au-vent* and roast veal. I'm hungry.'

'You can't be hungry yet,' Hannah said. But to Gavin, 'On a day like this, thank God for meal-times.' She braced herself to say what had been on her mind that morning. 'I was thinking.'

'What?'

'It must be dreary for poor Melissa, stuck in that little *pension*. And she was so good yesterday.'

'Yes, it must be. But I don't see one can do anything about it.' He looked pleased, though.

Hannah said, 'You could telephone, or I could. Have her up here to dinner. It would give her something to look forward to all day.'

'That's my good girl. But you said you didn't like her.'

How stupid she had been to raise the subject.

'That's not what I said. I said I thought she didn't like me.'

'I don't know anyone who doesn't like you,' said Gavin simply. He thought for a moment. 'Well, I suppose I could do that. It would be an act of charity. Of course, if it did stop raining I could go down there after lunch; God knows she's not likely to be out. Yes, that's what I'll do.'

'You are an optimist. It won't stop.'

It did not, not until three o'clock that afternoon, when a sour sun broke through.

'I could do with a breath of air,' said Hannah. 'Let's put on our macs and go there now.'

Giles, who had long tired of playing with Hans and Chloe and had been reading a Bunter book at their side, looked up. 'I'm coming! We could get in a round of Golf.'

'Darling, the course will be sodden! The balls will stick to it.'

'I want to. If you don't, I'll play by myself.'

Hannah hesitated. 'You could do that, I suppose, while we call on Melissa.'

'If she's out,' said Gavin, 'we can leave a message.'

Though the course was glutinously muddy, Michel was in his box and a few couples were playing as best they could, swearing as the balls got stuck half way up the fairways. They left Giles at the first hole. 'Don't be disappointed if you don't do well today. Nobody could,' said Hannah. 'We won't be more than twenty minutes, darling.'

They went towards Byronlaan, and down it to the Pension des Colombes. It was a gloomy place, permeated by the smell of stew. The proprietress came out to them and they asked for Melissa.

She replied in French that Mademoiselle Hirst had just gone out.

'Now what?' Gavin asked Hannah. 'Shall we go and look for her? She can't have gone far.'

'Better leave a note, in case we miss her.'

The proprietress supplied them with a scrap of writing-paper, ruled in violet. He wrote, 'Will you come to dinner with us tonight? It's such a dismal day and we should like it so much if you could. Make it about 7 o'clock.' He signed it 'G.E.'

'The Albert must seem like Claridges to her after this,' Hannah remarked, as they turned away. Though they did stroll as far as the deserted beach, there was no sign of her, so they turned back to pick up Giles. It was starting to rain again, large, slow drops starring the pavement. Hannah put on her headscarf.

Giles was only at the twelfth hole, attempting to drive a ball through a pipe embedded in concrete. They thought he was swearing to himself and wondered what words he used.

'Come on,' said Gavin, 'you'll have to give up. It's going to pour.'

'I don't mind.'

'Now come on,' Hannah pleaded, 'it may be all right for you, but we're not going to get soaked waiting.'

'Don't wait, then.' He was made fractious by the frustrations of the day.

'Darling, that's rude.'

He missed his putt. 'Bugger it!'

'*What* did you say?'

'Nothing.'

'Listen, you mustn't use such language!'

He walked away from them on to the thirteenth, teed his ball. This time, his shot barely went a couple of yards. 'Oh, do go away!' he said furiously, 'I can't do anything right while you're watching me. I won't be long, anyway.'

There seemed to be nothing for it but to go back to the hotel.

'He's growing up, at any rate,' said Hannah, with a sorry grin.

'Why? Because he says "bugger?" He says worse things under his breath. He thinks I can't lip-read.'

'Well, I don't like it.'

56

Back in the bar, they found the Vennings there.

'I say,' said Verna, 'wouldn't it be fun if we all had dinner together tonight? There's no one using that long table at the end. We'll ask M. Croisset to lay it for us.'

'Well,' said Gavin, 'I'm afraid we've got someone coming.'

'Bring him or her, then. Oh, do! John and I get tired of each other's faces. Don't be spoilsports.'

There appeared to be no good reason for refusal, or at least they could not think of one. They went upstairs to take their coats off.

'Be damned to that,' said Hannah. 'Why couldn't we have said no?'

'I don't know why not, but we didn't. Anyway,' he added guilelessly, 'it might be more fun for Melissa.'

At once she knew that it would not be, and she thought she knew why. The suspicion was no more than a slight one, but it lingered. The girl had got a schoolgirl crush on Gavin, as had happened with one or two of his students before. Now she would be hanging about all through the holiday, the plaintive waif-figure who had been so good with Giles, had given them their day alone. Hannah was not jealous – she knew she had no need to be – but she recalled the taste of old jealousies; they had tormented her in the early years of her marriage. But just as strong was the present feeling that she was, to Melissa, an outsider, unwanted, unliked. As Gavin had said, people did like her, and she was warmed by their approbation.

'What are you brooding over?' he asked her.

'Those Vennings.'

'What can't be cured, etc. Come on down, Giles ought to be back.'

'I wish I could get over the ridiculous idea that we need to police him everywhere,' she said, 'He's just beginning to resent it.'

But at that moment, he burst into their bedroom, all ill-temper forgotten. 'You were right, it did pour!'

'You're sopping wet, darling. Come on upstairs and I'll get you changed.'

'Good God, can't he change his things himself?' said Gavin.

8

When she came in from her walk, Melissa did not look at the letter-rack; there had been nothing for her that morning. But the proprietress stopped her on the stairs. There was a note. Had she seen it? A lady and gentleman had called while she was out.

She retrieved it. It was a single folded sheet of paper. For several moments she stood with it in her hand, not attempting to open it. It might be in his writing; she had never seen it. But it might be in Hannah's. Then she read it quickly, and an excited bliss ran through her. It was from him, his initials were on it. Running up to her bedroom, she shut herself in, and there she kissed the paper. He had a very neat spiky hand, the words looping each on to the next in a manner she had never seen before, individual and disturbing. She would know it among thousands.

She folded it, opened it again to repeat the initial shock of surprise. Again and again. She put it between her breasts and lay upon the bed, staring at the window down which the rivulets of rain were now running together. She would see him that night, and perhaps, if it was dark, he would walk home with her afterwards. But then, it would not be dark; she could not leave them later than half-past ten, and the lights would still be on in the shops, and in the lamps along the beach road. Yet he might still think it his duty to see her safely back; would she dare to hint at nervousness?

She said to herself, You must not hope too much from this. You know it is all in your imagination and not in his. You have seen how it is with him and Hannah. And then there is the boy.

But the words made no sense for her. She went downstairs for tea in the little dark parlour, and while she was drinking it, re-read the note several times. She lit a cigarette, but almost at once stubbed it out. She wanted her breath to be sweet. How lucky that she had brought with her a black afternoon dress, short-sleeved and plain! She had not really thought that there would be an opportunity for her to wear it.

At half-past five, she went to the bathroom, bearing with her the things of ritual; bath salts, scent for the skin, deodorant, razor, pumice stone, dusting-powder. It was too early, she thought, for anyone else to need the bath; she would be able to luxuriate.

She lay in the water, examining herself. Her flesh was pale, her breasts very small, her collar-bones sharp. If only she were a little rounder, but not so round as Hannah. Anger and envy, for the moment, swept over her. To have so much luck, to have him and his son! She envied Hannah that she could watch his dressing and undressing, watch him spread the lather over his face, watch him as he brushed his hair. And I, Melissa thought, have nothing at all.

But this mood did not stay with her, happiness superseding it. After dinner they would have coffee on the covered terrace, and she would pretend that she was alone with him. Rising from the fast cooling water, she dried herself and, her shoulders draped by the towel, put a foot up on the edge of the bath. Her armpits were smooth, but there were a few light hairs on her legs. She razored them carefully, then she pumiced the soles of her feet and dusted them with talc. She used the skin lotion lavishly, not worrying that it was expensive. A scent of lemons rose, fresh, enticing.

An English voice, behind the door, asked her if she were going to be there all night.

60

'I'm sorry, I'm coming now.'

Gathering her possessions, she slipped on a mackintosh – she had brought no dressing-gown and emerged.

Putting on her clothes was a sheer slow delight; clean underwear, her best pair of stockings, and at last the black dress. Her black shoes, she knew, would suffer on the muddy roads but perhaps she could wipe them with a Kleenex tissue before entering the hotel. Sitting before the glass of the dressing-table, she contemplated her hair. Should she wear it in the usual way or put it up? Would he like to see her as she always was, or just a little unfamiliar? She decided to coil it in the nape of her neck. Powder? A little, though she rarely used it. Lipstick, yes; rather a bright one. She looked long at the result. It makes me just a little older, nearer to his age. She took out a string of cultured pearls which had been her mother's, and put them on. Now I am ready.

But it was only half-past six; she had twenty minutes to wait before she could set off. I wish my handbag weren't so scuffed. I want to be perfect for him. If I count aloud, perhaps I can make the time go. One, two, three, four, five, six, seven . . . The rain seemed to have ceased, and the trees had stopped thrashing. Everything was very still. She read the note again, put it in the neck of her dress.

At last it was time to go. She went out into the muddy lane, stepping on the grass verges where she could, and along the road past the golf-course, optimistically flood-lit, though only a single couple were attempting to play, past the shop of 'Marcel, Traiteur', which was lit up until midnight, past the shop that sold children's shoes and beach-wear, and crossed the road to the hotel.

In her excitement, she had forgotten to wipe her shoes; she only noticed that they were dirty as she went up the steps. Hannah, motherly, was waiting for her.

61

'My dear, I'm so glad you could come! Hang your coat in the hall and come and have a drink.'

'It was very kind of you,' said Melissa. In a moment she would see him.

'We're all in the bar. We shall be quite a party tonight.'

Melissa's heart sank. A party? She would be less alone with him. She said, 'How nice. Would you wait a minute while I try to get the mud off my shoes?' She bent down, concealing her face, and scrubbed at them with a tissue.

'You look lovely,' said Hannah.

'Thank you very much. Hasn't it been an awful day?'

'Awful. But we have survived.'

Gavin rose to his feet as they went into the bar, and so did another man, a little one. Melissa was introduced to the Vennings.

They were all sitting in a corner, with Giles and a little girl; she too was introduced, and Giles smiled at Melissa warmly.

'We've heard about your miraculous meeting,' said the woman called Verna, with a glance that raked Melissa from head to foot. 'To think that you should have hit on Les Roseaux! Hardly anyone has ever heard of it.'

'Ah,' said the man called John, 'I suspect it was a plot.'

Melissa flushed.

'Do think what you're saying!' his wife said merrily.

'If there was a plot, I was in it,' Gavin said easily. 'I was luring one of my students away to the wicked continent. I'm sure she finds it wicked, though I don't know what she could have been doing today that was at all sinful.'

'I was reading most of the time.'

They asked her what she would have to drink, and she replied to them, but with a mind far from what she was saying. It seemed to her that she had been found out, and that he must know it. She turned to Giles. 'And how have you been spending your time?'

62

'Oh, playing with Hans and Chloe. And I did go to the Golf when it stopped raining for a minute.'

The bar was crowded, men from the town drinking on high stools, visitors packing the parlour and covered terrace. The lights were mellow behind golden shades, and the blueness of smoke floated below the ceiling. The tabby cat weaved by, rubbing between legs, at last making a jump for Madame's lap.

'Can Chloe and I—'

'May,' said Gavin automatically.

'May Chloe and I go and play?'

'Well, then, don't be long. We're eating at a quarter to eight.'

Hannah looked after the children as they went. 'What a very pretty child that is! Giles is too young to recognise it, though.'

'I should think he would be!' said Verna, with a little cream. 'You don't want a Don Juan of twelve on your hands, do you?'

'I wasn't such a slouch at twelve,' said John.

'Not such a slouch now.' But she said it sharply. She turned to Melissa. 'You know what we do?' she asked her.

'Why should the girl want to know what we do?'

'Stop it. – We tart up other people's houses. Gavin here knows all about art, but I don't believe he could colour-plan a kitchen.'

'I am quite sure I couldn't,' said Gavin placidly, 'my talents don't lie in that direction.'

'It must be interesting,' said Melissa.

'And do you know all about art, too?' Verna went on.

'Not much. I'm trying to learn.'

'Such clever people. John and I never went within touching distance of a university.'

They were maddening. Their chatter cut her off from concentrating upon Gavin. She dared not even look at him too often. Hatred and bliss swept over her, wave upon alternate wave.

'How nice to see the little black frock again,' said Verna, who seemed to have taken a fancy to her, 'one gets so tired of all that tat.' She sat in her own tat, this time a kind of poncho over a fringed skirt.

'Thank you.'

'Why don't you wear a little black frock?' John asked his wife.

'Because I just can't carry it off. Hannah could, I can't.'

Melissa caught Gavin's eye. He was staring at her, as if admiring. She looked away again. This evening, which had promised such wonders, was turning out to be a torment. She did not know how she was to get through it, yet dreaded the moment when she must leave.

Presently the children came down and they went into the dining-room. The table was laid for seven. Hannah had worked out some sort of *placement* – 'though it's an awkward number. Verna, you go here—' this was on Gavin's right – 'and Melissa on the other side. I'll sit at the other end with John here. The children can sit opposite to each other.'

Armand had set out flowers in a green vase.

'Festive,' said Verna.

He stood over them, himself with a festive air. '*Croquemonsieur*, roast chicken.'

'*Frites*?' said Giles.

'Certainly *frites*.'

'I don't like *croque-monsieur*,' said Chloe, who spoke rarely but with force, 'they've got cheese in them. I don't like cheese.'

'What a nuisance you are!' Verna exclaimed.

' Perhaps a little omelette?'

'No,' said John, 'she's just faddy. She can go without.'

'But I want a little omelette!'

64

'I assure you,' said Armand, 'that it is no trouble at all. Would you like that, mademoiselle?'

'Yes, please.'

John shrugged, but said nothing more.

Gavin asked what wine Armand would recommend, then ordered two bottles. 'Will you drink some, Chloe?' He turned to Verna. 'Does she indulge? Giles likes just a little.'

'I'd rather have fizzy orange,' said Chloe.

From a far corner of the room, Hans had turned to regard them wistfully. He waved his hand.

Melissa was in such a turmoil of emotion that she did not think she would be able to eat; but she found that she was hungry. The food was admirable. The skin on the chicken was crisp and gold, the piled potatoes golden on the big pewter dish. There was a sparkle over all things.

'No battery hens here, thank God,' said Verna. 'They're not only horrible, but they affect my conscience. Just think of them, spending all their lives in the dark!'

'Little tenderheart,' said John, unpleasantly.

'Oh, you.' She made a face at him down the length of the table.

'We're probably going to Ghent tomorrow, if it turns out better than today,' said Gavin.

Melissa felt desolate. Another day without him. 'I could take Giles for you,' she said, not wanting him to accept.

'Giles is coming with us,' said Hannah, 'he likes the Gravensteen, with all the dungeons and torture chambers.'

'There's nothing in the torture chamber,' said Giles, through a mouthful of chicken, 'it's just another room.'

Gavin said to Melissa, 'Would you like to come? You ought to see the Mystic Lamb, in Saint-Bavon. For my money, it's the greatest painting in the world.'

She saw Hannah glance at him, unable to suppress a

momentary surprise. Ought she to refuse? But she could not. She was too excited at the thought of it. 'Wouldn't I be in the way?'

'I don't see why, do you, Hannah?'

Hannah answered with her customary air of warmth, almost of embracement. 'Not in the least. Do come, Melissa.'

'Thank you very much.'

'Then perhaps you'll pick us up at ten, that is, if it's not pouring.'

She would have tramped along at his side in storm and wind and rain. She must pray for a fine day.

'You are rather a lucky one, aren't you—' Verna began.

'Thank you, no more wine. It's not much good to me.'

'Then I'll have to drink it myself.' Gavin was flushed; he had had more than his share already. He held up the bottle to the light. 'Do you think we might be dogs and have a third? Armand!'

'Darling,' said Hannah, 'it's rather a lot.'

'Let me have a special treat,' he pleaded. He looked at the Vennings with uncommon kindness. 'We don't have a party at Les Roseaux every day.'

Hannah smiled at him, but Melissa thought she did not look too pleased.

Verna returned to her question, 'I was saying, you've been rather lucky, haven't you, meeting up with the Eastwoods? I'd love a real expert to show me round. Now, furniture I do understand, but I'm no good on painting.'

Melissa intended no reply; she was by now deeply embarrassed and apprehensive. Verna persisted. 'No, it really was a remarkable coincidence.'

'But a coincidence,' said Melissa, and then wondered whether it would have been better not to speak at all. To dwell on the point might be dangerous; she fancied Hannah's gaze on her face. Damn the Venning woman. What did she

66

suspect? The truth, of course. But she couldn't know, couldn't possibly know.

She tried to quieten herself by thinking that tomorrow the Vennings would not be with them, yet feared every moment to hear them suggest themselves for the expedition. But they did not. And nothing more was said about coincidences.

When Gavin passed the wine to her – she saw that he passed it to the left, and people were supposed to help themselves – she took a third glass. It was more than she was used to, but she felt she needed it. Already she was a little light-headed, it seemed to her that all their faces were gilded.

After the meal, Giles asked if he and Chloe might play halma in the bedroom.

'Yes,' said Hannah, 'but not later than half-past nine. I'll come up to you.'

'Why make the kid go to bed?' asked John. 'He's on holiday, isn't he? We let Chloe sit up till we go.'

'Chloe is older than Giles,' Hannah said firmly.

'I sometimes sit up till twelve at home,' Chloe remarked, with an air of supreme satisfaction.

'Them's your customs and these are ours,' said Gavin, with a touch of tartness. Melissa guessed that, with his sudden likes and dislikes, he did not care for the pretty little girl.

When they had disposed of the children they went back to the bar, but there were no seats for them. Hannah said they would have coffee on the covered terrace – 'Though it's not so cosy there, really. I rather like dimness and fug.'

When half-past nine came, she went upstairs to see that Giles went to bed. Chloe came down, carrying a book. She sat down quietly to read it.

Melissa thought, I have only an hour more with them, perhaps less than that. Will they stay here for another hour? In Hannah's absence, she felt a glow of that pleasure she had dreamed about. Gavin was flushed and talkative, perhaps a little drunk. And I, I daren't quite shut my eyes without the room moving. Everything seemed very bright and clear, with a cavernous darkness beyond. He lit a cigarette for her, and for a moment their fingers touched. She felt the shock run through her.

Hannah came running down again, and the moment was gone. She swept them back into a party, into a general conversation, contriving to divert the Vennings when they showed signs of snacking and to make all things pleasant. They were still there, Gavin and the Vennings drinking beer, at ten-thirty. How long should Melissa stay? Should she wait just another half-hour? No. It was quite likely that they had all had enough of her. She stood up. 'I must go now. It has been lovely.'

They protested; she must not think of going yet. 'Night's young,' said Verna, who was winding a string of beads round and round her wrist.

But Melissa persisted. Gavin stood up. 'I'd better walk you back.'

She had not really dreamed that it could happen. 'No,' she said, 'I shall be quite all right.'

'It's pretty dark along that lane where you live.'

'You mustn't bother.'

'Let him, Melissa,' said Hannah. 'The air will do him good.'

'What do you mean, darling, do me good?' He looked a little huffy.

'She means, you're a trifle smashed,' said Verna, with one of her little screams of laughter.' But aren't we all?'

'You're not, anyway,' said Gavin, 'you didn't have your fair share of the wine.' He looked at Melissa, at Hannah. 'I shan't be long. Come on, get your coat.'

The night had cleared, and it was starry. They set off along the road. She was alone with him. Sometimes he put a hand under her arm to steer her past a puddle.

'We met those people last year,' he said. 'To tell you the truth, I don't greatly care for them; I don't like married couples who are rude to each other. You know what holiday acquaintances are, though. They go just so far, and you don't expect them to ripen. It's hell when they do.'

She said nothing. She was choked with happiness, almost to the point of tears. Gavin lost his footing for a second on a muddy patch, quickly recovered it.

'The Van Eyck really is wonderful. You'll enjoy it.' He began to describe it to her.

'You've been so kind to me. Both of you,' she added.

'Nonsense, my girl.'

She heard the note of intimacy with joy and incredulity. She dared to look at him, and in the light of a lamp saw that he was smiling.

He went on, 'I suppose it's pretty bleak for you to be all alone here, especially when the weather's bad.'

'Thanks to you, I'm not alone.' It was the wine speaking; she was grateful that it had so daring a voice.

'Careful, now!' He caught her again by her arm. 'If you'd gone into that, you'd have been up to your neck.' This time he did not let her go, for they had come to Byronlaan where there were few lights and the trees obscured the stars.

It is coming to an end, she thought, it is coming to an end and I cannot bear it.

They reached the Pension des Colombes, from which a lamp shone only in the hall. 'They keep early hours, these people,' he said, releasing her.

'I can't thank you enough,' said Melissa. 'Honestly, I can't.'

'Nice for us. And very nice for Giles, yesterday. Well.'

Then he stooped and kissed her lightly on the cheek.

'See you tomorrow.'

He swung off, and went away, lurching very slightly, down the lane.

She stood quite still, with her hand to her face. He had kissed her. Of course, she knew how casual these salutes between men and women now were; yet she would not have thought he would have been casual. Hope soared wildly in her. At last she rang the bell and was admitted, not without a sour glance from the proprietress.

'It's not eleven,' Melissa said to her.

She lay fully dressed upon the bed, her eyes closed, a hand still to her cheek. It was too much to believe. Yet it had happened.

The room swung round and she had to sit upright for a while, her back against the headboard.

9

As he shaved, Gavin damned himself for his silliness of the night before. He had not been unmoved by Verna's hints about 'coincidence,' and his mind was working busily. The invitation to Ghent, the kiss (he recoiled from the thought of that), had only been meant in kindness; he had kissed her as casually as he would have kissed one of Hannah's women friends. But he believed she might have taken it seriously. Somehow, this holiday was going all wrong. He wished he had never heard of her.

Hannah's voice came to him through the open door of the bathroom. 'Darling, did we have to ask Melissa to come with us?'

He peeled off a swathe of lather. 'You awake?'

'Obviously. I was asking you why we have to take Melissa to Ghent.'

'Just what I was thinking. I was simply in a charitable mood. And I admit that I was a little tight.'

'Let's say you were in a state of hyper-amiability.'

He came out to her. She was lying on her back, her hands clasped outside the bedclothes. She did not seem to be angry – anger was rare with her – but she looked perturbed.

'All right,' said Gavin, 'it was silly of me. But it's only for the day, and then we needn't see so much of her.'

'What is the weather like?'

'Cloudy, but not raining. It looks as if it might be chilly.'

She sat up, rubbed her eyes and reached for her cardigan. 'I've been thinking. Perhaps I'm being stupid, but I do think that girl followed you here.'

'The word for that is probably "fudge",' said Gavin. 'How on earth could she have found out where I was going?'

'I don't suppose you made much of a secret of it at the college. These things get around.'

'But what could she want with me?' This was disingenuous. He thought he knew.

'She is in love with you,' said Hannah, but without a smile.

'My dear girl, I'm twice her age!'

'Such things aren't altogether unknown.'

For a moment he said nothing. He sat on the edge of the bed and took her hand, seeming to admire the short, unvarnished nails. 'I think it's all rot,' he replied at last, 'but if there's anything in it at all, she must just get over it. It's ridiculous.'

'I do wish she weren't coming today. I tell you, it's not that I'm jealous—'

'That would be pretty absurd, wouldn't it?'

'– but I hate just being tolerated myself. I think she's looked me straight in the face just once.'

The maid brought her breakfast-tray. The smell of the coffee made him hungry. He finished dressing, but did not go downstairs at once. He had something else to say; she might as well know the extent of his idiocy.

'Darling, all being as you say, I did make a fool of myself last night.'

'Well, it wasn't all that noticeable,' she said placably. 'I suppose you had to see her home.'

'But I was fool enough to kiss her good-night, just as I would have kissed Anne, or Janet. She ought to know that it didn't mean anything.'

She was silent for a while, as she buttered a roll and put jam on it. Then, 'But she won't know, I'm afraid.'

'It was only because I had drink taken.' He attempted facetiousness. 'And so had she.'

'What sort of kiss did you give her?'

'Why, what on earth do you think? A peck on the cheek.'

'You must go down. Giles will be waiting, that is, if he's up.'

'Darling, this is all moonshine, isn't it? It's only because Verna kept hinting things. She has a very odd sense of humour. I dare say Melissa did come here by accident, and that she's no more in love with me than she is with the cat.'

'Let's hope so,' said Hannah, but still she did not smile.

When he was at breakfast, the telephone bell rang. It was for him. He went uneasily to answer it.

Melissa's voice was muffled, as though she might have been speaking through a handkerchief. 'I'm awfully sorry, Mr Eastwood, but I don't think I can come with you today. I seem to have caught a cold.'

'I'm sorry about that.'

'You won't mind, of course.' A pause. Then, 'Why should you?'

'It would have been pleasant to have your company,' Gavin replied with unnatural bluffness. 'Anyway, take care of yourself and keep warm.'

He raced upstairs to give the news to Hannah.

'Well, thank God for that,' she said. 'But I don't believe in her cold. It's just that, even for your sake, she can't stand a day with me.'

'Rubbish.'

'Not rubbish.'

'Oh, and Giles is saying he'd rather not go to Ghent, but I tell him he's got to. He's being high and proud and saying he'll be all right on his own, but he can't. We'd never have a moment's peace.'

73

'Fools that we are,' said Hannah, 'we shouldn't. Still, he's too young to be left yet.' She went into the bathroom. 'I won't be long.'

'Plenty of time.'

When he went down again, he found Giles and the Vennings in colloquy in the hall. 'Oh, Daddy,' Giles called to him, pink in the face, 'Mr and Mrs Venning say they'll look after me while you and Mummy go off. That'll be all right, won't it?'

Gavin hesitated.

'Oh, do let us,' said Verna, who could be good-natured. 'We're going nowhere ourselves and he'll be company for Chloe.'

'But I don't know whether I can put you to all that trouble—'

'What's one boy?' said John. 'The kids'll keep out of our hair.'

'Do you really want to stay, Giles?'

'Please, Daddy.'

Gavin turned to the Vennings. 'Then I suppose I can accept a very kind offer. But mind you give me a bill when you get back.'

'Bill nothing,' said John. 'We shall just go down on the beach and mess about.'

'And golf?' Giles enquired eagerly.

'Golf if you like.'

'Won't you be cold on the beach?' Gavin said to them anxiously. 'It's damned chilly.'

'Oh, we'll wrap up,' said Verna. 'It's sheltered against the windbreaks, if you get on the right side. Has he got a thick sweater?'

'Run for it, Giles, and get your raincoat. You ought to be O.K. This is very kind,' he added to the Vennings.

'Not at all,' said Verna, 'we know you'd do the same for us, if it was a matter of Chloe.'

74

He was not so sure of that.

He returned to Hannah with this fresh news. She was at the dressing-table, brushing her hair. 'Well,' she said, 'I suppose it will be all right. At least we know them, much as I wish we didn't. But we'll be obligated to them, as they say.'

'They're going back to England the day after tomorrow, so there won't be much time to be obligated.'

Taking the brush from her, he kissed the back of her neck. Annoyed with me? I think you are, just a little.'

'When am I ever annoyed with you?'

'On occasion.'

'On rare occasions, then,' She smiled at him in the mirror. He thought that she was still troubled.

But this time, freed from Melissa and the Vennings, and with their consciences easy where Giles was concerned, they set off for Ghent in better spirits than they had to Bruges.

Hannah was determined to enjoy herself, to put all thoughts of the girl behind her. She couldn't pretend that she had not, in fact, felt some touch of jealousy. Gavin, she knew, could be silly sometimes when he took some extra drink; it made him self-conscious at parties, where he would suddenly seem aware of his grace and his good looks, when he would obviously enjoy the admiration of women. She knew, or thought she knew, that he had been faithful to her during the twenty years of their marriage; they had spent few nights apart, and she had always been joyously responsive to his love-making. She knew that the attentions of Melissa had flattered him just a little; she would have been flattered in his case. But it must stop now, it must all stop.

Another day alone together. Bounty.

They went straight to the chapel in Saint-Bavon, where the Van Eyck was. They could hardly see it, so crowded was the room with guided parties; there was a cacophony of French, German and Flemish. Still, they managed to push past the groups and get a clearer view. Each of them had their favourite bits, Hannah the martyrs against their golden hedge, Gavin the madonna herself, with her crown of rubies, sapphires, lilies and roses. A custodian closed the *volets*, so that everyone could see the pear-shaped, mournful Eve with the fruit – not an apple – in her hand, the bearded, handsome Adam, in his eyes all sorrows to come.

Gavin suddenly called out to someone. He plunged into the crowd, returned with a short, red-haired young man.

'My wife. Hannah, this is Dr Crown, a colleague of mine. What on earth are you doing here, Jamie?'

'I might ask you the same. Or no, I mightn't; it's your department rather than mine. But isn't it splendid?'

'So splendid,' said Gavin, 'that I can hardly believe a human hand made it.'

'Do you think it's Supernatural, Mrs Eastwood?' said Crown. He bounced a little on his feet, and seemed a cheerful man.

'I think every great Work of art seems supernatural,' said Hannah. 'I've no creative power myself, I wish I had.'

'That's not true,' Gavin said fondly, 'you used to be creative as a teacher.'

'You know that's not the same thing.'

'Can you both come and have some coffee with me?' Crown asked. 'I'd like that.'

They agreed, and went out to a café. They sat inside, in the leathery brownness, because it was too chilly to be outdoors.

'Do you know a girl called Melissa Hirst?' Gavin asked. 'She's in your department.'

'Certainly I know her. I teach her. Why?'

'She attends my lectures. We came across her at Les Roseaux. Is she any good?'

'Good for a Two-One, just possibly a First. But I think not.'

76

Hannah was listening intently.

'What's she like otherwise?'

'Well, it's hard to say. Thin as a rake, not much personality. Quiet. Works like a beaver. It's all hard work, no real flair. She's an orphan, I believe. No people, or anything.'

'Little Nell,' Hannah murmured, making Gavin jump. She barely sounded hard.

'Oh, no,' said Crown, 'not even an aged grandfather. But I don't think she has a bad time. She lives with two other girls, and she's out and about a bit, I gather. Anyway, at weekends.'

'Do you like her, Jamie?'

Crown looked surprised. 'Like her? I suppose I do. You know, it's nice when they work. Essays in on time, no trouble.'

'I don't think she's altogether devoid of personality,' said Hannah.

The bells of Saint-Bavon clashed and clanged. The sky was clear now, ultramarine, ermined with small white clouds.

'You see,' said Gavin, 'she's attached herself to us somewhat. And however nice a person is, it can be a bit of a bore when you're on holiday.'

Hannah felt a wave of something like resentment, even of pity for Melissa, How mercurial he was! Suddenly to have found her boring, after all the encouragement he had given her. She fancied herself lonely and poor, in a Belgian watering-place, fancied, in her emphatic fashion, the small bleak bedroom, the hours hanging heavy, the constant glances at a watch the hands of which seemed to be unmoving. She determined that she would try to be kind. If this girl was in love with Gavin, so much the worse for her. Before Hannah had met him, she had had a young, greenstick passion which had been denied; she could not forget that, the awful heat, the awful chill. She looked at her husband in a moment's disenchantment, but a moment was all it was.

'Look, I have to be going,' said Crown, 'I'm meeting my wife for lunch. She doesn't like art. She's out shopping.'

'Shopping? In Ghent?' said Hannah.

'Oh, she's an expert at that,' he said. 'Lace, I expect.'

'I don't know what one does with lace these days. One goes to Marks and Spencers for underwear, or I do.'

The Eastwoods had their own lunch, and walked around the Béguinage. Gavin looked at Hannah intently. 'Do you know what?'

'What?'

'You weren't pleased with me a little while ago.'

'Don't be silly.'

'You weren't. It was when we were with Jamie Crown. You didn't like it because I said Melissa was a bore.'

'I only thought that perhaps we ought to be sorry for her.'

'You're something of a saint, aren't you? And saints make me feel very uncomfortable. Why can't you be an ordinary human being, and admit that she annoys you?'

'Because she's young, and I have so much.'

'All the same, we're going to dodge her, if at all possible, which I don't expect it will be. She put me in conceit of myself,' he said honestly, 'and now I'm out of it, and uncommonly wary.'

They arrived back at the Albert earlier than they had expected; Giles and the Vennings were not yet back. In the rack was a letter for them from Giles's headmaster, announcing a move to another building and regretting that the fees were going up. It went on, 'I hope you were satisfied with Giles's report, and that he was pleased. He has been putting his back into it more this term.'

Gavin laughed, and exclaimed. 'So we could have saved ourselves the great drama! Damn it, I wish I'd seen the thing. What shall we tell him?'

'Show him the letter, of course. He'll imagine that his report was better than it could possibly have been, but so much the better. He is a darling,' said Hannah, 'and he deserves that something should go right for him.'

They had half an hour alone before the others came back. Meanwhile, Madame came to them with stately tread, and gave Hannah a small packet. 'This is for you,' she said.

It contained some lace edging, very fine, very old; lace of Bruges.

'We were only talking about lace today!' said Hannah. 'How very kind of you! Thank you so much. It is lovely.'

Madame smiled, and withdrew to her chair which, in her occupancy, always seemed like a throne.

The Vennings came in, without the children. 'We've left them on the golf course,' they explained, 'they won't be ten minutes.'

'Did Giles behave himself?' said Gavin.

'Yes, of course,' said Verna, 'good as gold.'

'He's a queer fellow, though, isn't he?' asked John, crossing his stubby legs in the corduroy trousers, which were yellow this time. 'He and Chloe dug all the morning till Hans came along, and then they gave it up. In the afternoon we played two rounds of golf – God, I was puffed – and then went back to the beach. Your Giles wouldn't play any more but went up to the dunes by himself; he was there for ages. God knows what he does with himself there.'

'He sounds,' said Hannah cautiously, 'as if he'd been a little boorish. Is that so?'

'Of course not,' said Verna, 'it's just that he's something of the cat that walks by himself. Anyway, he and Chloe insisted on having another round before coming in.'

'I owe you for three rounds, then,' said Gavin, 'and Lord knows what for pastries. I take it he's been stuffing himself.'

'You should have seen him!' said John. 'But keep your money. Buy me the next beer when I've had a wash and brush up.'

When the Vennings had gone upstairs, when they had watched to see that Giles was really coming back, and had seen him strolling slowly along with the little girl, they wondered together what charm he could have found on the dunes. Chloe went to her parents, and when they were alone with Giles they asked him.

'Oh, I don't know. I can think up there.'

'What do you think about?' Hannah asked curiously.

'Things. Things I just imagine.'

'I hope you didn't go off too long for yourself. It wouldn't have seemed very polite.'

'I was polite,' said Giles. He seemed far away in a world of his own.

They showed him the headmaster's letter, and at once animation came back into his face. 'Oh, jolly good!'

'We didn't know you'd made this Gargantuan effort,' said Gavin. 'Why didn't you tell us?'

'I wasn't sure anyone would notice it.'

'Darling,' said Hannah, and felt the edge of tears.

'We saw Melissa this afternoon,' he said, 'on the front. But she only waved to us.'

IO

She was awakened at seven by a drumming headache. The pain was so severe that she did not at once think of what had happened the previous night. She reached for the aspirin bottle, took three tablets and lay down again, waiting for the pain to pass. Sleep once more overpowered her, and when she awoke half an hour later her head was a little better.

She would not go with them that day. It would be better not to have the strain of Hannah and the boy, more delightful to her to contemplate in solitude what had occurred. Besides, they would not then be able to say that they had too much of her. Not to see him would be a wrench; but she would have her fantasies, which did not seem to her quite so fantastical as they had been. Several times she changed her mind; first she would go, then she wouldn't. Then she made her decision. She could hear Hannah saying, Must that wretched girl go with us? Well, she would not. It would be a triumph over her.

Dressing slowly, tailing her hair once again into the pronged slide, she looked forward to the reviving coffee. She breakfasted early, and when it was time, went to the telephone. It might be Hannah who answered, or it might be he. When she heard him, she felt her heart slip. In a strangled voice, she told him that she had got a cold. (She could not bear him to think she had drunk too much). She would not be going to Ghent. She heard his sympathy lightly expressed, and thought that perhaps it would be less of a strain on himself if she stayed in Les Roseaux. She said, 'You won't

81

mind, of course,' then could not keep from adding, 'Why should you?' She was sorry the moment she had said it. It seemed to imply an intimacy, perhaps even a plea. But he replied heartily and at once, that it would have been pleasant to have her company. 'Take care of yourself and keep warm.'

As she put the telephone down, she had a sense of desolation. She thought she had been heroic: would he realise that? Or was she cutting off her nose to spite her face?

There would be a long and dreary day ahead of her, in which she could at least do some work, for she had brought several of her course books with her. She tried to concentrate. The headache had almost gone now, but she felt the after-effects of the aspirin. Work, however, was not so easy as all that, since his image persistently came between her and the page. The memory, of his brief kiss was almost palpable and she could not resist, from time to time, putting up her hand to her face. He, too, had been just a little drunk; she realised that; but didn't they say that in wine was truth? He must have meant something by it, he was not the sort of man to kiss everyone, she was sure of it.

You are banking too much upon nothing, the residual voice of common sense said to her. You are sure to be disappointed.

She felt her pulse, which was quick. Denying the voice, she told herself that there had been a breakthrough in their relationship; nothing could alter that. And I love him.

That afternoon she slept again, this time for two hours. It was nearly half-past four. She put on a warm jersey and a raincoat over her jeans and went out. The air struck damp and cold, but the sun had come through again and the poplars were enamelled by it. Going as far as the plage, she looked down over the rail. Despite the chill there were a good many people on the beach, many children playing. She saw the Vennings, sitting with rugs over their knees, and then she saw

Giles, digging in a desultory fashion with Chloe and Hans. So he had not gone. He looked up, caught sight of her and waved. She raised her hand, and passed on.

After dinner, when the sun was setting, she walked up into the town, taking care to hurry past the Albert, not to look for them. A fair was in full swing, naphtha flares under a green sky; the dodgem cars screamed on their overhead rails, and the barkers of the various booths were whipping up custom. Children ate *beignets* or fried potatoes from paper cones, and queued for the helter-skelter. Just beyond the fair, though, near a row of lighted shops, were several vans from which men were unloading incomprehensible paraphernalia. She supposed it was for tomorrow's 'Mechanical Circus,' which she had read about on the bills.

For a moment the effect of gaiety, of excitement, took hold of her. As a child she had loved fairs, had been intrepid on swings and switchbacks. She even spent a few centimes at a sideshow where one caught bouncing balls of many colours in a net, but did not catch enough to win a prize. All at once she felt ecstatically happy. The long day had been endured somehow, and tomorrow she would see him, perhaps on the beach or the golf course, certainly at the Circus. Everyone was sure to go; there was too little entertainment in Les Roseaux for anything new to be resisted. She began to sing under her breath, realising that the tune was one which had come through the piped music on the terrace the night before. A Beatles song, tart and sentimental at the same time. Did he listen to music? Would it mean anything to him? It was rarely that she did not have a tune running through her brain, sometimes one most inapposite to her mood; the Eton Boating Song, or 'Sail, Bonny Boat'.

On her way back, she paused in the darkness of some bushes, and this time she did look across to the Albert, but she could not see him. Dinner was long past, the terrace too crowded for any particular person to be discernible. She went to the beach again, and to the Star Café. Here, there were rows of people sitting motionless, watching television. She found a seat at the back of the room, to be a little out of the range of it, and soon M. Van Damm came to her.

'Good evening, mademoiselle! It hasn't been a very bright day, has it? But it's cleared up now, and it will be lovely tomorrow. You'll see. We never get more than one day's rain here at a time.' Like everyone in the town, he was a meteorological optimist.

She ordered beer. When he brought it, he sat down for a while for a chat. Business had slackened off, and now, despite his dapper cheerfulness, she thought he was looking tired.

'Have you known Mr and Mrs Eastwood long?' he asked her. She knew a stab of joy at the speaking of his name. 'They're old customers of mine.'

'I've known Mr Eastwood for some time,' she said, 'but not very well. I'm just a pupil of his.'

'You are at the University? My elder boy is studying in Brussels. He is reading law.'

She made some comment. She did not want to talk about his son.

'Giles is a nice little boy,' she said, hopefully.

'Very nice, very nicely brought up.'

'You work very hard.'

'Well,' he said, 'you must look at it like this. In October we close for the winter, and we don't open again until Easter. So my wife and I, you see, we have a long rest.'

He told her something of his life. He had been a prisoner-of-war in German and Russian hands, but it had not been too hard for him; he picked up languages very quickly, and had often been used as an interpreter. 'But perhaps I am boring you?'

She assured him that he was not; yet she had to drag the subject back to Gavin. Yes, said Van Damm, they were very nice, very pleasant people, and a handsome couple. 'But you? You are all alone here?'

'More or less, but I don't mind.'

'Mademoiselle would think me impertinent if I told her that a nice young man, now – but I expect there are a hundred young men back in England.'

She passed this off with a joke. 'Well,' he said, 'I am wanted again. You must have a drink with me before you go.'

She accepted it, and sat for half an hour more absorbed in her own thoughts. The end of the day. Deep sleep to come, and then tomorrow.

The next day was fine and warm, the promise of the massed and smoky roses over the sea having been fulfilled. Melissa put on a cotton dress and coiled her hair.

She was on the beach by ten o'clock, though she did not take a chair between the wind-breaks at the foot of the stairs, but chose a shelter further along.

It was not, however, a great while before Giles found her.

'Hullo, Melissa! How's your cold?'

She made some play with a handkerchief. 'Better, thank you, It was one of those one-day affairs. What are you doing with yourself?'

'As I usually do. Dodging Hans,' he added, with a grin. 'Mummy and Daddy are in their usual places. Aren't you coming to join them?'

'Well,' she said, 'I've got some work to do.'

'Work? You mean to say, you work on holiday?'

'Certainly I do,' she said, and put her arm around him.

'Coo, I wouldn't,' he replied. 'But did you hear that I'd got a good report?'

'How should I have heard it?'

'Well, I have. The best in ages.'

She congratulated him.

'I'm going to bathe. soon. Mummy says it's not warm enough yet, but I don't feel it. Are you going to give me a swimming-lesson?'

'I'm afraid I haven't brought my things down.'

'Oh, that's a shame.'

She had the warmth of his body, delicate and small, in the crook of her arm. So like Gavin, in the cut of his head, the set of his shoulders. He would be a graceful man. He went away, and shortly afterwards Gavin and Hannah came to her.

She saw them out of the corner of her eye, but would not look up from her book until they were upon her.

'Well!' Hannah was breezy. 'How's the cold? We were so sorry for you.'

Again she made play with a handkerchief, and answered them as she had answered Giles.

'Mind you don't catch another one,' said Gavin, 'we can't have that.' He was breezy too; well, as they were, so should she be. He took the book from her. '*Beowulf*! Labouring in the vineyard?'

There seemed almost a vulgarity in his heartiness. She felt her legs trembling even as she sat.

'We won't disturb you then. Are you coming to this grand circus tonight? God knows what it will be like, though.'

'Nonsense,' said Hannah, 'it will be superlative. You'll see.'

'I expect I'll be coming,' Melissa said.

'We'll probably see you there, then,' said Gavin, 'even if we don't before. Good-bye for now. We mustn't interrupt this hive of industry.'

She thought that they were giving a display of solidarity aimed against her. To avoid them that afternoon, she went by a circuitous route to the hills behind the town, and there she lay under the trees watching the sun shifting between the leaves and giving herself up to her imaginings. This time she went further than the embrace and the impassioned kiss; they were together, naked, in the high bright room and he was making love to her, gently at first, and then to the piercing climax. She was carried away by this to the point of shock, almost shocked to her senses: she sat up. She was surrounded by a crowd of children from the local orphanage, in charge of a teacher. They played touch around her in their yellow, blue and red jerseys, crying in their little shrill voices. When they had been called together and shepherded on, she lay down again and tried not to think at all.

It was almost nine o'clock before she went to the market-place. Everyone seemed to be there, and the noise was deafening. There was a kind of low metal caterpillar built along three sides of it, and on this a team of motor-cyclists, helmeted and goggled, were screeching and roaring round, as though dangerously stunting. In the middle of the square they had erected a great ship's mast, painted crimson. It towered against the paling sky, the top of it floodlit from a window over the chemist's shop, and at the foot stood Captain Keppel, as she supposed him to be, who was acting as a kind of ring-master. He was a short, strong, bandy man with fierce black eyebrows; he wore a white sailor's suit and a cap with gold braid.

Melissa looked about her, flinching at the din. Yes, there they all were in the front row of benches, Hannah and Gavin, the Vennings, the Fischers, and the three children. Hannah saw her. She cupped her hands to her mouth and shouted something. Melissa approached them.

'We've kept a seat for you,' Hannah managed to make herself heard. 'Move up, Gavin.'

He did move, making a seat for Melissa at the end of the row, on his right side. She sat down, wriggling to the extreme edge of the bench in an effort not to touch him. Memories of the afternoon's fantasy made her hot, tremulous, ashamed.

'We thought you weren't coming,' he said to her, easily.

' I forgot the time. Aren't they making a dreadful noise?'

'I think they're super,' Giles yelled across to her.

The motor-cyclists were doing somersaults now, revving their engines to ear-splitting roars. The crowd ooh'd and aah'd, standing up in their seats with excitement, and to get a better view. A tram clanged and clanked along the tracks.

'It's a bit on the monotonous side, isn't it?' said Gavin. 'But I expect Captain Keppel is going to do a grand turn of his own, as climax.'

Chloe edged along the row, to get out. 'It's giving me a headache. I don't like it. I'm going back to the hotel.'

'You'll miss the best part of it,' Verna yelled to her, 'but have it your own way.'

There was a sudden pause. A group of scurrying men were doing something or other to the caterpillar.

Hans was heard to say that he never had headaches. 'That is nothing to be proud of,' said his mother, 'that is something for which you must thank the good God.'

Now the sky was flushed by an apricot afterglow, and the rooftops stood black against it. A small band had burst into noise, marking the interval. The top of the mast, immeasurably high, glistened in the floodlight.

'How did the work go?' Hannah said, leaning over Gavin. Her tone was still motherly. Melissa thought, he could not possibly have told her. That was between him and me.

'Quite well. But you're right. *Beowulf* did seem rather deadly.'

The caterpillar burst-into violent flames, streaming up in yellow and orange, illuminating the faces of the crowd. Captain Keppel rapped out an order in Flemish. At once the cyclists sprang to their machines and went leaping through the fire. The sight of them was spectacular, even horrific, and one or two women cried out; but they seemed indestructible.

88

'Better them than me,' said Gavin. 'I should prefer a push-bike, without Gehenna.'

She was allowing herself to touch him now. She could feel the length of his arm against her own. Almost content, she wished the moment could go on for ever.

The flame riders, to applause and whistles, finished their turn. 'Now what?' said Hannah.

The fires were extinguished, making everything dark. The band played a drum-roll. Then the whole of the mast was lit up, and Captain Keppel stood glittering at the foot of it. The drum-roll continued, muffled. He saluted the crowd with grandiloquence and began to climb. The audience was hushed.

Melissa followed him with her eyes. Up and up he went, a figure tinier and tinier as he climbed the rigging. Her imagination was seized and grew wild. She would climb like that; all things were possible.

He was nearly at the top of the mast, this time no bigger than a doll. He attained it. He bowed. The drums ceased. Very slowly he turned over and stood on his head, Ms legs scissoring in and out. The applause this time was tumultuous.

'But,' said Gavin, 'if he is a sailor, heights shouldn't trouble him, and he could as soon stand on his head up there as anywhere else.'

'Don't be cynical,' said Hannah, clapping with the others. 'I think he's wonderful.'

The sky was dark now, the last of the sun drained away. The little figure continued for some minutes to scissor its legs, then straightened them out, and became a spire on a spire.

'An extraordinary way to make a living,' said Gavin.

Melissa was up there with Captain Keppel; she had attained. At last he reversed himself and stood upright, bowed again to the applause and then the band playing, ran down the mast, as agile as a monkey. The show was over.

'Well, I don't know that it was so very much,' said Verna, 'I like a circus with clowns and animals.'

'Don't be a fool,' her husband said, 'you knew that this was to be a mechanical one. You can't have mechanical elephants.'

They all began to make their way back towards the beach road. 'Come and have a nightcap with us,' Hannah said kindly to Melissa.

'Thank you, but it's rather late—'

'Do,' said Gavin, 'its only a litde after ten.'

As she went with them, she craned her head back to look once more at the miraculous mast. She would never forget it; it would be something he and she had shared. Gazing up, her head over her shoulders, she did not see where she was going.

She caught her foot on a tramline, and fell heavily.

II

As they all ran to pick her up she thought, They will think I did it on purpose.

But as Gavin and John Venning hauled her to her feet, she yelped in pain and collapsed into their arms. 'I've managed to wrench it,' she said.

She stood on one foot, unable to touch the other to the ground. None of them knew what to do for her.

'I expect it's only a sprain, not a break,' said Hannah, though they can be nasty. Can you move at all?'

'I think I could hop,' said Melissa, clenching her teeth. She felt the sweat break out on her forehead.

Gavin said, 'We'd better get a cab for you. But there won't be one in the square. If you leaned on my shoulder, do you think you could get as far as the Albert? We could telephone from there, or Armand might run you back in his car.'

The thought of putting her arm round his shoulders was so delicious that for a moment it overcame the pain; but Venning was quick. 'She'd do better if she leant on me,' he said, 'I'm shorter than you are.'

In bitter disappointment she allowed herself to throw her weight on him. She took a hop or two forward.

'I'll come on your other side,' Gavin said. 'It's not far.'

But the way seemed interminable. She had to stop almost every other minute to catch her breath. The smell of Venning's coat, the rough feel of it, were hideous to her. She was hardly aware of Gavin supporting her in her right armpit.

At last they came to the Albert. They helped her up the steps to the open terrace, where they sat her down, putting up her feet on a chair. The infra-red heating was working and it was not cold.

'I'll get you a drink first,' Gavin said, 'and talk to Armand at the same time. You need one.'

'You didn't half crash,' said Giles, staring down at her.

Hannah told him to go upstairs to bed.

She knelt down to inspect Melissa's foot. It was swollen and so was the ankle. She felt it gently, and Melissa shuddered at her touch. 'Don't worry, I won't hurt you. I did a little nursing before I taught.' She frowned. 'I don't think anything's broken, but I do think you'd better see a doctor.'

'Tomorrow will do.'

'But it'll have to be bandaged tonight.'

Armand came out, all concern, with a glass of brandy. 'I will take you back to the Colombes in my car, if you'll wait for a few minutes. I must get it out of the garage.'

Hannah asked whether he had anything in the way of bandages in the hotel, and he said he would look in the medicine cupboard. 'My mother may have one.'

Melissa drank gratefully. She was aware of them all crowding around her, but Gavin was the only one she could see clearly. He seemed to be ringed in a light of his own.

'Look, I shall go back with you,' said Hannah, 'and get you into bed. You can't do it by yourself.'

'But I'd much rather you didn't.' The thought that this woman should touch her flesh was unendurable.

'Don't be silly. There's nobody there to help you, is there?'

'Perhaps Madame Poiret—'

'From what I know from a glimpse of her,' said Hannah, 'she'd be no more use than a sick headache.'

'We are truly sorry,' said Frau Fischer. Her husband was hardly known to speak at all. 'What a misfortune!'

'It'll be down tomorrow, you'll see,' said John Venning, and Verna agreed that this would be so.

'She made a big bang,' said Hans, 'I saw her.' He, too, was sent off to bed.

Melissa wished they would all go away. Her foot did not pain her much while she had it up on a chair; but in fact, she did not know how she was to do without help.

She did not have to. Armand came along with the car, and he and Hannah helped her into it.

'Can I be of any use?' Gavin asked, standing at the head of the steps.

'Not in the least,' said Hannah, 'I can cope.'

They drove off in the dark, the short journey to Byronlaan.

As usual, there was a light only in the hall, and Madame Poiret opened up to them with obvious reluctance. Hannah told her what had happened. 'I'm going to put her to bed now, and I'll send a doctor tomorrow. Will you have her breakfast taken up to her room? M. Croisset, perhaps you'll help me up the stairs with her. Which room is it?'

'Second on the left,' said Madame Poiret. She greeted Armand, whom of course she knew, rather sourly.

Between the two of them, they managed to help her up; and Armand left them.

'Now then,' said Hannah, with a bluff, nurselike manner. 'You sit there on the edge of the bed, and I'll get your things off.'

'I think I can manage.'

'No, you can't. Stockings first.' She made a face as she saw the puffy redness of the flesh. 'Come on, now your dress. I'm glad you weren't in those tight jeans.'

Melissa tried not to let her mind dwell on the stripping, on her own meagre breasts exposed for the moment before the nightdress fell over them.

93

'You lie back while I bandage this as best I can. I expect I'm out of practice. – Too tight?'

'No.'

'Sure?'

'Quite sure.'

'Tuck down, then. We'll put your foot outside the bedclothes, it will be more comfortable. Aspirin? – Yes, I see you've got some. You'd better take three.'

'You're very kind,' Melissa said with an effort. It had all been horrible, the pulling-down, however decorously, of her pants, the exposure of her flat stomach, her thin shoulders. She knew the repugnance of the flesh.

'Comfortable as you can be?' The nurselike manner was complete; it was not so that Hannah had spoken to her husband. She too, Melissa knew, was embarrassed, that she too was hating this. 'Then I'll be getting off. I do hope you have a good night. We'll send the doctor round to you about half-past nine.'

'Thank you.'

At the door Hannah turned, smiled and waved. 'Bless you, then, and try to sleep.'

Alone again, Melissa moved her foot. The bandage *was* too tight; it sent shoots of pain up her leg. She fiddled with it, slackened it a little, then lay down again, a little easier. But it must get well quickly, she thought, or what am I to do? Lie in this featureless room, hour after hour? And if I have all my meals sent up, it will cost me more than I can afford. She burst into tears. They were a source of relief for everything which had happened that day, the dream on the hills, the soaring dream of Captain Keppel's mast, the accident at the tram-lines, the torturing journey to the Albert. She cried until her pillow was wet, and she had to turn it over. It was a long while before she got to sleep, comforted only by the thought that on the morrow he would surely look in to see how she did.

94

In the morning, the doctor came. He was blond, semibald, had a double-chinned face like an inverted pear, and spoke tolerable English. He was Armand Croisset's own doctor.

Not fully revived even by her breakfast, Melissa let him deal with her. After examination, he said there were no bones broken, and strapped her foot expertly for her. What he would like her to do, whenever she could bear it, was to try to walk on it: he believed she had friends in Les Roseaux: could they, perhaps, get her a stick?

When he had done, she asked what she owed him. She asked it in trepidation.

But he would take no money. 'We must send our visitors home well, must we not?'

She thanked him elaborately, for she had been afraid of his bill.

'I will call upon you at this time tomorrow, and we shall see how you are then.'

She heard him talking to Madame Poiret in the hall, and heard his car drive away.

Sitting cautiously on the edge of the bed, she swung her feet down. The sprained foot was less swollen, but she could only stand on the toes of it. She got back between the sheets.

In a little while she heard the bang of the front door, and Gavin's voice. Not Hannah's. She felt the blush rise over her face and down her neck. She waited for his knock.

He called to her. Could he come in? She tried to answer him in a natural voice. 'Wait just a minute,' she said, and groped for her cardigan. 'It's all right now.'

He was wearing an emerald tie, broad and flowing. At first he seemed to be alone; but behind him was Giles.

'How nice of you!' said Melissa, the blush subsiding. She could have cried out with this fresh disappointment.

He said it was not nice at all, that he had simply looked in to see how she was. 'We're on our way to golf. What did the doctor say?'

Giles, who seemed impatient, greeted her briefly and went to stand by the window.

She told Gavin the doctor's opinion.

'That's good. Hannah sends her best wishes. Old Madame Croisset had a bit of a turn this morning – nothing much, I fancy – but Hannah thinks she ought to sit with her for a while. She'll be calling in on you this afternoon.'

Now he was here, she did not know what to say to him. His thoughts did not show on his good-looking face, which remained cheerful and bland. If only there could have been some tension between them! But all the tension was flowing outward from herself.

'This is rough luck on you,' he went on.

She pointed to the chair, on which Hannah had neatly folded her clothes. 'If you take those off, you could sit down.'

He did so, then seemed at a loss.

Melissa told him, for the sake of something to say, that the doctor had said she should have a stick. Then, perhaps, she could manage to walk a little.

Giles turned from the window. 'I can get her a stick! They've got them in the souvenir shop. I could run up there and back in no time!'

Hope filled her. But she said, 'You mustn't do that. No, Giles.'

'Do let me go, Daddy. I won't be long, I promise!'

He looked doubtful, and, somehow trapped; but it was obvious that he did not know how to refuse.

'Daddy, please.'

'Oh, all right, if you really do run.'

'Let me give you some money,' said Melissa, 'I don't know what a stick would cost. Could you pass me my bag, Gavin? It's just behind you.'

His name had slipped out before she could check it. She

96

looked at him in fear, but he seemed to have noticed nothing.

'I'll give him the money,' he said, 'and you can pay me later.'

Taking some francs from his pocket, he gave them to Giles. 'Cut along, now, and be as quick as you can.'

When they were alone, she held her breath.

'Do you mind if I have a cigarette?' he said.

She said no, of course not. She would have one too. The smoke calmed her nerves: she drew deeply, and inhaled it.

Outside the window, the sky was bright. It would be another warm day.

He asked, 'How old are you, Melissa? Twenty-one? Two?'

It was the first personal thing he had ever said to her.

She told him. 'No great age,' he said. 'I wish I were twenty-one again. I admit that I don't like being elderly. Such a dreadful word.'

'You're not elderly,' she whispered, 'or I don't think so.'

'The generation gap,' he said lightly, 'it weighs on one.'

'I don't believe in a generation gap,' said Melissa, 'I think it's all a matter of talk.'

'Maybe. Oddly enough, I don't feel any gap between Giles and me. I expect I shall when he's fifteen or so. The awkward age.'

What was he trying to do? To speak in intimacy, or to make an unbridgeable gulf between them?

He changed the subject. 'Have you got anything to read? I don't expect you'll feel like *Beowulf* today.'

She said she had brought nothing else with her.

'Well,' he said, 'take Ngaio Marsh. Hannah has finished with it, and I haven't started. No, you needn't worry; we always take a book bag with us. I've got Ruskin, and another Trollope.'

She thanked him.

97

He said abruptly, 'I worry about you, you know.'

'Why? Just because I've sprained my ankle?'

'No, not that. But you do seem solitary. Perhaps you like it that way. Where do you live in London?'

'With, two other girls.'

He didn't tell her that he had already heard.

She saw that he pitied her, and was glad. Pity was better than nothing, and pity might lead to something more. She brushed the long, light hair back from her face, and waited.

'That sounds all right. And one of these days, I expect you'll get married.'

'I don't think I shall.'

'Oh, come! Marriage is a splendid thing. At least, Hannah and I have found it so.'

He was trying to tell her something, and she did not want to hear it. Putting down the instinct to cry, she assured herself that even this show of interest in her affairs had been encouraging. After this morning, things would not be quite as they had been between them. She did not reply to him. Leaning forward a little, he peered into her face.

'Woebegone?'

'No.'

'I know it's tough on you, stuck in here. But you'll be miles better tomorrow.'

'Mr Eastwood,' she began, not knowing what she was to say but hoping the words would come.

'You can call us Gavin and Hannah, if you like,' he said.

This was so wonderful a concession, that she felt the blush rise again.

'Gavin,' she said.

'Do you know, I'm more than old enough to be your father? More than old enough.'

'Why do you say that?'

'I don't quite know. Age weighs on me this morning.' He cocked an ear. 'Is that Giles?'

But they still had time left to them.

'Shall you come to my lectures next term? I'm giving a course on the Sienese painters. They're so magnificent, and so few.'

'I don't know,' she said, 'I've got to get my nose to the grindstone.'

The minutes ticked away.

He said, 'You always seem to be on your own at the college. I never see you talking to anybody after lectures. You just pack up and go. There are plenty of people around.'

The thought that he had observed so much emboldened her. She said in a whisper, 'I don't go to see people.'

'You just come for art's sake,' he said, with an attempt at heartiness.

'Not only that.'

He did not say, as she had hoped, "What, then?" Had he done so, she believed she could have answered.

'You've no parents, have you?'

'No.'

'You must be lonely. I don't like to think of that.'

'Not when you are here. And Hannah,' she added.

And then Giles did come back with the stick. He was hot with running.

'Oh, you are kind!' she exclaimed. 'I'm so grateful to you, Giles. How much did it cost?'

He told her.

'You can pay me tomorrow,' Gavin said. 'Don't bother about it now. Well, we must go. We'll see you again.'

He had been, and now was gone. It was Sunday morning, and church bells were ringing far off. She went back again over every word he had said to her, trying to recapture the sound of his voice, weighing his meanings.

She managed, with the aid of the stick, to walk a few paces across the room to the mirror. Sitting before it, she found she had a long smudge of ash down the side of her nose, and she wondered how long it had been there. She scrubbed it off.

'Will mademoiselle be having her lunch up here?' asked the maid, who had just come into the room.

Melissa said no; she would get downstairs somehow. It seemed to her imperative that she should make a complete recovery as soon as possible. It was not far to the beach; next morning she would try to go there, if only as far as M. Van Damm's. For the rest of this day there would be nothing, only the church-bells, the unwanted visit by Hannah.

Why should he have said so much about age? She thought she knew, prayed that she was mistaken. He was trying, in his gentle way, *to discourage her.* Then had he suspected? But she had wanted him to suspect. It was now no longer enough for her, as she had imagined that it would be, just to love him.

12

Hannah had returned from her afternoon visit. She and Gavin were sitting on the beach.

'She was stiff with me, I'm afraid. Oh, dear, she is becoming an embarrassment!'

'I don't see,' said Gavin, 'what we can do but show her a sort of hearty united front, as you suggested that we should do.'

The sea was calm and it was still warm, but the clouds were gathering and the blueness had gone from the wet sands. 'It's going to rain again, I suppose,' said Hannah, 'but I don't think just yet.'

'Listen.' He turned upon her a look both comical and apprehensive. 'I tried to put her off this morning.'

Hannah banged her book shut. 'Have you been the soul of indiscretion again? I bet you have. What did you say?'

'I told her how old I was and how young she was, and hinted that she ought to get married. Do you suppose she can build anything on that?'

'Yes, I do suppose so! It was a pity you had to be alone with her. You could have perfectly well have gone with Giles to get her damned stick.'

'Don't be cross with me. I'd only been there five minutes then, and I couldn't see any way out of staying. Giles was getting fretful, too; you know how children hate anything in the way of a sick-room. For that matter, so do I.'

'I'm not cross with you, but I suspect that you were very

silly. You know, you can't help being just a little flattered by the whole thing, can you?'

He paused a while before replying. 'Let me search my soul. Yes, I suppose I am, in the most ignoble part of me. I am nearly fifty, and it *is* a bit flattering to be claimed by youth.'

'I think you are the most honest man I ever knew,' said Hannah, and this time she smiled at him.

'Let's hope her foot keeps her out of the way for some time,' Gavin said callously.

'It won't. She'd crawl on all fours for you.'

'You are cross.'

'Not with you. But with her I am.' She added, 'and for something she can't possibly help, I know that. I, too, used to have a funny feeling when I heard your key in the door. For that matter, darling, I still do.'

He took her hand for a moment. 'Let's not think of her any more.'

'But I have been a little cruel,' said Hannah. Indeed, she was having a struggle with herself. It was preposterous to suppose that he would respond in any way to a girl nearly thirty years younger than he; she was in no way threatened. But in the even tenor of their marriage, nothing of the sort had ever happened before. Though she thought little of her person, she was vain about her capacity for empathy. She tried, though it was an effort, to put herself in Melissa's place. Suppose I wanted him, and could never have him? Damn, here comes Verna.

Verna was alone; she told him that John had wanted another round of golf. 'But What he sees in that game, potting a ball through those ridiculous hoops and drain-pipes, I shall never know.' She plumped down. 'Well, here today and literally gone tomorrow. Back to the grind. Do you know, he always does all the packing? He says I'm no good at it, which is a comfort. Has anyone seen Melissa today?'

'We've both looked in,' said Hannah. 'She's getting about a little with a stick.'

Verna pulled some swatches of brocade from her beach-bag and studied them frowningly. 'You know,' she said to Hannah, 'I sometimes think John and I are losing our grip. Not being quite with it. Oh, we like to dress trendily, but I'm sometimes aware that our slang is a bit old-fashioned, and that the trendier jobs don't come to us. Tell me, which of these would you choose for a set of fake William and Mary dining-room chairs? The walls are white, and the carpet's dark grey.'

Hannah pored over them for a while, then returned to her book. She thought she began to understand what had made her become friendly to Verna the summer before.

An hour passed. Verna looked at the sky. 'Blast it, it's going to rain again. I don't want to be caught. I'm going up for some tea. Are you two coming?'

'We'll follow you,' said Gavin, 'we have to collect Giles first.'

'John and I had a week in Tunisia last winter. Now that *was* weather. Well, see you.'

They watched her as she made her way up the beach. 'And by the by,' said Gavin, 'where the devil is Giles?'

They stood up, and shading their eyes, inspected the foreshore. The cloudbank was heavy now, and the light upon the flat miles of coast might have been cast by the moon rather than by the sun.

'I think I saw him go towards the dunes,' said Hannah. 'We should have kept him in sight. What a worry he is! Though what harm he can come to, I don't know.'

'Listen' said Gavin, 'I'm going to spy on that boy. There's some attraction up there, and I want to know what it is. You wait here, and if he comes your way, get a grip of him.'

They knew the old fret of worrying about Giles; he was always getting lost, or, at least, taking his time even when sent on the simplest errand. They were eternally torn by the desire not to coddle him and the desire to protect him at every turn. There had been the dreadful business of whether or not to let him have a bicycle; even now, he was only allowed to ride in one or two side-streets.

Gavin went up the slope on to the dunes. Already a few big black drops of rain were falling, making miniature craters in the sand. He had to walk quite a way, his apprehension growing with every step, until he saw him at last, crouched in a hollow, apparently trying to catch something again and again, and talking to himself. He was a small and solitary figure, nobody else near him.

Gavin moved softly. The boy was not talking to some imaginary being, he was counting aloud: '– five, six, seven, eight.'

'What are you doing?'

The boy jumped violently. He turned round and saw his father. 'You needn't have come up here,' he said, as if with hostility.

'You've been gone ages, and it's going to pour. Don't you want some tea?'

He saw that Giles was playing with jacks, little metal objects taking a dull glow from the sky.

'Where did you get those?'

No answer.

'I said, where did you get those?'

'Oh, I just found them.' Sulkily he exhibited a small cotton bag. He began to gather the jacks together into it.

'Buck up.'

'I can't find one of them.'

'Then you must let it go. Do come on, we're going to be drenched.'

'I was all right,' Giles muttered, 'I'd have come down soon.'

Gavin said, 'Why don't you want me to come here?'

'Because.' Giles rose and began to walk along with him, turning back now and then as if reluctant to be gone.

'Look here, old boy, "because" isn't enough of an answer.'

He could hardly catch the reply. He bent down. 'What did you say?'

'It's my place.'

'I see. Private?'

Silence.

'Well, I don't mean to poach on your preserves, however odd they may be, but your mother and I were getting worried about you.'

'You're always worrying.'

It was the tone rather than the words that Gavin found irritating. 'You're being rude. What would you think of us if we never cared where you were?'

'I'd be all right.'

They returned to Hannah, who scolded Giles and then tried to comfort him with the promise of pastries. They gathered up their beach things, their bags, books and towels, and just gained the shelter of the café before the rain fell heavily. Verna and John were at a table for two, and the only other table free was at the far end of the room. The Eastwoods were relieved that they had not to join them.

Giles went up to brood over the jewelled counter.

'Just what was he doing?' she said.

'Playing with some jacks. He didn't like me to come for him, he said it was his "place". He got into something which, in a less quiet child, I should have called a tantrum.'

'I don't know,' said Hannah, 'when I was little I often used to have "places" of my own. The desire for privacy comes in very young, and I suppose he has as much right to it as anyone else.'

Aimé Van Damm came by, rushed as ever, but he paused by their table. 'Very disappointing,' he said, indicating the rain that was coursing down on to the terrace, 'but it won't last long. You'll see. Where is Mademoiselle Hirst?' Like Armand Croisset, he never forgot a name. 'I haven't seen her today.'

They told him of her accident, and he commiserated. 'But it may not be very bad,' he said with professional optimism, 'these things clear up quickly.'

Giles returned to them, his plate laden with a slice of cherry tart and *mille-feuilles*. He seemed to have forgotten all about the incident on the dunes.

'I tell you what,' said Gavin to his wife, 'if it does clear up, I think we'd better go and look in on Melissa after dinner.'

'No, you *won't*,' she said, 'we've done quite enough for one day.'

His smile was sheepish.

M. Van Damm had been right; after the heavy storm the sun shone again, and when they came out on to the terrace they found the stones steaming from the heat of it. They walked up into the town. The mast had been taken down, the caterpillar dismantled and packed into trucks.

'I thought it was super,' said Giles with a sigh of regret. 'I wish he'd come and do it again. Perhaps I'll see him next year. May I play golf before dinner? They've got something called a *carbonnade* tonight. What's that?'

'I'll come and have a round with you if you like,' Gavin said. 'I don't suppose the rain's made it too tacky. It only lasted for about twenty minutes.'

While they were getting clubs and balls, they saw two men making their way to the first tee. Both were dressed in bright jackets and striped trousers, both wore small flat caps. Both were fat. They were carrying their own clubs, which seemed to be specially designed for them.

'Experts,' said Hannah, who was not playing herself. 'We shall see something now.'

The taller of the two men teed his ball, and addressed it with a double-ended club, which he waggled intently back and forth, looking towards the hazard and back again, taking his time. Obviously an expert.

'Let's start on the second hole,' said Giles, 'they're going to be all night.'

'No, wait,' said Gavin, 'this I must see.'

At last the expert hit the ball, and sliced it. It did not even hit the hazard; it jumped over on to the grass verge.

Giles gave a yelp of laughter, which was rewarded by a glare. 'Sh-sh,' said Hannah. 'You mustn't.'

The second man, after interminable delay, took his shot. This one did hit the hazard, rolling back precisely on to the tee. Giles was in fits of silent mirth.

They watched until they had both taken five shots apiece.

'So much for experts,' said Gavin. 'You're right, we'd better go ahead. We'll start at the third, and play the first two off at the end of the round.'

As they drove off, he felt very happy, very much father-and-son. The boy certainly had a knack; they would have him taught to play real golf one of these days. It was useful to have at least one game in one's power. He watched as Giles climbed the mound from which it was necessary to take a chip shot on to the green; this was always a difficult one. But Giles got the ball cleanly on to the bank which surrounded the hole, and it ran within a few inches of it.

'Well done.' Gavin took his own turn, but went straight into the bunker. He felt all the proud sweetness of being bested by his own son.

The moments of perfect felicity in this life come unexpectedly, and seem to be without causation. So Hannah thought that evening, as she went to tuck Giles into bed. He was already undressed and Hans had left him. 'I've had a bath,' he said.

'So I see.' She went to pick up his clothes from the floor and the wet towels.

When she came back he opened his arms to her. He smelled, he was very fresh, with the freshness of soap and youth. She felt a wave of great love, of protectiveness. She kissed him.

'Mummy,' he said, 'Mummy.'

Life must be made easy for him; the sun must not shine too hot nor the wind blow too cold. She caressed his small-boned arms, smoothed the hair back from his brow. She put her lips to the palm of his hand.

'Mummy. What are you and Daddy going to do?'

'Just sit by ourselves. Thank Heavens the Vennings have gone out.'

'Don't you like them?' His sweet breath rose to her nostrils.

'Don't you think they're a little noisy? I don't care for them very much.'

'Then I don't either. I like people you like, and I don't like people you don't.' He was trying to make her talk, to delay the hour of sleep a little.

'Good. That will do for now, but you'll feel different later. You'll have your own likes and dislikes.'

'No, I won't.'

She kissed him again, tucked his arms away beneath the sheet. 'Good-night, Sleep well.'

'The golf was fun today. I liked those silly men.'

'Yes. Good-night, my darling.'

Outside the door, she hesitated for a moment or two, not knowing why. Then she heard his feet crossing the floor, saw the light spring up in the glass panel above the door. She waited. There was a long pause. Then she heard, Click, click, click: and the murmur of his voice. She opened the door again, and he started guiltily.

'Giles!'

He was playing with his jacks. 'Only one more game. Then 'll go to bed, I promise, really I promise.'

She thought for a moment. 'Well, just for this once I'm going to let you. I feel very happy tonight, for some unknown reason, and you shall have the benefit of it. Hurry up, now; I shall send Daddy in fifteen minutes to see you really are down.'

'You don't want to disturb yourself, Mummy. I can look after myself.' He sounded very grown-up.

'Perhaps you can. We'll see. Good-night again, then.'

She went down to Gavin.

'Think of it,' he said, 'no Melissa, no Vennings. And no Vennings at all from tomorrow on.'

'Yes,' she said, 'it's peace. What a wonderful evening!' It was encrusted with stars, and smelled of the sea. 'Isn't he a lamb?'

'Who, Giles? That goes without saying. Though he'll grow up to be a sheep, and don't you forget it.'

They were both so filled with happiness, with a sense of celebration, that they had a bottle of wine brought out to them on the terrace. 'We only had a half-bottle at dinner,' he said, 'so we're not really sousing. What shall we do tomorrow?'

'Well, after we've paid a call on Melissa – I suppose we must – I thought we might take the tram to Knokke, or somewhere like that, just for the ride.'

He thought it a good idea.

'Perhaps you'd better go up to Giles and see that he's in bed,' she said, 'I left him playing with his jacks. I felt indulgent tonight.'

'Perhaps I had.'

When he came back to her he said, 'All well. All quiet. All dark. I gave him a hug and he said, "You smell of drink." I felt degraded.'

'Let's both be degraded for once,' said Hannah. 'Anyway, we're not really.'

They sat so long over their wine that the crowd on the terraces and in the bar had thinned before they had finished it. 'We are having a good holiday, after all.'

'Nothing shall spoil it for us.'

13

That afternoon she read a little of the detective story and wrote a letter to each of her flat-mates. They would not be here when she returned; better off than she, they were taking their holidays in Norway. She mentioned her accident, but said nothing about meeting the Eastwoods.

Time hung down like a curtain unstirred by a breeze. She tried to read some more, but could not; her mind went back again and again to what had happened that morning, and the more she thought about it, the more meaningful it appeared to be. When at last six o'clock came she thought she would make the effort to dress for dinner, though nobody at the Pension des Colombes did so. Hobbling to her wardrobe, she took out the black dress. She fancied he had liked her in it; his eyes had seemed to admire. Surely he – or they, for he could not come again alone – would call on her that evening? After all, there could be nothing else for them to do. This time she used a little colour on her cheeks as well as on her lips, for she was very pale. Idleness and emotion had exhausted her, making her feel that the second journey downstairs would be almost more than she could achieve. She just managed to squeeze a sandal over her bandaged foot, letting the straps hang loose.

When at last she made the difficult descent, clinging closely to the banisters, and went into the dining-room, she saw that there was a young man sitting at her table, with Madame Poiret standing by.

Madame explained. The young monsieur had just come from Brussels, the room was full and there was nowhere else for him to sit. Would mademoiselle mind sharing, just for this one meal?

Melissa said no. He had risen to his feet, was beaming at her and introducing himself. 'Bob Conrad,' he said.

She responded.

'Here, let me help you, let me take your stick. There! I'll hang it on the back of the chair.'

He was of about her own age, an inch or two shorter. He was pretty rather than handsome, bullet-headed, with a turned up nose and fine blue eyes, dark enough to appear black. His light hair was cut short, growing in a Caesarian fashion over his brows. His tight striped jersey displayed a well-muscled body beneath.

Solicitous, he had her seated. 'I hope you really don't mind. But I only came here by chance. I'm on a hitch-hike. I've been through France and Belgium, and I'm going on to Holland and Germany.'

She asked him how he had found the pension.

'I called in at the Syndicat d'Initiative. It seemed about the cheapest place they'd got.' Then he seemed to realise that this might in some way be uncomplimentary to her, making her feel that she, too, was doing things cheaply. 'Not all that cheap, of course,' he added, 'but it's bang in the season.'

He had a direct stare, which seemed to have liking in it.

First he wanted to know how she had come by her accident. Then, plainly given to chatter, he told her that he was at the London School of Economics – 'but I don't demonstrate, I'm too lazy' – and that he was, in fact, nearly twenty-two. He lived in digs with a friend called Oliver. 'I haven't any right to be away at all, we've both got our Finals coming next year, and Oliver is spending the vacation swotting himself silly. But I couldn't resist it. Wanderlust.'

She told him, then, about herself, where she was studying, what she was doing.

After the potato soup, came *blanquette de veau*. 'A white sort of meal, don't you think?' he said. 'But I'm starved.' He ate hungrily, had a second helping. 'Rough luck on you,' he went on – they had all said this – 'being crocked up like that.'

'I'll get to the beach tomorrow, I think, or at least to the café on the promenade. It really isn't far.'

'Are you all alone here?' His manner was concerned, just a little flirtatious.' It can't be much fun.'

She replied a little shortly that she had friends in the town. 'How long are you staying?'

'Well, I can do with a short rest. Three nights. Four. Five. No, I don't suppose so much as five.'

He looked round, to catch a glimpse of the pudding. It was a rice tart, and he ate two helpings.

Afterwards – 'Do you smoke?'

'I won't take yours,' she said.

'Oh come, please. Pretty please.'

Coffee was put on the table; nobody used the small parlour until the meal was quite over. She hoped he would go away soon. She did not want Gavin to find anyone with her, lest he thought she had taken her mind from him. And she wanted him to know this could never, never happen, not so long as she lived. Yet again: this young man seemed to be taken with her, and would it not be good for Gavin to see that she, too, could be admired? She even had a fleeting thought that he might feel a touch of jealousy.

Conrad followed her into the little parlour, bearing the rest of his coffee with him, a course somewhat disapproved by Madame Poiret, since it meant that the maid might have another room to clear. It was a dingy room, papered in beige, with orange-painted tables somewhat scratched, and easy chairs, the springs sagging, of which the colours had long smudged together.

'Do you mind if I stick with you for a bit?' he asked her. 'I don't want to go out, anyway, not yet, and it's nice to have somebody to talk to.'

'It's a beautiful night,' she said.

'It will keep.'

He began to talk about the things that had happened to him on his journeys. He was an amusing talker, apparently in a permanent state of euphoria. 'And here was I, ten miles out of Paris, in the middle of the night, laden like a pack-mule, with not a hitch to be had. So when I saw a light in a house in the middle of a field, I went there and knocked up the household. They weren't pleased. A great bristly chap in pyjamas came to the door, and I thought he'd slam it in my face. "We've no beds here," he said, "and I'll thank you for getting us up at all hours." So I pleaded with him – Oliver says I'm good at pleading – and at last he took me down the garden and showed me a shed with the rain coming through – I forgot to tell you it was raining, it would be – and told me I could stay there for the night if I could find anything to sleep on. Not the soul of hospitality. Anyway, I had my sleeping bag and it did well enough for me, though there was an enormous mastiff who kept prowling in and sniffing at me. I fancy he'd had instructions not to attack; still, it was dodgy.'

She laughed at that, feeling better, but still watching the clock, undecided whether to stay where she was or to go back to her room. 'I should never dare to take a holiday like that.'

'Oh, it's not for girls. Especially for pretty ones. – No, don't be cross. Never know how to watch my tongue, that's me.'

Madame Poiret was standing by the door, watching them with an unexpectedly beneficent, almost a pimping smile.

After all, she did like her guests to be happy, and she did, Melissa guessed, like young men.

'Pretty or not,' she said, half-accepting his compliment, 'it's dangerous for us to hitch rides. Some girls do go in pairs, though.'

He leaned across the table, arms crossed, looking at her with wide eyes. When he opened them like that, she could see the rim of white right round the iris.

'Tell me, what do you do when you aren't soaking up English?'

'I like music. Not Pop.'

'I like Pop and everything else. But I like the theatre best.'

'Open-space?' Melissa asked him, feeling sophisticated.

He ducked, as if she had hit him. 'Oh, you'll be shocked by me. I like seeing some of these old stars, grand old troupers. Hermione Gingold. Beatrice Lillie. I've got an L.P. of hers. There is nothing to beat them – what is your name, Melissa? – they've got something the others haven't got, and never will. Of course, I keep it as quiet from Oliver as I can, but he knows all right. He's all for those plays where the actors insult the audience, I think he's a masochist. He sits there as quiet as mice, while they tell him what a shit he is – Excuse me, but that's what they do say.'

'I don't get to the theatre much. It's too expensive.'

'Well, I don't spend money on much else. Melissa's a pretty name.'

She was glad to have this acknowledged. 'But a little ridiculous, I've always thought,' she said insincerely, 'I should have liked to be Susan or Joan.'

'It wouldn't have suited you. Melissa suits you perfectly. It is *just* right. Don't mind me,' he said, as she flushed faintly, 'I always say what I think. Which is a curse of course, and brings me every kind of unpopularity.'

While they had been talking, time had gone by. But it was not yet the hour for Gavin to come; dinner was half an hour later at the Albert.

'Well,' he said at last, 'I think I might go out for a drink. Could you come out with me, if we made it very slowly? You know where to go and I don't.'

She refused. 'I'm too tired to do any more hopping around today. Tomorrow will be better.'

'Then I won't go.'

'Don't be silly. You don't want to be stuck indoors.'

'I shouldn't mind.'

'I would, if you did it for my sake.'

He seemed uncertain of his next movement. 'Can I get you anything, then? A book? More coffee?'

She shook her head. 'I'm accustomed to brood.'

'You ought to be doing it on a rock in the harbour in Denmark.' He made the ducking motion again. 'Speaking out of my turn.'

'No,' she said, easy for the first time with him, 'it was a nice compliment.'

'I shan't be long.'

'When you get back, I shall be in bed.'

'Then I'll see you tomorrow, shan't I? That is, if you're not going out with your friends.'

'Tomorrow,' she said.

When he had left her, She began to wait once more.

She thought of Bob Conrad just a little. She had liked him, but had sensed some ambiguity; he was too easy, too accomplished. She thought of the students she knew, and decided that he was not like them. Still, it had been pleasant to have his attention, to be complimented, above all to be distracted from Gavin. Somebody turned on the television set and she listened to a girl singing in Flemish.

Nine o'clock came. She gathered that the grey and flickering face was reading the news. Very carefully she mended her make-up, and waited. Half-past nine, and no one. She knew he was unlikely to come now, thinking she might have gone early to bed; yet still she waited, till ten o'clock and a quarter past. Her eyes were aching; she was deadly tired.

Then at last the sound of the front door, and a man's voice in the hall; she could not hear it clearly, since too much noise was coming from the television set: but she jumped up, forgetting her foot, and lurched upon it painfully. Madame Poiret came in chattering, clinging to the arm of a stranger. They were obviously old friends. They sat down together in a corner.

Hope gone, Melissa reached for her stick and made towards the stairs. She could almost, but not quite, stand on both feet now, but to climb up was worse than climbing down. Be patient, she said to herself, you must be patient. He will come tomorrow.

Next morning, she found herself breakfasting with Bob Conrad. Having passed a troubled night she was eased by his prattle; he was a life-giver. He had made a thorough exploration of the town and had found out a surprising amount about it. He had gossiped with Mr Van Damm, and had found out that Einstein had lived for a month or so at Les Roseaux in 1938. 'They've got a Byronlaan, and a Dantelaan, and so forth, why not an Einsteinlaan? Shall we do something about it? I wonder whether one writes to the Burgomaster. Don't you think it must be very grand to be a Burgomaster? I think of them in long red robes with gold chains. What are you doing this morning? I could help you get down to the beach, if you liked?'

She told him that she would have to wait in for the doctor.

'This afternoon, then?'

'I don't know. I may be going out with my friends.' She had barely said this when she felt comfortable, assured, as though that was something she would certainly be doing.

'Isn't your hair long,' he said, 'I like it. More jam?'

His eyes were sparkling. This was a nice little place, Oliver would like it. 'See you at lunch, then?'

'I expect so. I'm not sure.'

The doctor did come, and was pleased with her. 'You ought to get about more comfortably now. So not very much time lost, no?'

Then there was nothing to do but wait. She could not stay in the bedroom, there would be no excuse for it. She went into the parlour where, fortunately, there was no one about.

Gavin came in a rush, he was alone. This, he told her, was simply a flying visit. 'Just to see that you're all right. Will you be able to get out today, do you suppose?' He did not come right into the room, but stood in the doorway.

Her pulse was very rapid. 'I'm sure I shall.' (With them?)

He said, 'We're going off to Knokke, just for the ride. I think Giles will like the change.'

It was a blow to her; she had believed so strongly that he would want her. Now she was to be deserted, for many more empty hours.

He added, and she thought he seemed a little concerned for her, 'I suppose you couldn't get to the Albert for a drink with us after dinner? I'm sure Hannah would be pleased.'

(Oh, would she?) Melissa wanted to accept, but the thought of the long road made her hesitate. 'That's very kind of you. I suppose I could try.'

'Well, don't make it too much of a strain. We'll look for you about eight-thirty, and if you don't come we'll know why.'

'I could telephone.'

He told her not to bother. He looked at his watch. 'I must be getting back. Have a nice day.'

A nice day! She looked after him with love and something like scorn. However, there was something to look forward to,

118

after all, and she might manage the road if she took it very slowly. She would manage it.

At lunchtime she saw Bob again. His hair was damp from bathing, and the jersey stuck to his body. 'Your friends not come?' he asked her guilelessly.

'They've gone to Knokke. I'll be seeing them tonight, I expect, if I can get as far as the Albert.'

'Is that that place in the town, with turrets, and two terraces? I had a drink there last night. Look here, I could help you along and deliver you, if you like.'

She pondered. If she arrived with him, she would have to introduce him and Hannah would be relieved. Gavin might feel she was no longer any affair of his, and be relieved also. (What am I doing, fretting after this middle-aged man? He is going grey, he has a wife and child. He is as far from me as the moon.) Yet it seemed to her that she might not be able to manage the ten-minute walk entirely alone. She thanked Bob, and said she would see how she felt when the time came.

'What about the beach this afternoon, though? That's not very far and it would give you a bit of practice. I could settle you in a deck-chair and then not bother you at all, if you didn't want it. Oliver says I talk too much and I know I do, but I can't help it. The world seems so full of things to talk about, doesn't it?' He looked at her with the eagerness of a puppy about to lick one's face.

'Yes,' she said, 'I'd like to do that. Do you think the world's so interesting?'

'Horrible, perhaps. Interesting, yes.'

'Do you think a lot about politics?'

'In the abstract, in so far as my work makes me. But nothing seems to touch me much; it all seems so far away. *Gaudeamus igitur, juvenes dum sumus*, that always gives me a kick. Go on, tell me I'm selfish! You know what I'm like, or you must do after three meals of me.'

'She smiled, and shook her head.'

'Well,' he insisted, 'tell me. Do you bother about things much?'

'Quite a lot, only I don't know what use bothering is. I worry about other things, too, mostly about money.'

'Oh yes, but I make out. I'm not used to eating as much as I do here.'

She found herself telling him a little about her life, taking some comfort from his interest in her, about the loss of her parents, the cluttered flat, the occasional student parties which she did not much enjoy. He listened, and did not interrupt her.

When she had finished, he asked her if she were happy.

'That's such an extraordinary word, I think,' she said, 'can one really be happy for more than moments? A constant state of happiness is inconceivable.'

'Are you in love? Don't mind me, that's just my cheek.'

She did not answer.

'Brick dropped. Sorry. Only I thought that if there wasn't some ragingly jealous regular incumbent, I might see you sometimes when we're back in London. I'm harmless, I promise you.'

Though his manner continued to be intimate, her instinct told her that he was not really absorbed in her. She was just someone met casually on holiday; they had been thrown together.

'I should like it,' she said. Better him than nothing: to go through the motions of friendship with, to impress Sally and Marina. They were always going out and about, always borrowing each other's clothes.

She let him help her down to the plage, down the iron stairs to the sands. It was an easier matter than she had expected; still, it tired her, and she was glad to be at rest. He bathed again, but otherwise did not leave her side.

'Do you know,' he said, 'I have a hankering after a bucket and spade? I should like to make sand-castles. I'm having a very early second childhood, I think.'

He began to burrow with his hands, throwing up a sand-heap. He had not yet replaced his shirt, and she was able to admire the strong muscles of his back. She wondered how many girls he knew, whether he was fond of any one of them, but she did not really believe it.

'There! Is that something like a fort? Let me have your stick a moment, I can make some holes for the guns to come through. Do you know, I've still got boxfuls of toy soldiers? I've got hundreds. I believe some of them are collectors' items by now.'

It was a soft day, the breathing of the sea remote and gentle.

She asked him what he would do after he left the university.

Lying back on the sand, his fort abandoned, he answered her. 'That's the worst of it, I haven't the slightest idea. It drives my old man mad. What about you?'

'Teach, I suppose.'

'Do you like children?'

'I like this child or that. In the mass, I'm indifferent.'

'Then poor kids. I imagine them needing to be lapped in love. I had buckets of love as a child, all sorts of over-indulgence. Every minute of it was bliss.'

'I suppose I shall give them as much love as I can.'

'Left over from what?' he said sharply. Then, 'Don't mind me. Cheek again.'

She made no reply, not because he had offended her but because she did not know what to say. It seemed impossible to take offence with a labile character such as his; it was only someone like this who could at all have distracted her from the aching hours.

That evening, she let him help her along to the Albert. She did not really want his presence, since she guessed that he would ingratiate himself with the Eastwoods and spend the rest of the evening there; which meant that it would be he who would see her home. But she could not face the journey alone.

14

When Hannah and Gavin saw her, through the terrace window, come limping up the steps, supported by a young man, both were relieved. Had she found a friend? They sincerely hoped so.

She introduced them, making the distinction. 'Mr and Mrs Eastwood, Bob Conrad. He's been kind enough to propel me along; I don't think I could have done it without him.'

'Well, we're delighted that you could get here at all,' said Gavin. To Bob – 'Sit down and have a drink with us.'

'No, really, I mustn't do that. I'm only an escort.'

But they urged him. Both were eager to have the pressure of Melissa lifted from them.

He needed little persuading. 'Well, just one, then.'

Melissa told them how they had met. 'It was a piece of luck for me. Mr Conrad—' she was stiff – 'has been acting as a crutch. We got down to the beach this afternoon. Did you enjoy Knokke?'

Hannah studied her. She was neither flushed nor excited, as a girl might have been about a new young man. However, casual or not, this acquaintance was to be fostered. She asked him what he would have to drink. He would have a *gueuse*, he replied, it was a bit sticky but stronger than the light stuff. When it came, he thanked them elaborately, and began to prattle about his journeyings. 'I went to India last year, overland, in a shocking old truck. It didn't cost much, but it wasn't

exactly comfortable. Have you ever been to the East, M
Eastwood?'

Gavin said he had never been out of Europe. 'But then,
can't do these things cheaply, as you young people can.
have to have a modicum of comfort.'

He, too, was studying Melissa, noticing for the first tim
that she really did sit half-turned from Hannah. He ha
begun to feel guilt.

Hans came up. 'Good evening, Mrs Eastwood. I can't finc
Giles.'

'I think he's upstairs, Hans.'

He stood stiffly. 'I think he runs away from me. I do not a
all know why he should. It is not friendly.'

'Oh, come now!' Hannah exclaimed. 'You mustn't say
that. He's been playing with you almost every night.'

'You do not know why he should avoid me?'

'Don't be silly.'

'Perhaps he does not like German boys.'

'That really is all nonsense.' Hannah was severe. 'Why
don't you go up and talk to him?'

Everyone is getting betrayed, Gavin thought, even poor
Giles.

Hans went away, his shoulders drooping, plainly thinking
himself a martyr to xenophobia.

'These holiday friendships,' Gavin said to Bob, 'sometimes have very little to commend them, Our small boy can'
stand Hans simply because Hans bosses him.'

'And don't I know what that can be like! When I was a
school I had a best friend who was bossy. I loathed him.'

Melissa laughed at this. 'Then why was he a bes
friend?'

'Because I couldn't escape. I have a heart like putty, don'
you think I have?'

'I wouldn't know at all,' said Melissa.

'Don't you think she ought to?' Bob appealed to Hannah, his eyes admiring her. 'She has had me for – what is it, – four meals, now.'

Armand came to them, and exclaimed to find Melissa there. 'You must have made a very good recovery, mademoiselle.'

'You were so kind to me that night,' she said. She made enquiries after Madame Croisset.

'It was nothing. Nothing at all.'

When he had gone, Bob said, 'What a good place this is!' He had settled back in his chair, was sipping his beer slowly.

'It's very modest,' said Hannah.

'I don't know about that. Are you like Mr Eastwood? Do you like to have your creature comforts?'

'Now that I'm my age, yes.' He made a dismissive gesture. His gaze dwelt on her face and hair, and she felt a momentary embarrassment. 'When we were young, we used to rough it. But no more. Do you remember when we hiked along the Seine valley, Gavin?'

'Do I not! Pont de l'Arche, Caudebec-en-Caux. There was a very good inn at Caudebec, very cheap, where we had lots of pâté and Calvados.'

'And I drank too much of the latter,' said Hannah, 'I was extremely sick.' She had, in fact, made herself ill, had spent most of the night retching in a cold bathroom; but now all this seemed part of the wonderful times.

'You make it sound sordid,' Gavin said.

'Well, it was.'

'Nothing Mrs Eastwood could do would be sordid,' said Bob, 'would it, Melissa?'

She said No, rather loudly. Hannah watched her, wondering whether she was interested in this young man at all. She might come to be so, it might break her obsession. But supposing we have been wrong all this time? She did not think she had been wrong.

He turned upon Gavin an engaging deference, asking him about his work, implying that he himself knew a little of the subject. 'I've just been reading Friedländer's *Art and Connoisseurship*. I thought it was wonderful, but of course I wouldn't know. Is it?'

'You're on safe ground with that,' Gavin said, 'it's a fine work. You like painting?'

'As an absolute ignoramus, yes. Poor Melissa says she isn't going to get to Bruges or Ghent this trip. Isn't it a pity?'

While he was talking, he was watching Melissa out of the corner of his eye. He saw that she was staring at Gavin with intent and sorrowful gaze, that she was watching the movement of his lips.

Hannah said she must go up to Giles.

When she had gone, Bob said to Gavin with an air at once naïve and daring, 'Mrs Eastwood is charming!'

Gavin was somewhat at a loss. 'I'm glad you think so.'

'But she is! I admire her enormously. Just my cheek.'

Gavin thought him impudent, but with a calculated impudence, going just so far and no farther. He could not help a mild liking for him.

But he felt Melissa was being left out of things. He turned to her, and as he did her eyes fell. 'Was it very tiring, coming up here tonight?'

She replied that it had been, a little, but that all should be well next day. 'Anyway,' she said, 'it was worth it.'

There was a stir and bustle from the bar. Armand, on a step-ladder, was putting up fairy lights, red, yellow and green.

'Oh, I like that,' said Bob, 'it looks so festive!'

The barmaid was framed by them; they made her already pale face a good deal paler.

'*Bar aux Folies-Bergère*,' he said.

'I don't think that one had fairy-lights,' said Gavin.

'Oh, you know what I mean.'

126

Hannah came down. 'He's very tired. He'll drop off soon.'

'How old is your little boy?' Bob asked her.

'Eleven. Nearly twelve.'

'The only one?'

'Unfortunately, yes.'

'I'd like to meet him. I get on with kids, though you mightn't think it.'

'I don't know why we shouldn't think it,' said Hannah, 'but I expect we shall all meet on the beach, if the weather holds.'

'It will be wonderful, just you wait,' he said. He was full of optimism; his spirits raised their own. 'I suppose I couldn't come and see you both in London? – All right, tick me off.'

Hannah said, 'I see no need to tick you off. We should like to see you.'

They exchanged addresses, and Gavin did not altogether approve. This boy might be a limpet.

'I'm going to look Melissa up, aren't I?'

She tried to smile. But it seemed to Gavin that she was apart from them, that she had withdrawn into some shadowy place of her own.

'Have another drink,' he said.

'Thank you, I don't think so.'

He pressed her. It would liven her up.

But this was a mistake, one of his many mistakes. The colour rose up her neck, unbecomingly. 'I didn't know I wasn't being lively.'

'I only meant, the walk has tired you. Come on. Are you fed up with beer? Would you like anything else?'

She said that beer would do, but when the glass came she scarcely touched it.

She is becoming heavy in the hand, Hannah thought, and it is because of Gavin. She had tried not to let Melissa irritate her, but now irritation rose, filling her with a kind of restlessness. It was hard to keep her hands and feet still. 'I don't think,' she said, 'that we ought to keep Melissa up late. She's looking very fagged.'

'I'll take you back whenever you like,' Bob said to Melissa. 'We'll go very slowly.'

But at that moment, Armand came to lean over them. 'I have my car outside. If I could run mademoiselle and the young man back to Byronlaan, it would be no trouble at all. It is only five minutes.'

Hannah was relieved. 'That would be so kind! But you're very busy here.'

'I am not too busy to spare five minutes. See, I have done my decorating!'

'It looks very pretty.'

Melissa rose with obvious reluctance; Hannah wondered how long she would have sat with them in a brooding silence. 'Well,' she said warmly, to make up for the moment in which she had expelled her, 'we shall see you, of course. Both of you.'

'I hope so,' said Bob with enthusiasm, 'this has been very jolly. Thank you so much for everything.'

When they had gone, Gavin said he would have just one more beer before bedtime.

'You'll be going back and forth to the bathroom all night,' Hannah said practically.

'Nevertheless. Now the strain's off.'

She said to him slowly, 'I suppose he will take her off our backs.'

'He seemed more attracted by you.'

'That's silly. I'm old enough to be his mother.'

'That's what I told Melissa. That I could be her father, I mean.'

'I am always suspicious of the attentions of very young men. It seems to me that they must want something.'

'Do many young men attend to you? That is something I must know.' He was teasing her.

128

She laughed. 'No, I suppose they don't.' Her mood changed. 'But Gavin, I do think things are working up with that girl. She hardly took her eyes off you the whole evening. It begins to worry me.'

'I don't see why it should. It will all be over when we get back to England.'.

'We are having a very curious holiday, I must say.'

'Oh, come,' he said euphorically, 'you must admit it's an original one. I could never have imagined anything like it.'

'Is it being spoilt for you?'

'I should ask you that. Nothing can be spoiled for me when you are around. And Giles.'

He looked at her with love, full, unremitting. There had never been a day in his married life when he had not consciously loved Hannah; if she was touched with joy by the sound of his key in the door, so was he by hers. It seemed to him that they had enough felicity to spare a little compassion, even a little encouragement, for the Melissas of this world – if, he thought, there are any more of them.

'Poor girl,' he said. 'No, I don't mean you.'

15

Melissa dreamed that she was climbing a great crimson mast, up into the sky. She could see above her an octagonal lantern, like that of a lighthouse; her feet were bare on the glittering rigging. She was climbing; and yet she sat in the square below, watching herself. It was perilous; she was afraid all the time that she might fall, but knew she must go on. To reach the lantern, to grip on to it, to crawl inside it, where joy awaited her; she must do this. Her feet were bleeding; she saw her other self, quiet on the benches, watch the slow black drops splash on to the cobbles. Her body ached; all her bones were strained to the ascent.

At last she came to the octagon, but it had diminished, to nothing greater than a street lamp. He was small inside, but she could not go to him. She tried to peer through the smudged glass, to call to him, but could make no sound. Her hands, slipping in rain or blood, gave way; she fell, but slowly, cushioned by the air, wrapped in its comfort. Soon, like a parachutist, she would feel the comfort cease, and would rush down on to the stones. She tried, as she fell, to catch at the rigging; it eluded her. The crowd was rushing up at her, faster and faster, white faces like so many expanding moons.

She awoke, sweating and trembling, sat up in bed to shake off the dream. The curtains were only half-drawn, and the moonlight shafted in. Where was the mast, where were the crowds upon the cobble-stones, greedy for her fall? She was not yet fully awake. Knowing this, she switched on the bedside lamp. Her watch lay on the table like a coiled snake. Four o'clock. Groping down beside the bed she brought up her handbag and took out a cigarette. As she smoked she became quieter, her heart pounded less, the vision receded. But it was a long time before she dared to lie down again, for she was frightened of re-entering the dream.

She slept heavily, and did not awake until nine. When she came down, Bob was just finishing his breakfast.

'Don't get up,' she said.

But he rose courteously, giving her the full benefit of his bright smile. 'It's going to be hot today. Can't you feel it? I think we should go swimming.' He asked her about her foot, and she replied that it was almost back to normal. 'Good. I expect we'll see the Eastwoods down there, shan't we? I think she's marvellous, so trim, not a hair out of place. I like him, too. You do, don't you?'

She said that of course she did, and tried to sound surprised.

'I thought so,' he said casually, as if he meant nothing by it. 'Anyone would. They're a nice couple.'

'Don't you wait for me. I slept rather late.'

'I never can sleep much after seven. I just lie on my back, yearning for breakfast. I eat like a horse, did you notice? But I can also eat like a fly, if I have to. I had to in India, when the money ran short. Moderation in nothing, that's me; that's why I like the Eastwoods. They do seem so moderate.'

She asked him not to wait for her, but he sat on until she had finished.

It was a beautiful day, blue hazy. Already crowds were out on the golf course, and the tennis-players were busy on the courts beyond. M. Van Damm in his white coat was standing by the door of his café, from which the hot sweet smell of coffee and pastry was emanating. They waved to him, and he shouted, 'Have a good time!'

Gavin and Hannah were not yet down, but Giles was. 'I'm keeping chairs for them,' he said proudly.

Melissa introduced him.

'Hullo,' said Bob, and shook hands. 'Are you going swimming? Can you swim?'

'Melissa was teaching me. I can, a bit.' He added, 'Only a bit.'

'I'll teach you too, if you like. I'm used to it. Shall we go in now?'

'I think I'd better wait till Mummy and Daddy come.' Melissa said she would go and change; when she came back, Bob was wriggling out of his jeans into bathing-trunks behind a towel.

Giles admired him. 'Don't you look strong!'

'Little, but tough. I used to box a good deal at school. Do you box?'

'The doctor won't let me, because my chest used to be weak. It's all right now, though.'

'Hard luck. Though you mightn't like it, I know boys who don't. How old are you, Giles?'

'Nearly twelve. They say I don't look it, though,' he added regretfully. 'I'm not very tall. There are chaps in my form who tower over me.'

'You'll spring up all of a sudden, you'll see.'

'My feet are big.'

'That's a good sign. Mine never were.'

Melissa thought that he was indeed good with children. She still wondered what he thought of herself, whether he found her too thin. She supposed he did. But for all his liveliness, his gaiety, it was hard to know what went on behind his head. She fancied that he would have a host of friends and treat them all alike.

Gavin and Hannah came at last, and were obviously relieved to see that Giles was in company. 'You're going to bathe?' asked Gavin, 'If you are, I will too.'

'Are you coming, Mrs Eastwood?' said Bob.

She shook her head. 'I don't. To tell you the truth, I'm getting past the days when I care to appear in a swimsuit.'

'Oh, what nonsense!' he cried, kneeling in the sand at her feet and looking up into her face. 'Look at all these women, hundreds of years old, all sunbathing.'

'Yes, and I don't care to look like them.' She could not really resist his teasing.

'You are prim,' he said. 'Isn't she, Mr Eastwood?'

'Live and let live. Give me a minute to change, and I'll be with you.'

Bob and the child ran down to the sea, Melissa and Gavin walked behind them. She felt curiously calm that morning, it was something to do with the dream she had almost forgotten. She dared not look up at him, only at his long legs moving with her own. A time would come when she must speak to him, no matter what happened then; she was quite sure that she would speak. They walked together into the water, wading out; it was cold, as always round northern coasts, and she shivered. By the time they reached the other two, Bob was giving a swimming-lesson, and Giles was obeying him with far more confidence than he had obeyed herself.

'You've got to breathe steadily, Giles. You can't swim if you're gasping all the time. Take it easy now; remember, the water will bear you up. It would pretty well bear up an elephant. Now, feet right up, that's right. Don't worry, I won't let you go, not till you're ready, and then I'll give you good notice.'

Gavin watched them for a moment or two. Then he said to Melissa, 'I'll race you to that boat. Is it too far for you?'

'Not a bit,' she answered joyously.

They swam together through the blue, swelling water. She stopped to disentangle her hair that had wound like seaweed about her face, and so gave him the advantage. He was at the boat first, and as she came up to grasp it, their bodies touched.

The shock wave went through her so violently that for a moment she ceased to breathe. She longed to put her arms around him; it would have been so easy. He moved away from her, not with haste, but by passing his hands along the side of the boat, and the contact was broken.

'Well, that was a swim and a half,' he said. 'Do you feel like going back? We'll take it pretty slowly.' He turned on to his back, and she saw that the hair on his chest was grizzled. He floated for a while, paddling his hands at his sides. They might have been alone in a world of sky and sea.

He said, 'I'm ready when you are. Right?'

They struck out, and swam easily side by side back to the shallow water.

Hannah was waiting for them at the sea's edge, her white dress all light and sharp shadow along the pleats. She called to them as they waded in. 'I thought you were going out a bit far.'

'Not too far for Melissa,' said Gavin, 'she's a damned good swimmer. I wish you'd have got over your inhibitions and come in with us.'

'Too cold. Even today.'

The three of them walked up the beach.

'Where's Bob?' Melissa asked.

'He's still giving Giles a lesson,' said Hannah, 'I think it's so devoted. But they ought to come in now.'

Melissa went to the cabin to change. It was very hot there, and smelled of seaweed. Her feet made wet tracks on the sandy floor. Still her sense of calm, of purpose, persisted. She was sure, now, that the thought of her must have moved him, and that he was no longer indifferent. She towelled her hair vigorously; it would soon dry in the sun.

When she came out again, Bob and Giles were back from the sea and Giles was triumphant. 'I did five strokes, by myself!'

'Give me time, arid I'll have him swimming like a fish,' said Bob, sitting down wet on the sand, and stretching out to let the sun do its work.

'Come and let me give you a rub,' said Hannah to her son. 'Why, you're cold! Your fingers are all wrinkled.'

'If I let him stay in too long, I'm sorry. But we were getting on so well. Do forgive me, Mrs Eastwood.'

Hannah was towelling vigorously. 'Get your shorts and your jersey on, and be quick about it.'

'Don't fuss him so much,' Gavin said mildly. 'It's as hot as hell. He'll come to no harm.'

'I'm taking him up to the café to get some hot milk. You can follow on, if you like.'

When Hannah and the boy had gone, Bob said regretfully, 'Mrs Eastwood is cross with me.'

'No, she's not,' said Gavin, 'but she always gets overanxious. He had a good deal of asthma between the ages of five and eight, and though there's been no sign of it since, she always thinks there will be.'

There was a stir and a bustle around them. The Vennings, with Chloe.

'Turned up like a couple of bad pennies,' Verna cried, 'we didn't like Liège, and the weather was so fine that we thought we'd have the benefit of the beach for the rest of our stay. Hullo, all.'

'I liked Liège all right,' John said, 'but you can never get Verna to settle anywhere for five minutes. It's a bore, if you want to know.'

Gavin introduced Bob. 'Well, we're getting to be quite a party, aren't we?' said Verna, 'I'll fetch a couple of chairs.'

Melissa sat hating her. She was a loud-voiced intruder into the miracle of this day. But the emotion did not last long, the felicitous calm overwhelming it.

The seven of them met again on the beach that afternoon, as if by prearrangement. It was still very hot, though there was a thundery tinge to the sky, a steely blueness, and a haze around the sun. Melissa had hoped Gavin would bathe again, but he did not.

At half-past three, abandoning a lackadaisical game with Chloe, who was a good child but very silent, Giles went off on his own.

Hannah was a little disturbed by this and would have followed him; but Gavin checked her. 'Leave him alone. He says it's his private place, and so it shall be. He'll be back when he wants his tea.'

'Don't encourage him to become a hermit,' said Hannah, 'or to become anti-social.'

'Oh, they're all anti-social at one time or another,' said Verna. 'No, Chloe, you can't bathe again. No One's going in with you, and I don't like you miles out there on your own.'

'I will go, if you like,' Melissa said, reluctantly. She wanted to impress the Eastwoods with her *usefulness*. She might become indispensable to them in time.

Verna would not let her. It was going to thunder later on, and anyway, it was too late.

I must not sit here looking at Gavin, Melissa thought, I do it too much. It seemed to her that they were ringing her with their eyes, Bob most of all.

Chloe had found a very small crab in a pool. She was trying to make it climb up the shaft of a spade which she had stuck in the sand. 'It's Captain Keppel's mast,' she said.

'Poor little brute,' said her mother, 'it doesn't want to climb. Let it go.'

Melissa was reminded, in a shadowy way, of the night's dream. It was so strange that so ugly a thing, for though she could not remember details she knew that it had been ugly, should have been the foregoer of such a blissful day.

'Penny for them,' said Bob. 'Come on, I really want to know.'

'I wasn't thinking of anything in particular.'

'But you do think a lot,' he said intimately. 'I've been watching you. Me, I really don't think, that is, it feels as though I don't. The time just goes by.'

'I agree with you,' said Gavin, stretching his legs. He threw up his hands behind his head and stared at the sky. 'Les Roseaux is the place where I don't have to think.'

'Het Riet,' said Bob, with satisfaction. 'Not so pretty, though.'

'Oh, I think,' said Verna, 'and so does John. We think about the business, which seems to make it no better.'

'Defeatism,' John said. He caught her hand. 'Messy. You were just going to drop ash all over yourself.'

'I was not!'

'Yes, you were. Chloe, we told you to let that crab go. He doesn't like it.'

'Where is your shop?' asked Melissa, with difficulty averting her eyes from Gavin.

They told her, speaking together.

'I think it must be wonderful to do a job like that.'

'It would be, if there were many jobs. Too much do-it-yourself going on, and how badly most people do it,' said Verna.

Bob began to tell them how he had decorated his own single room, but they were not very interested; unlike the Eastwoods, they did not find him specially attractive.

If only I could fall in love with Bob, Melissa thought, but then, he would not fall in love with me. She thought of the morning's swim with Gavin, the touch of his body beneath the water. I could not have felt it as I did if he had not felt it too.

She almost believed that he must come to love her, the force of her own desire being so great.

16

Giles knelt in the soft white sand, holding his jacks but not playing with them. He was waiting.

There were many people on the dunes that afternoon, picnicking, stretched out rose and bronze to sunbathe. Too many.

The shadow fell across him, the other.

'Oh, you've come!'

The other replied in Flemish; he spoke no English, but somehow Giles felt that he understood him. Giles pointed to the jacks. 'Thank you,' he said, and then, '*Merci*.'

The other laughed, and nodded.

'Shall we play? You go first.'

The other crouched on strong haunches. He held out his hand, and Giles put the jacks into it.

He was fascinated by his new friend, fifteen or sixteen, he would be, by his fair blond face, the skin untouched by the sun, by his blond hair. He never came on to the dunes in shorts or bathing trunks, but was always dressed, no matter how hot the weather, in shirt and jacket. He wore a narrow tie with a pattern of green snakes upon it. Giles touched this and laughed.

The other shook the ends of it at him, and said something.

'I like it,' said Giles.

The jacks rose and fell, were neatly caught, three, four, five, six. It was Giles's turn. He, also, caught them skilfully.

They played several more games, of which Giles won one; he would have been displeased if his friend had not bested him.

He said, 'You were very late today. Now I've got to be going. They'll only send to look for me.'

As if he understood this, the other rose. He said the one word he did know, 'Good-bye.'

'Good-bye. Tomorrow?' Giles pointed to the spot on which they stood.

His friend nodded. He jumped up from crossed ankles to his considerable height. He waved and walked off, without a backward glance.

Giles went back to his family.

17

Bob Conrad liked to be beneficent towards his fellow-beings, if this did not incommode him. For that reason he had protracted Giles's swimming lesson, so that Melissa and Gavin Eastwood might have some time alone. His genuine admiration for Hannah did not prevent him from doing so. He thought she was sufficient unto herself, she could spare half an hour of her husband's company that this love-sick girl might be comforted. For Bob, of course, had noticed everything; he always did.

He was so detached a young man that he had plenty of time to spare for other people. Except for Oliver, he had no intimate friends; just a great many friends. He was dazzlingly aware of his own *persona*, of the effects it made upon others, of how he could always make it work for him. He did not think much of Melissa, though she was pretty enough in her skinny way, but he did want to give her pleasure. He did not believe the Eastwoods could be altogether blind to her condition; she was, poor creature, so obvious. But it delighted him that he could have given her this happiness; he had seen her face when she came back from the sea, and it was transformed.

He thought he would stay on in Les Roseaux for another two days or so. This was a human drama, and he wanted to see some more of it; drama he could never resist, and his time was his own. He did not even object, if the opportunity arose, to helping it on its way.

He was not feckless. In term-time he worked hard, and in the vacations he occupied himself with equal vigour. He had no obsessive habits; he drank very little, smoked very little, and, as he had told Melissa, could eat like a horse or, if need be, exist on very little food. His dominant interest lay in the affairs of other people, and his pleasure in the attempt to manipulate them.

As he lay on his stomach on the beach, he wondered what he could do in this situation. His mind was busy with all of them except the Vennings, on whom he knew he had made no impression. Giles, for instance, whom the Eastwoods were trying so hard not to over-protect. Hannah, whose sidelong glances at Melissa had denoted irritation, Gavin, who must surely have suspected Melissa's state. Very interesting.

Least said, soonest mended, he thought. But I do like things to be said, and there is so much to say.

Though it was not yet four o'clock, he asked Melissa to go up with him to the café. 'I could do with a cool drink, couldn't you?' He saw that she did not want to go with him, that she could not bear to spare a moment away from Gavin, but that she did not see how she could refuse. She rose slowly and followed him up the beach.

They sat outside on the terrace, and M. Van Damn came to them rubbing his hands, his face bright because they were together.

They ordered lemonade. 'But I can't let you pay,' Melissa said.

'Oh, come, what's mine is yours, until it runs out. Don't be silly.'

She sat silent, her gaze constantly wandering towards the promenade.

'You like Gavin, don't you?' he said abruptly.

'You asked me that before.'

142

'But you do. All right, it's just my cheek. I can never keep my nose out of other people's business.'

'Anyone would like him.'

'He troubles you.'

'I don't see why you say that.'

'You're happier today, aren't you? Did you enjoy your swim?'

'You should have come along.'

'I wasn't going to butt in. Listen, let me tell you something. A couple of years ago, I had a tremendous thing about a woman a good deal older than I was, an actress. I used to go to her show night after night, and get into her dressing-room whenever she'd let me. I couldn't get her out of my mind. Of course, she treated me like a kid, did everything but pat me on the head and say Diddums. It was hell while it lasted, but it passed. That's what I want you to know; it passes.'

'I don't know why you're saying all this to me.'

'Just a story.'

The sky was perceptibly changing colour, not with any coming of cloud, but by a process of its own.

'I think,' Melissa said, 'that you're trying to be kind. But if you mean what I think you do, you're all wrong.'

'About Gavin?'

'I hardly know him.' Her hand, lying on the table, suddenly trembled, and she hastily withdrew it.

'I want you to be happy,' he said. 'I've an avuncular interest in you. I've had it from the first.'

This time she smiled. 'An extraordinary uncle,' she said.

'Do you know, you have a very nice smile? Only you don't use it enough. It lights you up, as though someone had pressed a switch.'

He saw that she was flattered, but also uneasy. He wondered, not for the first time, whether he had gone too far. But he was persistent.

'I think you're in love with him. All right, all right, tell me to mind my own business. You know me.' He saw a wave of emotion overcome her.

She said, 'I think if I can't have him, I shall die.'

Now that it was out, he did not quite know how to answer her. At last he said, 'There's no future in it, is there? He's pretty stuck on Hannah.'

'I think he has noticed me.' She wanted to talk of Gavin now, perilous as it was to do so.

He said gently, 'It's all right for us to talk like this, you know. We've one thing in common; our generation.'

'Please forget what I've told you. I know it sounds mad.'

'How can I forget it? Don't you feel better now that you've let it out to someone? You can't feel so alone. And I'm discreet, you may be sure of that. What attracts you to him? He's old enough—'

'Yes, to be my father. He tells me that himself.'

Bob's attention latched to this. Gavin would not have so spoken to her had there not been a degree of intimacy; intentionally or not, he had encouraged her. 'Maybe,' he said, 'he has noticed you a little. As you say.'

He was now encouraging her dream. Why he was doing it, he did not know; it was partly experimental, to see how she would take it, and partly benevolent. He wanted to give her a few moments of joy.

'Look,' she said flurried, 'I honestly don't want to talk about it.'

'But it's nice to talk about him, isn't it? I know I'd only to hear my actress's name to get goose-pimples. I was quite crazy while it lasted.' He rather liked the story he had invented to console her. He could almost visualise the actress in her dressing-room, see himself bearing flowers for her.

'We'd better get back to the others.'

'Don't bother, they're coming up now.'

Gavin and Hannah, Giles following, came up to the terrace. 'No room for us,' Gavin called, 'at least, I don't think so.'

M. Van Damm said he would find some chairs; he had a gift that was almost magical for fitting everyone in.

So they sat rather squashed together, Giles next to Melissa.

'What are you both drinking?' Gavin asked, 'Lemonade? Let me order a couple more.'

'No, thank you,' said Melissa, 'I really couldn't.'

'Pastries, then?'

She refused.

'There's a band concert in the Market Place tonight,' said Hannah, 'Will you two be coming?'

Bob noted that it eased her to lump them together. 'We might. If the weather holds up.'

'I hope there's going to be a thunderstorm,' said Giles, 'they're so exciting.'

'Well, I hope there won't,' said his mother, 'because if there is the weather will break and it will be horrible again.'

'We might walk up to the concert,' Bob said, knowing that they would.

'They will play *Maritana* and *Light Cavalry*,' said Gavin, 'both perfectly beastly. But it should be a lively atmosphere.'

He took Hannah's hand and held it for a second. Bob saw Melissa turn her head away, and he knew that Hannah saw it too.

Bob and Melissa had dinner at the *pension*, and afterwards they did walk up into the town. The weather was hot and very humid. Flares had been lit, and a stand had been built for the bandsmen who had not yet appeared. He had said nothing of Gavin to her since that afternoon, and she had been thoughtful. He knew she regretted her confidence.

'I'm mad about these little places,' he said. 'I feel I could spend my life in one, just lotus-eating.'

'But you're not a lotus-eater by nature, are you?'

'I like to think I am, sometimes. But no, I suppose I'm not.'

The crowds were gathering; there was as yet no sign of the Eastwoods.

'We're very early,' said Melissa, searching about her with her eyes.

'Don't worry,' said Bob, 'he'll come.'

'Please.'

The bandsmen, in their green uniforms, were entering the stand, the lights sparkling on the brass. 'It's going to be noisy,' Bob said.

The first number, not *Light Cavalry*, as Gavin had predicted, but *Poet and Peasant*, was almost over before the Eastwoods and the Vennings appeared, but without the children.

'They're playing chess,' Hannah said, as she joined Bob and Melissa. 'They're not very musical.'

'This is not very musical,' said Gavin.

They all stood together on the cobbles. The band was not too loud to preclude a degree of conversation.

'Beastly noise,' said John Venning.

'Don't spoil things,' Verna snapped back at him, 'it's romantic because it's Abroad.'

'It's romantic to me,' said Hannah, and she smiled directly at her husband.

She is doing that on purpose, Bob thought, she is giving Melissa no hope. He wondered just how much Hannah did mind the situation, whether she was too old to care seriously. She and Gavin were now standing arm in arm.

The band began to play a somewhat gloomy tune, and a singer stepped up to the microphone. The crowd applauded; this was a popular item. She sang in Flemish, her voice easily dominated the brass.

'I wonder what that's all about?' said Gavin. 'It sounds like death and disaster.'

'It is about a famous wreck,' a bystander kindly informed him.

'Thank you.'

'What have you two been doing since tea-time?' Verna asked Bob and Melissa. She had a meaningful air; she was again intent on making a pair of them.

'We played golf,' Bob said, 'and then we had dinner.'

'Who won?'

'Bob did,' said Melissa. 'I'm really not much good.'

She looked at Gavin, and to Bob, this time, her expression was frankly piteous. Yet she had been so happy that day, buoyed up by whatever had happened on her swim. Bob thought, It is high time Gavin realised what's up. This is not a usual thing. His restless mind sought for a means by which he could drop a hint. But it is ridiculous; he knows, and Hannah knows, and the Vennings know. He could see into all their minds.

Yet why should he meddle at all? He could simply go off next day and forget all about them. Nevertheless, temptation was strong. To go now would be like coming out before the end of a film.

Drop a hint? That would be to betray Melissa; but he felt she was already betrayed.

John's loud voice in his ear made him jump. 'This bloody row is giving me a headache. I'm going back.'

'I'll come with you,' said Verna, 'my feet are killing me.'

'We'll be coming soon,' Hannah said. 'Would you be very kind and look in on Giles? He ought to be with the other two.'

The four of them, Gavin, Hannah, Melissa and Bob, stayed on for a while; the band played *Star of Eve* in an ear-splitting fashion. When it stopped they could hear, far away, a roll of thunder. Gavin, almost as a matter of course, asked

Bob and Melissa whether they would not come back to the Albert for half an hour.

But she said no. She was tired, her foot had begun to ache again, she did not like thunder; she wanted to be back before the storm began.

'I'll go with you,' Bob said, but she cut him short. She would be perfectly all right by herself. She would see him in the morning.

He, as he said good night to her, wondered what had happened. He knew, though, that a day begun in joy could end in disappointment, even though the cause of it was not apparent. She wanted to be alone, so that she could cry in bed. He imagined her there, her eyes and her nose red, the long hair dripping over her shoulders.

'Isn't she well?' asked Hannah. She and Gavin had barely received Melissa's good night.

Bob said he thought she was all right, but that the long day on the beach had exhausted her. He accepted their invitation to the Albert, and they went to sit on the open terrace. Hannah went upstairs to Giles.

'That's a queer girl,' Bob said. 'Don't you think so, Mr Eastwood?'

Gavin said he hardly knew her well enough to think anything.

'But she is. I don't know what to make of her.'

'You've only had a couple of days or so to make anything of her. Unless, of course, you're something of a psychologist.'

'Oh, I'm not that. I never seem to see much.'

'I should have thought,' said Gavin, 'that you did.'

'Well, I see that she's in a state about something.' Bob had taken this hurdle. He waited for what was to come. For all he knew, he had said too much.

But Gavin said without interest, 'It's her age, I expect. Girls like that can be moody.'

'I shouldn't think Mrs Eastwood had ever been moody. She's so serene, isn't she?' Bob felt that his eyes were properly shining with admiration.

'Pretty serene.' Gavin changed the subject. 'I wish I could always think that Giles was. He broods so much to himself that I never know what goes on in his head.'

A nice family conversation, Bob thought. He felt that intimacy was creeping between them, like a twilight. Perhaps after all, in a day or two, he would be able to drop that hint.

Lightning flashed faint across the sky, and the storm came a little nearer, but still no rain fell and none of the visitors left the terrace.

Hannah came out to them, looking a little disquieted. 'Giles had already put himself to bed. Isn't that an odd thing for him to do?'

'It is, a bit,' said Gavin. 'Did you ask him why?'

'He was almost asleep.'

'Shall I go up to him?'

'I think there's no point in that,' said Hannah, 'he'll be quite asleep by now. Oh, Hans!'

He was sitting with his parents at the next table.

'Yes, Mrs Eastwood?'

'Were you playing long with Giles this evening?'

'It was only for a little while. He said he was tired. He seemed very tired. We were playing chess, but he could not – what is the word – con-cen-trate.'

She thanked him and let him go. 'I hope he isn't sickening for something,' she said to Gavin.,

'Don't. If you think of that, he will be.'

'He was all right this afternoon,' said Bob, 'and full of go this morning. I really don't think you ought to worry.'

'Well, we can't worry right now,' said Gavin. 'I'll get you a beer, darling. Bob and I are having ours.'

149

The storm crashed round them suddenly. The terrace began to empty.

Bob said that he must go; he thanked them, heard their distrait good nights.

As he went down the road, between the shocks of lightning, he congratulated himself. He felt nearer to them all. He felt that he had been a success.

18

The rain came down and the storm blew itself out, carrying July away with it. Several times during the night Gavin or Hannah went up to the child, but though he tossed about and threw his arms above his head, he did not wake. They touched his face gingerly; he did not seem to be hot.

But when they went to him at half-past seven next morning, he was awake; his face was very red and his eyes bright. 'Let's take your temperature,' said Hannah. She always carried a clinical thermometer with her.

'I don't want a temperature. I want to get up.'

'It's nothing like breakfast time yet. Come on, under your tongue.' She spoke cheerfully, a little louder than usual. Both she and Gavin felt sick.

Giles moved his head to and fro, protesting. He muttered over the silvery tube.

'Don't try to talk, darling,' Hannah said, 'just keep quiet for two minutes.'

She went to the window; she could not bear to look at him. Outside it was very grey, but the leaves were still.

'Surely you can take it out now,' said Gavin restlessly.

'Just a few more moments. We've got to let it cook properly.'

They waited. 'Here, take it,' said Giles.

Hannah took the thermometer. She turned it this way and that. 'I can't read it,' she said, panicked.

Gavin took it from her. 'Here, let me.' He saw the mercury standing in the glass. 'Just on a hundred.'

Giles began to cry.

'Well, my darling,' Hannah said to him briskly, 'I'm afraid that means you'll have to stay in bed, just for the present. I expect it's only a cold, but we'll get the doctor to you later on.'

'I want to go out this afternoon.'

'It's a horrid day, you won't be missing anything. How do you feel? Is your throat sore?'

'I don't know. A bit. Nothing much.'

'Do you think you could go to sleep again, for half an hour or so? I'll bring up your breakfast.'

'I only want milk.'

'Well, even if you do, that's nothing to cry about, is it?'

'I don't want to waste any of my holiday.'

'Listen, old boy,' said Gavin, sitting on the bed and taking Giles's hand. He surreptitiously felt the pulse. 'The quicker we can get that temperature down, the sooner you can go out. As your mother says, it's a horrible day and I don't suppose we'd be going anywhere. You seem to have caught a chill, but we'll soon get you over it.'

'It was that damned Bob,' Hannah muttered, 'I knew he kept him too long in the sea.'

'Come to that,' said Gavin, 'I should have brought him in sooner, or you should have.'

She was guiltily silent, knowing that in her own preoccupation she had taken no thought for Giles.

'And anyway,' Gavin said, in a conciliating voice, 'I don't suppose it was that. It was very warm out there.'

'It wasn't the swimming,' Giles said, his voice breaking.

'Daddy and I must go and get dressed. Would you like a book?'

'No.'

They both stood above him, rent by tenderness and fear.

'You go first, Gavin,' said Hannah, 'and have your breakfast. I'll have mine later. Would you like your milk now?'

Giles nodded, and shut his eyes. In bed he seemed very small, two years younger than his age. His body made only a small mound beneath the blankets. She kissed his cheek, testing his heat with her lips. She thought he did not seem so very hot. Gavin went downstairs.

'I don't want to see the doctor,' Giles said.

'But he'll give you something to make you better quickly.'

'It *is* a nuisance, on holiday, isn't it?' The childish note had left his voice.

'An infernal nuisance,' she replied, 'but worse things happen at sea.'

He smiled a little. 'Not very much worse, I don't think. You won't let Hans come up?'

'Certainly not. Anyway, aren't they going home today?'

'Not till tomorrow.' He slid out of bed. 'I want to go to the loo.'

She told him not to be long. 'And put your dressing-gown on, it's chilly.' She waited anxiously for his return. When he came back he seemed a little unsteady on his feet, glad to return to the shelter of the blankets.

'We love you so much,' she said, trying to speak lightly, 'you're the tops, you're the Tower of Pisa, you're the smile on the Mona Lisa.'

At the familiar quote from an old song, he smiled again.

'I'll tell you what, Daddy and I will play games with you all day, just to break up the boredom.'

'All right,' he said, 'but perhaps later. When will the doctor come?'

'Daddy will see to it.'

Gavin returned at last, after a hasty breakfast. He was carrying a glass of milk. Giles only sipped at it.

'Croisset has called the doctor, he'll be coming about nine. He wants to know if there's anything else he can do.'

'I don't see what, do you? Look here,' she said, 'I'd better get into my clothes now. I can eat later, when they send up my tray.'

She wanted to get away from Giles, from the panic he aroused in her, as people do need surcease from the sick.

As she washed herself, she tried to believe that her fear was unnecessary. She was almost angry with Gavin that she had seen fear on his face; she felt he should have been stronger for her sake, to make light of it all. For did not they always get into this state when there was the least thing wrong with Giles? Their nerve had been broken by the years of recurring asthma, and they could not regain confidence. This was probably an ordinary feverish cold; he had been very resistant to infection for some time past, was, despite the slightness of his build, strong enough. Her heart was hot against Bob Conrad, though she knew he had not been to blame.

She returned to Gavin and Giles. Giles was dozing now, or half-dozing, a slit of light beneath his lids. She believed, when she touched him, that his temperature had risen, but forced herself not to take it again.

'Do you think we might give him an aspirin?' Gavin said, following her thoughts.

She said, in a nurselike manner, not before the doctor came; it would only bring his temperature down unnaturally.

They waited; the time seemed very long. A wind had sprung up, sighing in the poplars. It would be grey on the beach, and only the hardiest would go there.

She began to whisper to Gavin, encouraging him. It was sure to be nothing; it seldom was. They were silly to worry as they did. 'I can't help it,' he said, again failing her, refusing to pretend.

They heard a step on the stairs, a knock on the door. It was the doctor.

154

'Well,' he said, 'and what trouble have we here?'

He was all optimism. His pear-like face shone.

'Let us see, young man. We will have a good look at you.'

Hannah roused Giles gently. 'The doctor's here, darling.'

They watched the examination in terror, the temperature-taking, the spatula inserted for seeing down the throat, the pyjama jacket stripped down for the sounding of heart and lungs. Then the doctor helped Giles back into his jacket, and laid him gently back on the pillow.

'How old is he?'

'Eleven,' Hannah said, 'nearly twelve.'

'He is not a big chap, is he? But he seems very healthy to me. We'll have him on his feet in a day or two.'

'What is it?' she said, almost shouting.

'A slight inflammation of the larynx. The lungs are clear. Nothing wrong with the heart. But we must bring that temperature down. I will give you tablets; one of these every four hours.'

They would have cried with relief, had they believed him, but they couldn't quite. 'At night too?' she said.

'That will not be necessary. Give him his last tablet at ten. Well, well, old man, I'll look in again this evening. Nothing much to eat, madame; I do not suppose he will feel like it.'

'When can I get up?' Giles asked, in a stronger, more hopeful tone.

The doctor said cheerfully that they would have to see about that. Not today. Perhaps for a little while tomorrow. They thanked him, and he said good-bye.

Gavin said when he had gone, 'Thank God, it seems like nothing much.'

'I thought he was very careful.' She gave Giles the first of the antibiotics, which he swallowed without fuss; he had always been good about medicines.

Hannah felt real relief for the first time, and it made her hungry. 'I expect my tray's come up. I must go and have something to eat. Will you stay here?'

'Of course,' said Gavin, 'where else should I be?'

'I shan't be long.'

'Take your time. We've both had a shock.'

'Why was it a shock?' asked Giles drowsily.

'Oh, you know how we always fuss about you, like a couple of old hens with a chick.'

'Daddy's a funny sort of hen.'

She was glad to go to her room, to drink the hot coffee. Apricot jam today: it tasted good. So did the cigarette.

Before returning to her husband and son, she went downstairs in search of Armand Croisset. He greeted her with concern.

'You were very kind to send the doctor,' she said. 'He thinks it's nothing much. Just a matter of a day or two.'

Madame came up, her face grave, and asked in French for news of the little one. She smiled when she heard it, but said that it was hard for him to miss anything of his holiday. If there was anything either she or her son could do, they had only to let them know.

'You must feel that this is your own home,' said Armand. 'Nothing is too much trouble.'

'We do feel that. We always have. We shall always come back here.'

Most of that morning, Giles slept. Gavin read, and smoked. Hannah, for something to do, set out the chessboard and moved the pieces about. She never played now, though some time ago she had been quite good at it. Now and then, she rose to lay a testing hand on Giles's cheeks and forehead. The awful sickroom tedium almost overwhelmed her apprehension.

The maid came up to say that a gentleman wished to speak to her, and she went down into the hall. It was Bob.

'I've heard about Giles from M. Croisset. I thought I'd look in and ask about him, as you were a bit worried last night.'

'We don't think it's anything much.'

He said openly, 'Did he catch a chill because I let him stay in the sea too long? Are you angry with me?'

'She answered with fairness, 'No. It was all my fault. I should have been keeping an eye on him. Anyway, we don't know it was that.'

'You look done in. Sit down for a moment and let me buy you a drink.'

It was a temptation, and she hesitated. She did indeed feel as if she had been awake all night.

'Please,' he coaxed her.

She said she did not suppose fifteen minutes would hurt. They went into the bar. The Vennings were there and she answered their enquiries briefly, but led Bob off to a table in the corner.

'You look as if you could do with a glass of wine. That beer's such very cold wet stuff.'

'Thank you.'

When their glasses were brought, he said to her confidentially, 'I'm so sorry about all this. Poor Giles. 'It's ridiculous of me, I know, and it may be cheek, but after these few days I almost feel a member of the family.'

She did not answer.

'And you are so splendid.'

She knew that he was trying to persuade her into mild flirtatiousness. 'That's very nice of you.'

'No, but I mean it. I do like calm people, with not a hair out of place.'

'I wasn't calm this morning. I was terrified.'

'You're calmer now, aren't you?' His tone was caressing. 'Say you are.'

'A little. But with an only child, one does get like this. How is Melissa this morning?'

'She? She's all right. She's waiting for me to bring back the news. You know, she'll miss it awfully until she can see you and Gavin again.' He paused. 'You do know she's become fond of you?'

Hannah said, before she could stop herself, 'Not particularly of me.'

'I suppose she's a bit jealous,' Bob said. 'You seem to have so much, and she had got so little. Your colour's coming back, Mrs Eastwood.'

Hannah said nothing. She recognised the young man's impudence and could not help being a little allured by it.

'Melissa's a strange girl,' he said.

'I don't know that she is.'

'Hard to get to know. And I can usually get to know anybody in two days.'

Hannah said that she was sure of it. She could not help smiling upon him.

'You're not hard, or you don't seem so. I expect there's an awful lot to know, in fact.'

She indulged him. 'I'm not complicated. Gavin and I lead pretty quiet lives.'

'I'm not complicated either,' he said, and this she doubted.

'I must go back to Gavin. It's almost time for Giles's pill.'

'May I look in again this evening, just to know how you all are? Just after dinner?'

'Do, if you wish.'

'But say if you don't wish. I'd hate to butt in. My God, here comes Hans.'

'Mrs Eastwood, may I go up and see Giles? I am sorry he is ill.'

'I don't think today. He's sleeping most of the time.'

'We are going home tomorrow.'

'Then perhaps before you do go. He will probably be better then.'

'I thought he would like me to play with him. It must be very dull for him upstairs.'

'No, not today, Hans, he's not up to it. And now I must go up to him. Good-bye, Bob, and thank you.'

She went up to Gavin and Giles. She gave the latter his tablet, and she took his temperature: it was down to ninety-nine. 'That's better!' she said bracingly. 'You'll feel miles fitter tomorrow.' She asked him if he would eat anything, but all he wanted was a Coca-cola. 'You shall have it. We'd better take our lunch in shifts,' she added to Gavin. 'You go down first.'

'You and Daddy can go together. I'm all right. I think I should like a book.'

She asked him which one, and he said, *The Tale of Lal*.

Propping him up on the pillows, the dressing-gown round his shoulders, she gave him the book. 'Are you sure you don't mind if we leave you?'

He shook his head. The flush had subsided, and his eyes were not so brilliant.

'Thank God he's more himself,' said Gavin, stretching and yawning as they went downstairs, 'it was quite a morning.'

'It only goes to show that we shouldn't worry so much about him. In his own way, he's quite tough.'

'I can't help worrying, darling, and neither can you.'

When they were at lunch, she told him she had seen and had a drink with Bob.

'What did he have to say?'

'He came to enquire about Giles, really. He'll look in again tonight.'

'Well, I don't think I'll be quite equal to him. I'll probably go for a stroll after dinner, I don't like being shut in all day and we shall have a long afternoon with Giles. Was he oppressive?'

'Who, Bob?'

'I'm beginning to find him so. He has a detective mind.'

'He has detected Melissa.'

'Oh I'd forgotten about her.'

'He hasn't. I haven't. I find her the more oppressive of the two.'

It was a relief to be talking of something other than the boy, a feeling almost of being out of school.

'It's only for a few more days,' Gavin said, helping himself to another prawn *croquette*. He peered at her. 'Surely you don't think I ought to do anything about her?'

'It is what she'll do about you.'

After a moment or two she added, 'We've got to admit it's so.'

'I hate to. It looks like such absurd vanity on my part.'

'Well, I can't think of anything *you* ought to do.'

Giles was livelier that afternoon. They played interminable games of halma, draughts, snakes-and-ladders. As they had done in his infancy, they let him win.

The doctor came, and was pleased with him; his temperature was almost normal. 'If it keeps down, he may get up for a little while tomorrow afternoon.'

'Can I go to the beach?'

'No, I'm afraid not.'

Giles's face clouded.

'I'll come again tomorrow morning, and we will see how you are. But you must not go out, not for twenty-four hours.'

'I want to,' he muttered.

'Ah, old chap, we cannot always have our own way.'

That evening Giles fancied an omelette, and Gavin and Hannah had their dinner as usual.

'What else was Bob talking about?' Gavin said. 'You were gone quite a time.'

'He was going through his routine of flattering old ladies,' she replied.

'It seems that we each have our admirer. I'll get out of the way of yours, though, if you don't mind. My head feels stuffed up. I won't be long.'

'Be as long as you like, when I've got Giles to sleep. What a day this has been!'

'And we have scared ourselves into fits about nothing at all.'

'As we no doubt shall again.'

'As we shall again.'

She stood in the dark bedroom above the breathing boy for quite a while. She could smell his sweetness, could no longer smell his heat. Peace descended upon her, and a great tiredness.

She went down to spend the evening in the bar.

19

Gavin walked along the beach road. He had put on a scarf, turned up his collar, for a cold wind was blowing from the sea. Near the golf course, floodlit for the few who cared to play, he met Bob Conrad.

'I was just coming up to see you, sir. I wanted to know how things were.'

Gavin blinked at the formality of address, paradoxically concluded that it was meant to be more informal. He told him about Giles, how he was much better, but that it had been a long day. 'I wanted a breath of air. You'll find Hannah in the bar.'

He would have walked on, but the boy did not appear disposed to move.

'Melissa's gone for a walk too. She's gone to the beach. I think she's rather miffed.'

'What's the matter with her?' asked Gavin, though he really should not have.

'Oh, one thing and another. She missed her breakfast this morning.' Bob said in a rush, the whites around his eyes glittering in the floodlights, 'I think something ought to be done about her.'

Gavin, apprehensive, said he did not see what he could do.

'An older person,' said Bob.

'An older person, what?'

'If you could have a word with her.'

'Look,' Gavin said, unnaturally robust, 'I don't know what this is all about.'

Bob glanced over the hedge. 'Oh, good shot,' he said, as if distracted.

Michel was still in his box, where he had been for twenty years, framed like a Rembrandt in the chiaroscuric light.

'That's rather a good game, sir, isn't it?'

'I think you're trying to tell me something,' said Gavin, with a note of exasperation.

'Me? I've no right to stick my nose in, go on, tell me I haven't. Only it seems to me that she depends a lot on you.'

It was an extraordinary conversation, on this cold night, the hedges lit about them, the grass verges a ferocious green. Gavin tried to think quickly. He knew perfectly well what this was all about, knew that he ought to walk on, was allured by the thought of what might be said next. Like Bob, he had an irresistible sense of drama.

'I don't see why she should depend on me. Hannah and I scarcely know her.' It made him feel safer to speak Hannah's name; that, and the thought of his age, gave him some security.

'If you could have a word with her. No—' Bob lifted his hand as if to ward off a blow – 'I know it's no business of mine. But if you could.'

'I can't think of any word to say,' said Gavin, 'and I won't keep you standing here, in the wind.'

'I worry about her. Again, no business of mine. But,' Bob added, with an appearance of frankness, 'I can never mind my own.' He said good-bye and walked on, briskly, towards the Albert. Gavin walked on to the sea.

The Star Café was full of television viewers. He did not go in, but peered through the glass. He both hoped and feared to see Melissa. Though he told himself that it was his duty to say some word to her, if it could be of any good, he was really motivated by the desire to know what would happen next. It had always been a desire with him, as long as he could remember. When Hannah and he went to the cinema, and found the film boring, she would want to go out before the end; but he had to wait and see what the end would be. Despite the placidity of his life with her, it seemed to him that most things were exciting enough; there was so much to be known, always something which could happen even though it did not. He was not quite sure whether he liked Melissa at all, though he knew he had in some innocent measure responded to her feeling; mixed with his emotions towards her there was perhaps a touch of repugnance. And certainly of pity. He knew himself easily cajoled into bizarre situations, but rationalised the knowledge; he was, after all, a teacher, he was here to help when he could.

He saw her then, standing by the rail, wearing a long coat. Her tail of hair was tucked into the neck of it. She was look-ing out into the darkness, unmoving.

'He could have gone away then; but he did not. 'Hullo, Melissa. It's a cold night for you to be out.'

She started violently, turning upon him her white, aston-ished face, her large and shining eyes. 'Gavin!'

'I've just come for a walk. It's too smoky in the bar, and sitting all day with Giles has given me a bit of a headache.'

'So have I, come out for a walk, I mean. How is Giles?'

'He should be up tomorrow. Up, but not out. Would you like a quick coffee?'

She said no. She had just been going to take a turn along the promenade. She pointed vaguely to the road which ran past the villas, unlit, save for random lights that shone through the shutters.

'I'll come with you,' he said, knowing he should do no such thing, that vanity and curiosity were both playing a part. She seemed to him very young and very harmless. What harm

164

could she do? He would walk with her for no more than five minutes; Hannah would be closeted with the Vennings, and with Bob's ingratiating chatter.

'I met Bob just now,' he said, as they walked together down the dark road. 'He said you were down in the mouth. Is that so?'

He could see her face in the lamplight from the houses.

'I don't know what Bob thinks he knows about me,' she said clumsily.

'Well, I'm sorry if you were. It's no fun being shut up all day. And I don't see much hope of the beach tomorrow.'

She said, in exactly the same tone of voice, light, neutral, 'I am in love with you.'

Gavin stopped short; so did she. 'Don't be such an ass,' he said.

Now he saw that there were tears in her eyes. He bitterly regretted the impulse, self-indulgent, that had made him come with her.

'I had to tell you. I know it does no good.'

'Melissa. You must get all this out of your head. You know it isn't real.'

'It is real. It is real.'

'I am double your age.' He did not say by how much more.

'Age, age, age,' she said, as if in pain, slapping her hand against her side.

'You must see how it is with Hannah and me.'

She said passionately, 'Oh, I know it's no use, no use at all. But I just wanted you to know, it would be something I had, to think you knew. I don't want you to do anything about it, just to understand a little. I have been in love with you for more than a year.'

'Then, my dear girl, you have got to stop it.' Indiscreetly, he had admitted knowledge of her love; he was not lightly brushing it aside.

165

'I shall never stop it. Nothing has ever been like this before.'

'Come, there hasn't been much time.' He was trying to relax the tension.

'Nothing will ever be like it.' She was trembling.

'You're cold. We'd better be getting back.'

'Not for a moment. Please. This is all I have. And I think you knew.'

He paused for a moment before replying. Then he said, honestly, that he had believed she had some feeling for him; but that it could not have gone deep. 'And of course, it hasn't. This is an absurd situation, and you'll soon realise it. There are plenty of men your age, and unattached. I'm an old married man, brutally set in my ways.'

'Age again!'

'Yes, but not the only argument against all this. Look, Melissa, we shall have to go on seeing each other while we're here, so don't let things be more awkward than they must be.'

'You'll tell Hannah.'

'I tell her most things.'

'You think I'll be afraid to face her. I shan't.'

'I don't suppose I shall tell her this.'

'Then we shall have something between us, that is only for us.'

'Let it be the only thing, then.'

She turned her face up to his, put her hands on his arms. He moved them gently down again.

'That's no good,' he said.

She said in a breaking voice, 'Will you kiss me? I have so little.'

'No.'

'Just once, and the only time.'

But instead, he tucked his arm beneath her own, and made her retrace her steps. They went past the café, down the little hill past the shops and across the motor-road, and on to the road back to the town. A blur of lights lay ahead of them, swivelling in the damp air; the golf course.

'Do you know,' he said, trying to soothe her, for though he did not look at her he thought that she was crying, 'when I was a small boy I believed so strongly in God that I believed He could put the clock back, that is, if I didn't like what happened on Wednesday, put me back to Monday and let me try again. He could have, I suppose, but I must say He never did. We could put the clock back, though, to yesterday.' He fancied something parsonical, unnatural, in his own manner. Nevertheless, he went on talking. 'We'll have to, you know, for your sake and mine. I don't believe for a moment that what you now feel is going to last, and I think you wouldn't, too, if you gave it a little reflection. So cheer up, and tell me you'll try to forget it all.'

'Why should I try?' It was almost a wail. 'If this is all I have, or all I'm ever going to have, I don't see why I should try. I don't see why you should ask me. In a way, it is nothing to do with you.'

Irritated, and feeling repelled, he answered her sharply. 'No, it's damn all to do with me. So stop it.' He looked at her then. The tears were pouring down her cheeks. They were at the corner of Byronlaan, and they stopped. 'Don't do that,' he said with compunction, 'please dry your eyes. You can't go back to your place like that.'

She took out her handkerchief and put it into his hand. 'You dry them. You made them.'

'Don't be silly, Melissa. This has gone on long enough.' Yet pity for her caused him to scrub briefly at her face before returning the handkerchief. He wondered whether he should deliver her to the *pension*, decided not to. There, they would be in the shade of the trees and he feared another outburst. He could feel now nothing but apprehension and pity; what was he going to do with her, what would she be

167

like when they met again, as they were bound to do? He wished the holiday were over and he were safely home. He knew that a part of this, if only a small part, had somehow been his fault.

He wanted to leave her, but felt he had to stay while she tried to ride out the surge of emotion. She was shaking violently. They were standing in the light of a street-lamp, so he drew her a little away from it lest a passer-by should see her. At last she pulled herself together.

'You think I ought to say I'm sorry. But I can't be sorry for what I couldn't help, I had to get release somehow.'

He said, but not unkindly,' I don't think you ought to get such release, as you put it, at my expense, do you?'

'I can't care about anyone except myself. And I had to say it. But I won't again.'

'That's a good girl,' he said, as if to a child. 'You go home to bed now, and in the morning it will all look quite different.' He could only speak to her in clichés. She turned abruptly and left him, walking quickly down the shadowed lane.

Gavin went back towards the Albert. He was shaken, perturbed, and was aware of feeling strangely randy. He would want Hannah that night.

He did not find her in the bar. The Vennings were there, but there was no sign of Bob. He realised that he had been gone for nearly an hour.

'Hannah's gone to bed,' Verna called to him, 'we told her the night was young, but she was tired. Giles was O.K. when she went up to him last. Have a drink?'

'No thank you,' said Gavin, 'I'd better join her.'

He found her in bed, but not asleep. 'Sorry,' she said, 'but I'd really had enough. The Vennings were squabbling as usual, and it's been a heavy day. You've been a time.'

'I'm sorry. I met Bob on the way down, and Melissa on the front.'

He was aware that his tone was forced, and that she had noticed it. He meant to tell her everything, after all. It meant throwing Melissa to the lions, but he needed Hannah's help. He went to the bathroom to wash and undress. He realised that during the whole of their married life, he had never kept from her even the most petty secrets; I am an unusual sort of man, he thought. But he had confided in her not so much out of loyalty, though there was that, too, but because she always knew what to do in all manner of situations. 'A safe way round, out, or under,' he said to himself, recalling *Stalky and Co*.

Her voice came to him through the open door. 'What did Melissa have to say? Come on, I know there's something.'

'Wait a minute.' He shaved himself rapidly, knowing she would realise what *that* meant. For all the fineness of his hair, he grew a stiff beard. He came to her with lather on his face, and she smiled at him.' I won't be long,' he said.

He came out to her, switching off the bathroom light but leaving the bedside lamp on. He got in beside her. 'Plans for me?' she said. It was one of their joke-phrases.

'Later. I must tell you about Melissa first. I'm in somewhat of a fix.'

He put his arm round her and she rested her head on his shoulder, listening.

'Poor Gavin,' she said, when he had done. 'And I suppose I ought to say poor Melissa. Yes, I'll be decent, and say it.'

We are so secure, he thought, that nothing can touch us. Not really.

'But we should have a plan of campaign,' she went on. 'What do we do when we meet her again?'

'Perhaps we shan't meet her. She may keep out of our way.'

'She won't,' said Hannah, 'she's only got one thought in her head, and that gives courage. You'll see.'

'We shall try to behave just as usual.'

'Did you give her any encouragement this time? I have to know that.'

'No, I didn't. Except that it was silly for me to stay and talk to her at all.'

'Yes, it was silly. Idiotic. Do you know, I should think you felt some kind of response? It would be extraordinary if you hadn't.'

'I did feel some response. I felt put off. It is irritating to be loved, when one feels nothing in return.'

'A mild word,' said Hannah. 'How I wish we'd never come here! Will she go on haunting your lectures next term, do you expect? It may tend to put you off your stride.'

'I sincerely hope she won't. If she does, I shall just have to ignore that owlish gaze.'

He knew that to Melissa this conversation, so light in tone if not in feeling, would have seemed an ultimate betrayal. Yet he also felt that she could, in some strange manner, endanger Hannah and himself, and that the only help for them both was for Hannah to have his complete confidence.

'Let's forget it if we can,' she said.

He kissed her, gently at first, then with intent. He pulled back the sheets so that he could see her rounded body, which was still young. The randiness, which had not left him since he had parted from Melissa, was now intensified. 'Plans?' she said.

'Plans. You know I love you?'

'I like to hear you say it, but I don't need reassurance.'

He knew that, in some measure, she did.

'There's no one but you,' he said, playing with her body. 'Quick, I want you.'

As he entered her he found, to his dismay, that the thought of Melissa was exciting him. The struggle to get rid of it made him fail, at first, and for a few minutes he lay quiet at her side.

'I'm tired, I suppose.' Then, with renewed energy, 'But I still want you.'

This time all was well, though he was aware that she had come to a climax before him.

'Nice?' he said.

'Wonderful.'

Their bodies were damp. He smelled the peculiar scent of her flesh, and was comforted. Putting out the light he said, 'Shall you sleep?' 'I shall. I wonder—'

'What?'

'Whether either of us should go up to Giles.'

He put on the light again. 'I'll go.'

He thought the day would never end. When he came back, had reassured her about the boy, he lay down a little apart from her. Music was still arising from the terrace, faint but disturbing. A classical record this time, after all the pop; he thought he recognised it. Yes, he did, Satie's *Gym- nopédies*. He had had an old 78 of it once. He knew he would always associate it with this day, with Giles, with Hannah, with Melissa, and he damned the capacity of music to make itself into a theme-song. Memory was strong enough without its persistent interference. Hannah's breathing was just a little too deep, he knew when she was pretending to sleep; he wondered what she was thinking about. He had always felt that a certain amount of mystery lay in her calmness. Had she really so calm a heart? Had anyone? Tomorrow she would be quite serene, ready to cope with anything that might happen. He hoped nothing would.

20

Bob was lurking about for her in the hall. She made as if to walk past him, but he gripped her arm.

'I've been waiting for you. Come and have some coffee, they're getting it now. You look blue with cold.'

She did not want to look at him, not knowing how much her appearance had been altered. 'No, I'm going to bed.'

'You can't. I want to say good-bye properly, because I'm going off to Holland early tomorrow morning and you may not be up.' He coaxed her. 'Don't disappoint me.'

Suddenly she felt too weary to resist. She went with him into the little parlour, which was not too full, and sat down with him at a table by the wall.

In silence, he passed her a cigarette and lit it for her.

She took off her coat and he sprang to drape it over the back of her chair. She thanked him.

'I shall miss you,' he said, 'but we shall meet in London. It's been fun.'

She wondered with dreary humour what fun she could have been to him or to anyone. She realised that she would be sorry to see him go; however foolishly, she had confided in him and made him a part of her life.

'Did you meet Gavin?' he asked. 'I saw him going down towards the sea.'

'Yes, for a few minutes.'

'You've been crying,' said Bob, peering at her, showing her the whites around his eyes.

She denied this.

'Oh, but I think you have. Do you want to tell me about it? Don't, if you don't. But I might help.'

The coffee came. He poured it for them both, sweetened hers as he knew she liked it, and watched her assiduously as she began to drink. She said, 'You were right, I was cold. What made you decide to go so suddenly?'

He told her he had had a letter from Oliver, who was getting lonely all by himself. 'So I thought I'd better rush through the rest of my tour and get back a week earlier.'

'I'm sorry.'

'Are you? I'm glad of that, though I shouldn't be glad when anyone is sorry about anything. I thought I might have been a bit of a bore.'

'You know you never think that,' she said, making an effort to tease him a little, to put him off the scent.

'You mean, you think I'm conceited. Oliver says I am. But believe me, I've nothing to be conceited about. Unless it's that I'm a good listener. Go on, give me something to listen to, it will help you.'

'I don't need helping, and I've nothing to tell.'

'All right, all right, then. Just sit there, and let's be nice and quiet together. I can see you're in a state, and I want to get you out of it before you go to bed.'

She did not now want to go to bed; though she was determined to tell him nothing, the mere comfort of his presence was enough for her. He began to talk about his journey, where he would go, what he would see. She refilled her own cup. The room was warm; she had not realised how chilled she was.

He leaned across to her. 'We've only known each other for a few days, but it seems like years. At least, it does to me. What about you?'

'Quite a long time, yes.'

'We're friends, aren't we?'

She said yes. Her pulse had slackened, she felt the relaxation through her whole body. She knew that it might be different when she was upstairs alone.

'We can talk about things,' he went on, 'I feel I can say anything to you.'

'Only,' she replied, 'you don't. You want to know all about me, but you tell me nothing about yourself.'

His eyes widened. 'What should I have to tell? I work, I amuse myself, I get on well with my flat-mate, I take damn' all interest in politics, I let the world go by. I've got an elder brother, he's in Hong Kong. I can't think of anything else.' He paused. 'I'm very fond of you, Melissa. Come on, confide in me. Something's happened.'

'And I tell you that nothing has.'

'You were upset when you came in tonight. I thought you might be.'

She said she did not know why he should have thought anything of the kind.

'And I don't like to see you like this,' he went on, not heeding her. 'Come on, you saw Gavin. What did he say? – Just my cheek.'

'This and that. It was only for a moment.'

'Well, if you won't tell me, you won't. But I shall worry about you, alone here with something eating you up.'

She said there was no need for anyone to worry about her, 'I'll say good-bye to you now, if we don't meet in the morning.'

'Till London, then. We'll take in a flick.' He kissed her lightly, squeezed her upper arm. 'You're my girl, you know.'

She did not believe him.

Her calm persisted while she undressed and brushed her hair. She found herself wishing it were thicker, a shade lighter. She might have a cold-water rinse, as Sally and Marina often did.

It was only when she was in bed that her heart and her temples began to pound. She lay first on one side, then on the other, eyes wide open in the half-darkness. What was she to do tomorrow? For she was determined not to hide from Gavin; he might expect her to, but she would not. She would face him out, and Hannah too, be bright, be natural. Forget all about it, he had said; well, she would pretend she had forgotten. Beneath the strength of her emotion, a lesser emotion stirred; she was afraid she had made a fool of herself. But he was kind, he would not let her think that. Had he told Hannah? The thought of it made her sit upright in bed. The moon had risen, and a thin streak came through the curtains, falling across her hands. No, he would not have told her, he had promised. This would still be between the two of them. It must make a tie of some kind.

Unable to lie still, she got out of bed and paced up and down the room. What have I done? *What have I done*? She did what she had neglected since childhood, and said her prayers. Oh, God, if you are anywhere at all, listen; make me not love him. For I cannot bear it.

21

Hannah, happy because of the previous night and because Gavin had come to her with good news of Giles (temperature normal, as cool as a cucumber and claiming to be hungry), had her own breakfast, as usual, in bed. She gave a thought to Melissa, but did not let it trouble her; it had all been silliness and must be treated as such.

The weather was bright, but by the look of the rustling trees it was still chilly. When Gavin came up to her, she told him she had an idea: Giles had lost two days of his holiday, so why not stay for two days longer? They had nothing to get back for, and she was sure Armand could fit them in, even if it meant moving to the annexe.

'I thought you'd had enough of it,' he said.

'Well, I've changed my mind. And by that time the Vennings will be gone, and so will Melissa, and we can really enjoy ourselves.'

'I could ask Giles,' he said, but with some reluctance. 'He may not want to stay on.'

'I bet he will.'

She put on her dressing-gown and they went up to him.

He was sitting up in bed reading, the empty tray pushed to one side.

'That's more like it, darling,' said Hannah. She cuddled him. 'How are you feeling?'

'I feel fine. Can we go to the beach today?'

'Now look, I am pretty sure the doctor won't let you, not yet.'

His mouth drooped in disappointment. 'But Mummy, it's wasting time!'

She thought how childish he was, and as usual was a little disturbed. When would he grow up? She did not like to think that he was not quite as other boys.

'I know, and I'm sorry for you. But we've got an idea.' She told him of the plan to stay on. At once he brightened.

'Do let's do that! And the good weather might come back. It's better this morning, isn't it?'

'Yes, but if you go out too soon you risk another chill.'

'I can't just sit in the hotel.'

'Oh, yes you can,' she said firmly, 'and thank your stars that the Fischers have gone. So you won't have to be worried by Hans.'

'I'll have to play with that dumb Chloe.'

'No, you won't,' she told him, 'not if we tell her you'd just like to sit and read. She knows you've been under the weather.'

'When is the doctor coming?'

'Soon, I expect.'

'I shall ask him whether I can go out.'

'Perhaps a short walk later on wouldn't do any harm—' said Gavin weakly, but she frowned at him.

'There's no question of that. Giles, you must just make up your mind to put up with your father's company and mine.'

The doctor was, indeed, pleased with him; but said firmly that he must not go out of doors that day. 'Or you'll have more days in bed, old chap, and you wouldn't like that, would you?'

Giles sulked.

When the doctor had gone, however, he said anxiously to Hannah that she must see M. Croisset at once about the other two days; there might be lots of other people coming, he mightn't have room for them.

'I'll go down now, while Mummy's dressing,' Gavin said, propitiating him.

'Giles,' said Hannah rather severely, 'you don't take things well, you know. You must make up your mind that things sometimes won't go your way. We all have to.'

He flung himself into her arms, kissing her cheeks and her lips.' Please. Let me go out for a little while.'

'But what do you want to go for? Anyone would think you had a business appointment.'

He said nothing.

'Listen, my love, you simply can't.'

'Daddy said I might.'

'Daddy isn't as responsible for you as I am. And I say no.'

Detaching himself from her, he returned to his book. 'All right.'

'That's my good boy. I must have my bath now.'

Gavin came to tell them that all was well; they could keep on their rooms. He brought with him a solitaire board, made of mahogany with beautiful green marbles. 'M. Croisset thought this might while away the time for you.'

'Oh, good,' Giles said, seeming quite composed. 'And later on, we may see Bob and Melissa.'

'You won't see Bob,' said Hannah, 'because he's off to Holland this morning. He asked us to give you his love.'

Hannah took some time over her bath, propping herself on her hands, letting her legs trail in the water. It would be a long morning with Giles, she knew; perhaps they might at least let him get up for lunch. She wondered about the destroyed report, and wished that they had seen it; it would have been encouraging. The trouble was that he appeared to have no concentration, except upon things in his inner self; or upon some game or other, like the miniature golf. She wondered how it would be when he went to his next school, where they would be sending him as a boarder. Would it help him, to be under constant supervision? They had made up their minds that if he hated it, they would have him home again. But they would try it for a term or two. He had himself, surprisingly, seemed to like the idea, though she imagined that his image of it was drawn from the school-stories of which he was so fond. I shall miss him dreadfully, she thought, I shall hate to see his bed empty. She saw it in her mind's eye, neatly made up, the blue and green cover drawn up.

But one of these days he must go altogether away from us. She stood up, and dried herself on a rather scratchy bath-towel.

She did not hurry over her dressing or her make-up, taking extra care with the latter. She wanted Gavin to see her as still young, as she knew he had seen her last night.

Somewhat to their relief, Giles did not seem to want amusing that morning, but was content to play solitaire. Gavin left him his watch: 'At twelve o'clock, you can dress and come down. Put on your sweater.'

The bar was not crowded, the Vennings were nowhere to be seen. Even on a bright day it was rather dark, and the thin frame of fairy-lights was consoling. Madame bowed to them from her majestic corner.

'I do like it here,' said Hannah, 'we'll come back another year and pray to God that persons who shall be nameless will not.'

'Touch wood,' said Gavin. Then he said, 'Damn it, she's still got my Ngaio Marsh, and it's a library book. I'm not going to fetch it, after what happened.'

'You won't have to. She will make it an excuse for coming here.'

He looked at her sideways; he had heard the note of tartness in her voice. She pulled herself together. She must not let the slightest cloud come between them. Yet she was aware, now that the memory of the night was fading, that she had been hurt. She had been hurt several times during their life together, when women had admired him too openly, but had never let him see this. And it was true that he had never responded, by word or glance, to this flattery.

'Anyway, suppose she doesn't, I'll go along and fetch it myself,' she said, 'only not today.'

They settled to their reading. 'Ruskin,' said Gavin, 'was an old ass, but an exquisite old ass.'

An hour or so later, they saw the Vennings coming up the road, and between them was Melissa. They came up the steps into the bar.

'Hi,' said Verna, 'we found her alone and palely loitering – aren't I literary? So we brought her along for a drink.'

Melissa greeted them in a voice that was somewhat over-loud. She looked different that morning; she was wearing lipstick and green eye-shadow, and her hair was up. 'I wasn't loitering. I was coming to return your book.'

Hannah and Gavin exchanged a brief glance. 'Well, sit down,' Gavin said. 'What will you all have?'

' It's my shout,' said John.

'How's Giles this morning?' Melissa asked. She was holding her head high.

This is effrontery, Hannah thought; or she is driven so hard by wanting Gavin that she cannot endure not to see him. She replied evenly that he was better, and that he would be getting up that afternoon.

'Well, don't let him out yet, it's parky,' John said, using his obsolescent slang. 'Bright, though.'

'It'll warm up later,' said his wife.

'What do you know about it?'

She gave a heavy dramatic sigh. 'You see how he is?'

'It's how you are,' said John, 'the little weather prophet.'

Hannah turned her thoughts from Melissa to wonder about them. How had this marriage endured? Was this type of scrapping a cherished game with them? She wondered whether Chloe had ever noticed it. 'Where is Chloe?' she asked.

'We left her playing golf. She's getting the same mania for it that Giles has.'

'You'd better go back for her,' said Verna, 'she's been gone quite long enough.'

'Oh, stop badgering the kid. She's not six,' said John.

'Bob left this morning,' Melissa said brightly, addressing herself to Hannah. She was keeping her eyes from Gavin. 'He had gone before I was up. What with him and all of you, I'm having a better holiday than I hoped for. I expected to be lonely.' She sipped at her beer. 'You've all been very kind.'

'Not at all,' Gavin said bluffly. 'We've liked meeting you.'

She smiled at him then, as though nobody else was there. 'You make it sound very much in the past. It's not over yet.'

'We're staying on for two more days,' he said, 'to make it up to Giles.'

Ass, Hannah thought; now she may try to stay on herself. She believed Melissa would have the nerve for that. If Gavin had not spoken, the thought would never have entered her head. However, she might not be able to make her money last out.

'I was thinking of staying on for a day or so,' Melissa said, with an air of surprise. 'The Colombe's quite comfortable, and I feel, like Giles, that I've lost time.'

Hannah saw Verna and John exchange a glance; and it came to her suddenly that they had brought the girl with them out of mischief. She felt the stir of humiliation that other people should have divined the position.

'We may have the weather back again,' said Gavin, with the air of one making the best of a bad job.

Melissa was sitting back in her chair, with the gay appearance of someone quite unperturbed.

This *is* effrontery, thought Hannah, even though I don't suppose she knows that he has told me. It would be enough for her to face Gavin.

'Gavin's as much of an optimist as Mrs Venning,' Melissa said, using his name with an effect of ease. 'Aren't you, Gavin?'

I don't know how I am going to bear this, Hannah said to herself. But what else can I do? We must just go on pretending that nothing has happened. I must not let my guard drop for a moment. Anyway, what does it matter? She can make a nuisance of herself, but that is all.

Melissa was looking quite pretty, which made things worse. She was talking with unusual animation, her big eyes shining. Hannah noticed that she had a little lipstick on her teeth, and was unworthily comforted.

Giles came down, carrying the solitaire board. He was still a little pale.

'Hullo, darling!' Melissa cried, as if bound by affection to him also. 'How are you feeling?'

'All right. I can't get this out.' He showed her the marbles. 'I can never get down to less than three.'

She put a casual arm around him. 'Here, let me try. Though I was never any good at it.'

'Can I have a coke, Mummy?'

'Yes, if you'll drink it slowly.' Hannah went to order it. When she came back they were all engrossed in solitaire, Gavin, perhaps, a little miming his engrossment.

'No, no,' said John, 'you want to put this one *here*, or you'll have a space you can't hop over. Let me show you.'

'I told you I was no good,' said Melissa. There was colour on her cheeks and her neck, a striping, as on unripe currants. Leaving the board, she leaned back and spoke boldly to Hannah.

'What are you both going to do this afternoon?'

'Sit with Giles, I suppose. He mustn't go out yet.'

'For half an hour,' Giles pleaded, 'it wouldn't do me any harm.'

'I said no.'

'I could sit with him for a bit, if you liked. Then you and Gavin could go out together.'

'No,' said Gavin almost sternly, and Hannah was relieved by this, 'it's very kind of you, but we shan't do that. It would be a waste of your day.'

'It wouldn't, I promise you,' said Melissa. 'I should love it.'

But he still said no, he and Hannah would stay in together.

Giles intervened, to say that there was no need for anyone to stay in. He would be all right by himself.

Verna looked round, wildly. 'Oughtn't Chloe to be back by now? John, you simply must go and fetch her.'

'Do you worry about them as we worry?' said Hannah. 'I wonder at what point we ought to stop?'

'We ought to have stopped by now,' said John. 'They tell us that children mature more rapidly these days. And you needn't worry, Verna, because she's just coming along.'

'I'll go and meet her,' she said.

'And what's the point of that? If she sees you like an anxious hen, clucking on the porch, it'll destroy her confidence.' He pushed her back into her chair. 'Have another beer. You, Gavin? Hannah? Melissa?'

But Melissa refused. She must be getting back to her lunch.

'Come again this evening,' Verna said, cordially, and Hannah could have killed her. 'Go on, she must, mustn't she, Gavin?'

This was pure malice. Hannah wondered at the urge of some people to stir up trouble; she hated the Vennings, she longed for them to go.

'Of course,' Gavin said shortly, and Hannah as shortly echoed him.

'I might.' Melissa spoke directly to Verna, as to a host. 'Thank you.' She rose and Gavin rose with her; John did not. He had no formal manners. 'Good-bye for now, then.' Only John and Verna watched her as she left them.

Giles went out into the hall to inspect the luncheon menu.

'I feel sorry for that poor girl,' said Verna sentimentally, looking at nobody, 'I feel she needs caring for. I bet she lives in an awful hugger-mugger at home and doesn't bother to eat enough.'

'Probably stuffs herself like a pig,' said John.

'Well, I don't know where she puts it all, then. She's as thin as a rake. Don't you feel sorry for her, Hannah?'

Hannah paused before replying. It was necessary to be careful. Then she said, 'I suppose I am.'

'Gavin?' Verna enquired. She was breathing through her nose. Chloe came in, and her parents greeted her with false casualness.

'No, not particularly. I think she does well enough for herself.'

'Brute! How would you like to have no parents and live in some crummy flat with a couple of girls?'

'It's how most students live.'

'I said you were a brute,' Verna repeated, comfortably.

Giles came back. 'It's *fondus au parmesan* again, and roast veal. I love the veal here. We never get it so white, or cut so thin. Why don't we, Mummy?'

A beautiful smell was arising from the kitchen. 'God, I'm hungry,' said John. 'Is it time to go in?'

Hannah and Gavin could not, of course, talk much while Giles was with them. But immediately lunch was over, he left them to go with Chloe.

'Effrontery,' Hannah said, speaking the word that had been in her mind.

He did not pretend not to understand. 'I suppose so. You wouldn't call it bravery?'

'I might, if I were a more generous woman.'

'The most generous of women,' he said. 'What are we going to do?' As usual, he looked to her to take the lead.

'What we are doing. Trying to pass it off.'

'It's trying for you. And for me.'

'For both of us.' She watched the Vennings out of the dining-room. 'They did that deliberately, you know.'

'Who?'

'Verna and John. They want to see what happens next. It's human. It's disgusting.'

'I'm not devoid of that instinct myself,' said Gavin, thinking back to the night before.

'And now you have seen what happened next?'

'I don't want any more of it. Don't be acerb with me, there's a good girl.'

She told him she was sorry, that she was trying to be patient. All she had to do, she knew, was to go on pretending that she knew nothing. 'But she's going to stay with us, you heard that? We shall have no time alone.'

'If it's fine tomorrow, we might take Giles to Blanken-berge. We can just run away.'

'Yes,' she said. 'I wish I didn't have a sneaking feeling that it would be cruelty. Why should I care about being cruel to her?'

'Because,' said Gavin, 'she's a pitiable object. And you'd always be sorry for anyone like that.'

'How some girl of twenty-one can make our lives misera-ble, I don't know.'

'I should have thought it was self-evident. Still, let's not exaggerate. We're not miserable, simply feeling a bit hunted.'

They went into the bar parlour. The sunlight was filtering through the curtains deep-edged with grapes of Belgian lace, and between the leaves of the pot-plants. Giles was working at a jig-saw puzzle which Armand had found for him; he was absorbed, or they thought he was.

'I'd like a stroll,' said Gavin, 'but I'm almost afraid to go out.'

'Why are you afraid to go out, Daddy?'

'I may have a cold coming, that's all.'

'If you went towards the town—' Hannah suggested.

'I might do that.'

'Why wouldn't you make your cold worse if you went to the town?'

'Because it's more sheltered than the beach,' Gavin said promptly.

'I do wish I could go to the beach.'

'That's enough of that. Get on with your puzzle,' said Hannah. 'Look, if you put that green piece in here, you'll complete the top edge. Have you got the picture on the box? We can see what it will look like.'

'It's a cottage and a garden, with a windmill in the distance.'

He went on with the game.

Gavin did go out, leaving Hannah with the boy.

He had not been gone long when Verna came in. She signalled to Hannah to join her at the other end of the room. She wore a smile that was both jolly and secretive.

'Where are John and Chloe?' Hannah asked her, taking a chair at her side. She felt apprehensive.

'They're playing golf. They went out early, so that it shouldn't be crowded. Hannah, I want to talk to you.'

'What about?'

'Why, don't bristle! It's just that I've been keeping my eyes open, and I do think you ought to warn Gavin.'

Hannah asked her again what about. She tried to speak easily, but was aware of a defensiveness in her own manner.

'About that girl Melissa. She's got a frantic crush on him.'

'I don't suppose she has,' Hannah replied, 'but even if it were true I don't see what harm she can do.'

'I was watching her this morning. She either avoids looking at him altogether or she stares right into his face, as if she was taking photographs. He ought to be on the look-out, that's what John and I think. I suppose you think we're poking our noses in. – Yes, you are bristling! I wish I hadn't said anything.'

'I'm not bristling at all,' Hannah said, 'only I think you're making a mountain out of a molehill.'

'And she's so tense. Aren't you afraid there will be some kind of outburst?'

'Not with me here, at any rate,' said Hannah. 'Do stop it, Verna. If this were true, what on earth good would I do talking to Gavin?'

'To put him on his guard, that's all.'

Hannah said, exasperated, aware of duplicity, 'Anything you could notice he could notice too, I suppose. And I don't imagine it would worry him.' She felt that the secret was exposed to the whole of Les Roseaux.

'All right, all right. I only wanted to tell you. I know how I'd feel if someone was making sheep's eyes at John, not that I can possibly imagine such a thing.'

Hannah could not possibly imagine it, either.

'You know,' Verna went on, 'you wouldn't believe it, but I've always been mad jealous of him. Extraordinary, isn't it? Oh, I know we have our fights, but it means nothing. We've always squabbled. Don't you ever get jealous?'

Hannah resented this intimacy. She said shortly, 'No, I don't.'

'You're the lucky one, then. Why, if some woman comes into the shop and I think she's making up to John, it's all I can do not to tell her to take her business elsewhere.'

Hannah said, 'I'd better be getting back to Giles.'

'Now you're offended with me.' Verna's plump face was sorrowful. 'You mustn't be. John and I took to you both at first sight when we were here last year.'

'I'm not offended. Giles!' she called across the room, 'How are you getting on? Need any help?'

He shook his head. He called back, 'I've done all the edges.'

Armand came in. Hannah said with relief, 'How kind of you to find him the puzzle! And the solitaire. Do you keep a stock of things for occasions like this?'

'They belonged to my little girl,' he said.

Verna, not noticing the past tense, said, 'Oh, where is she? At school?' She had forgotten that it was holiday-time.

'She died.'

'I'm so sorry,' said Hannah, glancing over to Giles, giving him the protection of her heart.

He said, 'It was a long time ago.' He tried to smile at them, but it was not a success. Changing the subject, he said hopefully that it was sure to be milder next day, and fit for Giles to go to the beach. 'Alas, you go home tomorrow, Mrs Venning.'

'I'm afraid we do. We love it here, M. Croisset. We'll be back next year, I expect.' He bowed his appreciation, and moved on.

Hannah said, 'I must go and talk to Madame.'

She took refuge by the old woman's chair. 'How are you today?' Her French was rusty, but it served her.

Madame Croisset said she was very well.

'But very busy.'

'Only just before lunch and again before dinner. I only supervise the cooking now, you know. Once I did it all. Sometimes the days seem very long; it is always the same. I go to bed quite early, I do not like it when we get the crowd in the evening, I do not like all the smoke.'

Hannah, guiltily, suppressed her cigarette.

'You need not do that,' said Madame, 'it is only bad when it gets late.'

'The beautiful lace you gave me—'

'It was nothing.'

'I'm going to trim a slip with it.'

'Once upon a time I made such lace. But my eyes are not good enough now.'

Hannah saw with relief that Verna had gone away. She returned to Giles.

When Gavin came in, she did not tell him what Verna had said to her, for she thought he was sufficiently burdened. Giles had come to a difficult part of his puzzle, and they both helped him with it. He was content till about half-past three, when he began to fidget, and to look longingly out of the window.

'No, old boy,' said Gavin, interpreting the look, 'it's far too cold. The sun looks all right, but there's a beastly wind. Cut your losses and wait patiently till tomorrow.'

'I wasn't going to ask,' Giles said.

22

Bob never let his left hand know what his right was doing, and did not let anyone else know either. Arriving in Brussels, he did not go straight to Holland but went from the station into the Grand' Place.

He was sitting over coffee, when he noticed, on a nearby banquette, a familiar face. He tried to place it. He had seen it on television, in a donnish sort of quiz-game. He knew: James Crown. Dr Crown. He taught Melissa.

Bob wondered how this might be turned to acount, though why he should wish to turn anything to account he was not sure.

He decided to try his luck. He got up and made his way to the other's table. Affecting both shyness and diffidence, he said, 'It *is* Dr Crown? I've seen you on television. Do you mind if I introduce myself??'

'Why, no. It's flattering to be recognised.'

'I'm Bob Conrad, I'm at the L.S.E. I believe a friend of mine is a pupil of yours, Melissa Hirst.'

'Yes, I teach her. Sit down.'

Comfortably ensconced, contact made. Life, Bob thought, was very simple.

He remarked how good the programme had been. Crown said it was pretty silly, but quite amusing. They spoke of their travel plans. Crown was touring Belgium; he had brought his car with him. His wife had gone on to Paris.

'Do you know Les Roseaux?' Bob asked him. 'It's a little

place on the coast. As a matter of fact, I met Melissa there; we were at the same *pension*.'

'No, I don't know that. Where's it near?'

Bob said it was about twenty minutes from Ostend. He asked whether Crown by any chance knew the Eastwoods.

'Gavin? Certainly I do. As a matter of fact, I ran across them in Ghent.'

'They're staying at a rather nice hotel called the Albert. I've seen quite a lot of them.'

Crown spoke appreciatively of Gavin, whom he had known for some years. 'I believe Melissa attends some of his lectures; a work of supererogation.'

Bob deliberately gave an impression of disquiet, drawing on his cigarette then stubbing it out half-smoked. 'She's a nice girl,' he said, 'but odd.'

'Is she? I only know that she does her work.'

Bob was silent for a moment or two. Then he said, as if driven by an uncontrollable impulse, 'I'm worried about her.'

Crown did not look especially interested. 'Why?'

'Well, it's not my business to gossip.'

'Since you've started, perhaps you'd better go on.' This was uncomfortably dry.

Bob felt that perhaps his charm was not working with this man. He thought a lot about his charm, but not with much vanity. Since he was a child, he had felt it as integral to him as the shape of his nose and no more to his credit. 'I shouldn't have started this.'

'I'm human,' said Crown, 'better proceed. After all, she's one of my concerns, I suppose.' Interest was stirring now, very slowly, like an insect moving one leg.

'It's only that she's in such a queer state of mind. Something's getting her down.'

'I'm sorry to hear that.'

'Look,' Bob said in a rush, 'perhaps I'm sticking my nose in, but as I say, I'm worried about her. As a matter of fact, I think she's got some sort of fixation about Mr Eastwood.'

Crown looked startled. 'A what?'

'She follows him around. And she seems disturbed in her mind.'

'Does Mr Eastwood know about this?'

'I don't think so,' said Bob, 'he ought to. But I'm only a kid. *I* can't warn him.'

'And what does Hannah seem to think about all this?' Crown had forgotten to speak of her formally.

'I think she's worried too. She's certainly noticed something.'

'What did you say the place was?'

'Les Roseaux. The Albert.'

'You must excuse me, but I don't believe a word of this.'

'I should never have told you. You think I'm just butting in.'

Bob mimed acute embarrassment.

Crown called for his bill. 'Well, let's hope you're wrong. If you are right, I don't really see what harm this is doing anybody.'

'Only the harm to Melissa herself. I've become very fond of her.'

'In that case, I suppose you were right to say something. I'll keep an eye on her next term.'

'That's a long way away.'

'I must be going, anyway. Enjoy your travels. If you're going to The Hague, you must see the Vermeer. Where are you making for in Germany?'

They had some desultory conversation; then Crown left him.

He's hooked, Bob thought, he has asked for the address. He felt both triumphant and good. He could not be sure whether Melissa had lied last night; he fancied that anyway, by her manner to Gavin, she must have let the cat out of the bag. But if she had not? He was genuinely concerned for her, wished her protected. He was sure that it was high time someone spoke to Gavin, someone carrying more weight than he did. He thought to himself with a rare spurt of compunction, that he did like to try to run the lives of other people; but then, it had always been a hobby of his, as chess might have been. He imagined the chequered board with small figures being moved over it; Hannah, Gavin, Melissa, himself. Anyway, I do no harm; most people would rather be interfered with than strictly ignored. His personal imperialism seemed to him something that had always been put to the good of others. Oliver, for example, what would he be without me? A mess.

Of course, he did not know whether Crown would really bother to look Gavin up, far less say anything to him. Probably he would put it straight out of his mind. But he thought he was a man in whom, once interest stirred at all, curiosity would flourish. A good morning's work. Perhaps he might even have been instrumental in preventing a suicide. He could imagine Melissa, drowned in sweat and her hair, taking an overdose of something. Virtue flooded him. He went out into the square, walking slowly in the sunlight, past the bright flower stalls.

23

Melissa was counting her money to see how long it would last out. Yes, she could manage another few days, if they could have her. The shame and fear she had felt had now deserted her. She was filled with a brave and restless energy. She had carried off the morning well, she was climbing almost as steeply as Captain Keppel. She no longer missed Bob, had forgotten all about him. There was nothing she could not do, nothing she could not dare. He would come to her in the end, she knew that. He would not be able to resist the strength of love she felt for him. For Hannah she did not care; Hannah could share him, just this once.

It occurred to her that she was losing her sense of reality, and for a moment she sat still as stone, trying to recapture it. But, she thought, I have come too far to care about reality. This is real for me.

She put on the black dress, re-coiled her hair, renewed lipstick and eye-shadow, more heavily this time. I am young, which Hannah is not. I can even look quite beautiful. Nothing is going to stop me. I was asked there this evening, and I shall go.

She ate a hearty meal; she had never known such an appetite. It was good tonight, eggs and ham in a cheese sauce, a chocolate mousse.

I shall not go up there till nine.

The only thing that troubled her was the thought that they would again be paying for her drinks; she had taken too much from them already. Well, she could manage to stand them a round, if the Vennings were not there. She had just enough for that.

Something was telling her insistently that she should not go at all, but she did not heed it. I am brazen, she thought, I am quite brazen; and the word gave her strength. I am wonderfully, beautifully brazen. There is so little time left, and after that I shall not see him till the end of the summer. They would not grudge me that.

So, at nine o'clock sharp, she was on the steps of the Albert. They were sitting on the covered terrace; through the glass they were like figures of wax. The Vennings were not there, the children must have been sent to bed. 'Hullo,' she said, addressing herself to Hannah, ' I'm afraid it's me again.'

For the first time, she saw an expression of active alarm cross Hannah's face. She did not care. She sat down with them. 'You must have a drink with me, this time.'

'There's no need for that,' Gavin said, the bluff tone still in evidence.

'Oh, yes, there is. I've taken too much from you both.'

Stiffly, but brightly, they accepted her offer.

'There's nothing much to do here in the evening, but down Stellas,' said Hannah, speaking naturally. 'We thought of going to the cinema, but it's a Flemish film with subtitles.'

'How's Giles tonight?'

'Sleepy,' Gavin answered, 'it's been a bit of a bore for him today. He's clamouring for the beach tomorrow.'

'It's surprising how they manage to amuse themselves down there,' said Melissa, 'for hours and hours. I knew I did at his age. Where are Mr and Mrs Venning?'

'Packing,' Hannah answered. 'I believe he does it all for her, though. It seems to be a special gift. Are you good at packing?'

'None at all, I'm afraid. Everything comes out creased.'

It is all quite normal, Melissa thought, I am still carrying it off. She glanced at Gavin, who gave her a cordial, impersonal smile. But he is feeling, she thought, he is feeling deeply. He could not have forgotten so soon.

After a while, Hannah went upstairs on the routine visit to Giles. After a little idle conversation, Melissa said to Gavin softly, almost airily, 'You haven't forgotten what I said to you.'

He brought his fist down on the table, not in a swift gesture, but in one that was slow and restrained. 'Oh, my darling,' she said.

'You must listen to me. If you don't forget it, we shan't be able to see any more of you. I don't think you realise how badly you're behaving. It isn't fair to me, nor to Hannah.'

'She doesn't know. Or did you tell her.'

'No,' he said, wanting to spare her that, 'but it's obvious to everybody that there's something wrong with you.'

'Something wrong,' she whispered, smiling.

The bar was too crowded and too noisy for them to be conspicuous. Both were keeping their voices down.

'This must stop, I tell you,' he said,' I can't give you anything in return. And it's beginning to feel very much like persecution.'

For a moment she felt the cruelty of this; but she was still riding high.

'It's not a crime to be in love with someone. It's something that can't be helped. If I could help myself, I would.'

'Do pay attention. You're being childish, you know.'

'Is it a childish thing to do?'

'You're imagining the whole thing. Believe me, it will pass; you'll wake up one morning and wonder how you could ever have been so silly.'

'I wake up every morning and wonder that. But it still goes on.'

196

She saw that he had turned rather pale. She was sorry for him, in a way; but she could not stop herself. Hannah might be back at any moment, and she still had things to say to him. Still had things: but now she did not quite know what they were. 'I love you very much,' she said at last, 'it helps for you to know it.'

'I think,' he said, 'I'd better go up to Hannah. She's being a long time. And I think you'd better be gone when I come down.'

'I want to be with you while I can.'

He half-rose, but at that moment Hannah came in. Melissa saw that she was perturbed about something, too much so to notice the tension between herself and Gavin.

'What'swrong?' he asked quickly.

'Nothing much. Only he was having a nightmare, shouting about the beach. It was lucky I went in when I did, or he'd have wakened Chloe; she's next door to him.'

'Poor chap. Is he all right now?'

She said she had done what she always did in these cases; had woken him right up, talked to him quietly till he had shaken off the dream.

'You're sure he isn't hot, or anything?' Gavin asked anxiously.

Melissa knew a spurt of fierce jealousy that the child should so have drawn the whole of his attention away from her.

Hannah reassured him. Reseating herself, she asked for a cigarette. She said to Melissa, 'I suppose we're idiots to make Giles the sun, moon and stars. But he is the only one.'

'I can imagine how it must be,' Melissa replied, trying to sound concerned. The memory of the few minutes alone with Gavin was beginning to frighten her now. Had she not received her dismissal? She wanted to go, but could not bring herself to make the move. She felt that she had been breaching a wall, little by little, that she had come so much the nearer to him. Hannah, who had lost the air of strain Melissa had noticed earlier that evening, began to talk of her son.

The Vennings came in. 'All packed up,' Verna called to them, 'everything shipshape. Now I want some beer.'

Hannah shot at her a look of pure dislike. Melissa saw it, and wondered why; Hannah was not one to show her feelings easily, unless they were maternal ones.

'Gome on, drink up,' said John, 'we'll have another round.'

Melissa forced herself to her feet. 'I've got to be going now.'

'Don't,' said Verna,' sit yourself down.'

'I must, really. I've got some things to do.' She held out her hand. 'I won't be seeing you tomorrow, so I'll say goodbye now. Have a good journey.' She thanked Hannah and Gavin with what sounded to her like a child's politeness, and left them all in the warmth, the brightness, below the violet ceiling of smoke. Nobody, she thought, would bother to see her home now.

As she walked back down the road, the sustaining elation began to fall away from her. It had been a madness in itself, and she knew that she would pay a price for it. I ought to go back to England, she thought, but I can't bear to leave him. I must just carry on from day to day, being as easy as possible, not letting Hannah see that I care. She knew they would not ask her out in the evenings again, but on the beach, did not see how they would be able to avoid her. Persecution, she thought. It had been a brutal word. Did she really mean nothing to him at all? She could not really believe it.

It had turned warmer, and there was a half-moon. The golf course was phantasmagoric in the floodlights. On the impulse, she went in and paid for a round. Anything was better than the solitude of her bedroom; she needed to quieten her thoughts before she went to bed.

It was hard to play in these conditions, in the dazzle of light and shadow. She took three shots at the first hole, impatiently picked up her ball and put it on the far side of the hazard. Three more shots before she sank it. The other players were nightmare figures on the vivid grass. She moved on to the next tee: better, three shots only. But not a distinguished performance, she said to herself; and the words caught and repeated themselves in her mind. Not a distinguished performance. Not a distinguished performance.

A voice spoke to her, a foreign voice speaking with an American accent. 'All alone?' A tall young man had loomed up at her side. He wore jeans and an anorak. 'Play with me, then.'

'No, thank you. I'm all right.'

'It is a great shame to see you so lonely, with such a lovely moon.'

'I tell you, I'm all right,' said Melissa, 'I like to play by myself. I'm not much good.' She moved away from him, but he followed.

'Oh, come on, come on,' he said.

He followed her round the course, keeping a little behind her, cajoling. Unnerved, she began to play even worse.

'No,' he said, 'you want to get it up the side of the bank, half-way up, and it will run into the hole. That is not the way to do it.'

'Leave me alone,' she said, 'please.'

'Such a pretty girl, all alone.'

'I like being alone. Please go ahead, you can play through.'

She lost him somewhere on the course; he had melted into the other shifting figures. I can attract people, she thought, it isn't because I can't. I should like Gavin to see that I can attract them.

Geraniums glared, calceolarias were livid in the light. She climbed up the little mound to play the chip-shot, but sent it into the bunker. There were people behind her, impatient for her to hole the shot, and they threw her into a ferment of irritation, She picked up her ball and left the course, returning ball and club to Michel in the heat of the little hut. She was just leaving, when the young man rejoined her. 'Let me walk you home', he said. But she rejected him almost angrily, and went on with a rapid step, daring him to follow.

24

Next day they told Giles that they were going to Blankenberge, but met with unexpected resistance. He didn't want to go, he had lost two days of Les Roseaux, he wanted to stay where he was. Hannah and Gavin, who had hoped thus to escape from Melissa, pleaded with him. It would be a change, it was a nice day, it wasn't far on the tram.

He would not hear them, protesting with a babyish air that he wanted to play golf, he wanted to go on the beach, he didn't care about Blankenberge or anywhere else. 'All those places are the same, Mummy.'

'But we'd like to go. You can't always have everything your own way.'

' Then go,' he said rudely.

'You know we can't leave you all alone,' said Gavin.

'Melissa would stay with me, I expect. You could go and ask her.'

Gavin said feebly, 'We might all go tomorrow.'

Giles gave a deep sigh. He knew he had got what he wanted.

It did seem to Gavin that, without meaning to do so, the child had trapped them. He and Hannah looked at him helplessly.

Giles sprang off the bed, where he had been lolling. He was all animation now, his eyes bright.

'Well, clear up those jig-saw pieces,' said Hannah, 'and be downstairs in ten minutes.'

He hugged her. 'I'm so strong I could lift you right off your feet.' He strained to do so, but she pulled herself free.

When she and Gavin were alone, waiting for him in the hall, Gavin said: 'I'm damned if I'm going out this morning. You take Giles to the Golf, and I'll stay here. She's less likely to be there, and even if he is, I dare say she won't worry you. My God, I feel in a state of siege!'

He had not, for some obscure reason, told her of Melissa's behaviour on the previous night; they would have to put up with the girl until they went home, and it seemed to him that Hannah, if she were further angered, might betray herself. For she had felt anger, he knew, even though it was kept sternly under control. 'You don't mind going without me?'

'I suppose not, but we can't play golf the whole morning.'

'Well, take him to Van Damm's for the usual stuffing. And pray to be left alone.'

'That will mean the beach, though.'

'Then let him go alone, he won't come to any harm. You can stay in the café and read a book. You can keep an eye on him from there.'

Giles came down. He collected his shrimping-net and he and Hannah went off together.

Gavin took himself to the parlour, nodding to Madame on the way, and settled himself in a chair right at the back of it, well away from the windows. It was a relief to be by himself, even a relief to be alone, for a while, without Hannah and Giles. He thought he would take the opportunity to sort things out in his mind. Surely the situation was less horrific than ludicrous? They had been making too much of it altogether, treating as an obsession what was only silliness. It surprised him that he should have been attracted to Melissa even for a fleeting second – it had been no more than that; now, the very thought of her made him cringe. He was quite determined that she should not catch him alone again. If she continued with this, when they were home again, persecuted him, for instance, with telephone calls, he would forbid her his lectures. He wondered whether it might do any good for Hannah to talk to her. Perhaps not. He bitterly regretted their intention to stay on for two more days; he could not have believed that Melissa would decide to do the same. He even wondered if she were a little mad.

He returned to his book; nothing was good or bad but thinking it made it so, he told himself, and he would try not to think for a while.

At midday he had an unexpected visitor. Armand showed him in; it was Jamie Crown.

'Jamie! What on earth are you doing here?'

'I'm lucky to find you in, on such a morning. Oh, I was just cruising around, and thought I'd look you up.'

Gavin was pleased to see him; it was a distraction.

'Well, then, sit down and have a drink.'

'It was purely on the off-chance,' said Crown. 'It's a bit umbrageous in here, isn't it? Shall we go into the bar?'

Gavin thought it would be safe. Even if she came by, even if she saw him through the window, she would see that he wasn't alone. They went together into the light. It was a soft day, the sky a thin turquoise. The poplars over the way were unstirring. The crowds were again in holiday mood, the women, slim and stout, in their gaudy sun-dresses, the men with open shirts, the children weaving along on their coloured bicycles, red, yellow and green.

'How did you know where to find me?' he asked, 'I don't believe I told you where I was.'

Oddly enough, Crown replied, he had met someone who knew them, Conran or Conrad, he thought his name was. 'This is a nice little place,' he said appreciatively. 'Better than your stony vast hotels. Would they give me lunch here? It's not residents only?'

Gavin urged him to stay. Hannah and the boy, he said, would be back soon. He was beginning to wonder, with a stirring of suspicion, what Bob had been saying. But nothing intimate, of course, not to a complete stranger. 'Where are you making for next?' he asked.

Crown said Ostend; he wanted to see the Ensors before he went home next day.

Gavin called Armand over, and introduced them. He would be having a guest to lunch, he said, would that be all right? Armand was pleased. 'It is the *water-zooi* today,' he said, 'it is very good.'

'I've been hearing something about young Melissa Hirst,' Crown said, when he had gone. 'It sounded rather disquieting. But I thought you ought to know. Mind you, I expect the boy was making something of a production of it.'

Gavin was for a moment speechless with rage. That Bob should have told all this to Crown was intolerable; he was sure he had urged him to interfere. He felt ringed with peering faces.

'I feel some responsibility for her,' Crown said, 'if there's any question of her being ill, or something like that—'

'She is not ill. She is simply making a fool of herself. I suppose that damned Conrad told you as much.'

'Look here, Gavin, we've known each other for years. If she's putting you on a spot and I can help—'

'There's nothing you can do. Leave it alone.' He felt an impulse to hilarity; this was beyond comedy, this was turning to farce. He almost laughed in Crown's face.

'So it's not serious? The boy was talking about suicide.'

'That's rubbish. She's going through a phase, and she'll get out of it. I don't want to talk about it, Jamie.'

'I'm sorry. Perhaps I shouldn't have said anything.' He paused. 'Anyway, I didn't really come about that. I wanted to talk to you about the possibility of some inter-disciplinary lectures.'

A fresh topic, and a blessing. They talked about it till lunch-time, when Hannah and Giles came in. She was pleased to see Crown, and her cordiality turned the meal into a party. That is what we need, Gavin thought, distraction. He longed to ask her if she had seen Melissa, but could not.

'I won,' said Giles, 'we were playing hole by hole, and I beat Mummy by four. Then she sat in the café and I went on to the beach. There was a boy there just like Hans, only English. He wanted me to build a castle, but I wouldn't.'

Gavin said to himself, If he had seen Melissa he would have said so. 'Then what did you do? Go on your old dunes?'

'No,' said Giles.

'Is he interested in art?' Crown enquired. Gavin had often noticed that people tended to talk of Giles as though he were not there.

'I like some pictures,' Giles said. 'I liked the one in Ghent. I draw a bit, too.'

'And he's not half bad,' Hannah said proudly. 'Are you, darling?'

'I like this chicken,' he said. 'I wish we could have it like that at home.'

'Perhaps Madame Croisset will give me the recipe.'

Gavin thought he would tell her nothing about Crown's intervention. For one thing, it made him look slightly ridiculous; for another, the least said, the easier the whole business would be to handle.

'Would you like a drive after lunch?' Crown said to the boy, good-naturedly.

Giles hesitated. 'How long would it take?'

'Just as long as you like.'

'I want to go back on the beach, though.'

Gavin was eager for this, and he saw that Hannah was too. It would be another spell of escape.

So they drove through the dead-level countryside, past the cottages washed in rose, starch-blue and yellow, through the lanes of poplars, through other little seaside towns. As time went by, Gavin saw that Giles was straining in his seat as if to urge the car forward. But they were not long away. It was three o'clock when Crown brought them back to the Albert. 'I'll drop you on the sea-front if you like,' he said, 'it's on my route.'

They accepted his offer, pausing for a minute to collect their books and Giles's impedimenta.

'And now,' said Gavin, when they were alone, and Giles had run ahead of them, tumbling at full speed down the stairs to the sand, 'we may be for it.'

'She wasn't down here this morning,' said Hannah, 'or at least, I didn't see her.'

'Good. Cross your fingers for this afternoon.'

They found their usual chairs, and Giles went up to the dunes, clinking his jacks as he went. They soon saw Melissa, but she had made no attempt to approach them. She was going down to the sea in her white bathing-suit, thin as a stick, her hair bound round her head. She must have been sitting by the second row of wind-breaks, for she did not pass them on her way.

'It looks all right,' said Gavin, 'but we'll still touch wood.'

She came back from her bathe without a glance at them and disappeared from sight behind the canvas screens. Nor did she emerge when they went up to tea, Giles having come down from his private place. There was no sign of her.

When they returned to the hotel, Hannah took the boy straight upstairs; he had a small cut on his leg from one of the spiny reeds, and she wanted to wash and bandage it. Gavin lingered in the hall. Suddenly his eye was caught by a letter sticking out from a pigeon-hole; he was expecting none, and would not have thought deliberately to look there. It was for him. His heart sank; he guessed its source. Not wanting Hannah to see it, he locked himself in the lavatory and opened it. No superscripture. A spindly writing, with a strong right-hand slope.

'When I woke up this morning, I thought I must have been mad. I am very sorry I said all those things to you. I had no right to bother you and I won't do it again. I don't know what got into me. If you will forgive me, everything shall go on as before. Please go on letting me see you both, and Giles. I meant what I said, but I will try to forget it. *Please*. This is a very hard letter to write. I remember what you said about putting time back; we can do it, I'm sure we can. I promise you, it shall never happen again. I have control over myself now, and I feel very ashamed and ridiculous. Melissa.'

He drew a sigh of relief; it was not what he had feared. This he would show to Hannah, for it did not reveal the fact that Melissa had spoken to him again last night. He would have some time alone with her, for Giles did not care to come down from his room before dinner. He was still battling with the jig-saw puzzle.

Gavin went to sit on the outside terrace, before the fringe of geraniums, and waited for her to join him.

Seeing his face, she said at once, 'Now what's up?'

He gave her the letter and watched her while she read it.

'More effrontery,' she said, and passed it back. Her colour was high.

'I don't think so. I think she means it. We shall have to give her a chance, shan't we?' He did not really want to; he was still flinching from the thought of her; but sympathy was stirring in him. After all, it was not essentially displeasing, at his age, to have aroused a girl's passion.

'Why should we?'

'Because we can't go on lurking out of her way, or she out of ours. She's only young.'

'I feel unrelenting,' Hannah said. 'But I suppose I've got to go on seeing her. I'm not supposed to know anything.'

'Yes, it's awkward for you. Shall we just wait and see what happens?'

'I can't think of anything else to do.'

'You might say,' said Gavin, folding the letter and putting it back in his pocket, 'that this is a not unhandsome *amende honorable*. And as she remarks herself, it can't have been easy to write.'

'I think there is nothing handsome about her,' said Hannah, 'either physically or spiritually.'

'You're being unlike yourself. Please don't be.' He hated to see a harsh strain coming out; from Hannah, the magnanimous.

She turned to him, her face open. 'Yes, I know I am. But this business has upset me more than it should. All right, next time we see her we'll go on as we are, and I'll try to play up properly. We'll soon find out if her promises are pie-crust.'

'But for God's sake, don't leave her alone with me.'

'A nice prospect, policing you.'

'Darling.'

'Well, let's not stay here tonight, or go to Van Damm's; we'll go to the café just across the way. We shan't be far from Giles.'

He demurred at this; they need not run away from the places they liked best, just for Melissa's benefit.

'The wrong word,' said Hannah, 'it is not meant to benefit her.'

'She won't have the nerve to come up here. I think her nerve has been broken.'

'I would put nothing past her. Still, stay here if you like.'

It was a beautiful evening, the sky periwinkle under a flush of sun, and it calmed them both. 'I take it there's no need for me to reply,' said Gavin.

'No, there is not.'

They stayed on the terrace that evening, but she did not come in search of them. Darkness fell, and she did not even pass by.

Next morning, on the beach, she approached them shyly, almost humbly, her eyes averted from Gavin. They greeted her in a normal fashion. It was a Saturday, and crowds had come in from surrounding towns. The sea was pegged out with bathers.

Giles said, 'Are you going to bathe? You might give me another swimming lesson.'

She looked at Hannah. 'Would it be all right if I did? I'm going in, anyway. And he'll be all right with me.'

'Well, I don't know. It's rather soon after his chill—'

'Oh, Mummy, Mummy, Mummy, don't fuss!'

'Let him,' said Gavin, 'it will do no harm.'

'You mustn't keep him in too long,' Hannah said.

Melissa turned upon her with mournful and sincere round eyes.' I promise not to, Mrs Eastwood, we'll only be in about fifteen minutes.' Not Hannah: Mrs Eastwood.

Melissa and the child went up to the huts to change; they had to queue for a while.

Gavin said, when they had gone, 'I think it's going to be all right. She really has come to her senses.'

'You may be right. It may have been a kind of brainstorm.'

The morning passed naturally for them all, or so Gavin believed. She kept her promise and did not let Giles swim for too long; when they came out she raced him up the beach, to warm him up. The four of them went up to the café together.

'And where is the young man?' Van Damm cried cheerfully, when he had taken their orders.

They told him Bob had gone off on his travels.

'A pity. He was such company for mademoiselle. But, of course, she has company now.'

He was attracted by Melissa, Gavin observed and he let her see it.

'He has gone to Germany? Perhaps I have told you, I was a prisoner-of-war there, liberated by the Russians. I was lucky, I had no very hard experiences. One night, if you care to come in late, I will tell you about them.'

He turned to greet, in fluent German, a party which had just come in. 'Excuse me, I must go.'

'I won't let you both buy me coffee,' Melissa said to Hannah, 'you do it all the time, and it's dreadful to let you. Please let me pay for mine.'

'If you really want to,' said Gavin, 'but a cup of coffee isn't all the world.'

Melissa sat back in her chair, looking out at the plage, the beaches kaleidoscopic with colour, the glittering sea. She looked no longer shy, but calm, and at ease with the world. 'Oh, isn't this nice? I should like to stay here always.'

'It's very packed on Saturdays, though,' said Hannah.

Gavin was pleased to see that the touch of tension had left her.

'I love crowds,' said Melissa, 'I love people, really, especially if I don't know them. I don't mean you, of course, I only mean that it's nice to know a few people really well but to see plenty.' To Hannah she said, 'You've been kind. This has been a wonderful holiday for me.'

'Can I have another slice of cherry tart?' asked Giles.

'How he finds the appetite!' Melissa said, laughing.

The fevers of the last two days might not have been. She had, Gavin believed, accepted her situation; so long as she behaved well, they could not refuse to see her. It seemed to him that, with any luck, the trouble was over, and he drew a breath of pure relief.

25

The fair had come again to the market place. There were dodgem cars, helter-skelters and a great roundabout; Giles felt the music lurch round him. He had rushed off early from his lunch, in order to have a good time there, and then keep his appointment; the other had not kept it yesterday, and he had been disappointed. His friend had let him down, there had been no one to play at jacks with.

He wandered between the stalls, the various attractions, wondering how he should spend his money. His secret weighed with him; he knew he should have let his father and mother into it. But then, they might have spoiled it; he never knew what they might do.

He stood by the roundabout, waiting for it to stop; he would have a long ride. Then, as it ground past him, he saw his friend. He was sitting on a little green and gold horse, his hands clasped about the gilded, spiralling pole; he looked as big as a man, and his fair face was flushed with the sunlight. Giles waved to him frantically, and thought he had been seen; his friend made no sign, but went circling round, up and down, grave and unsmiling. Giles had never seen him away from the dunes before. The roundabout slowed down, and he clambered on to the footboard, waiting for his friend to alight; but the music stopped, and he did not. He waved his hand. Giles cried to him, 'Today? Today?' But the other shook his head. Had he understood, even, what 'today' meant?

Plainly he intended to go on riding. Giles climbed on to the horse behind him, a white animal with crimson flares in its nostrils. The man came round, and he paid. Everyone but his friend had got down, a new crowd were taking their places. The music started again. Slowly Giles's horse rose into the air and down again; he could see his friend's broad back, it was as if he, Giles, were chasing him, for ever and ever, without a hope of catching him up. He shouted above the noise, 'Today? Today?' but the sound did not penetrate. Faster now, still in the vain pursuit. On and on, a blur of faces upturned, surrounding him. Again they were slowing down, the music with them. His friend climbed down, circling with the platform, his hand on the horse's back. Giles clambered off, too, and stood beside him. 'Today?' Again a shake of the head. Giles knew one word he thought the other might know, he had learned it from Hans. '*Sonntag*?' This time a smile and a nod. The roundabout came to a halt. Giles touched his friend's arm, but felt his hand shaken off. They both got down. The other smiled, put a finger to his lips, and melted away into the milling crowd. It was as though he had never been there at all.

Would he be on the dunes that day, or not? Tomorrow, perhaps; he had seemed to understand Giles's word for Sunday, even though it was a German one. It might be the same in Flemish, he didn't know. This time he remounted, and rode alone. In the ring of faces, he saw Melissa's. Had she seen his friend? He thought not, hoped she hadn't. This was his secret, and no one else's. Riding along, up to the sky, down to the earth, he thought it was the first secret he had had from anyone; yet why should it be as secret as all that? He simply knew that it must be, that his friend expected it. He did not even know his name.

When the ride came to an end, Melissa came up to him. 'Hullo! That looked fun. Do you want to come on the dodgems with me? I'm always a bit scared to go by myself.'

'Why?' he asked. 'Aren't you good at steering?'

'Not much. I seem to get crashed into more than other people.'

'All right,' he said, 'I'll do the driving.'

They sat together, packed tightly in the little battered steel car, the blue sparks flashing overhead. He was expert at this, keeping them largely unscathed. Melissa kept crying out whenever they saw another car bearing down upon them on a collision course; this made it very exciting. All the time he was driving, he was looking out for his friend; but if he saw him again he would not speak. Melissa was grown up, she would be sure to talk. He had his dark, secret happiness. Yet what about? he thought, it is only playing jacks in the sand.

His mother and father were too much with him; he loved them, but he did not need them all the time. He was older now, he must have some things to himself.

'Well,' Melissa said shakily, when the drive ended, when she stepped unsteadily out on to the surrounding planks, 'that was a thrill. What do you want to do now?'

They went to the coconut shy (he won a dried-up specimen which he threw away) to the rifle range, where he had only one successful shot, to the helter-skelter on which she would not follow him. 'I'll stand at the bottom and watch you slide down.'

From the top of it, just as he was taking his place on the mat, he saw his friend once more: making his way towards the outskirts of the town, down an unfamiliar road. Giles soared down, and Melissa helped him up.

Well, it did not look as though he would come that day. He had understood, and the shake of the head had meant no.

'Let's go fishing for ducks,' said Melissa. This time she won a vase of pink plaster, which Giles rather liked though he knew by instinct that his parents would not. He was given a consolation prize, a ball-point pen. They both had a turn on the roundabout, Melissa beside him, her hair bobbing on her back – 'You look like Joan of Arc,' he said.

'I feel like it. How did you know?'

He saw his parents making their way towards them; he and Melissa waved. His parents waved back. They were walking arm in arm, as they so often did; other boys' people did not seem to do it so much. Giles was not sure whether he liked them to do it, since it sometimes made him feel like an outsider, a poor third. He thought about love, and was shy. He supposed they had been 'in love' when they first married, wondered whether they could possibly be so now; though they were getting old. A complexity of emotion stirred in him, of fascination, of revulsion. It seemed to him that his mother should be all his.

He swung down, Melissa following. 'We've been having such a time!' she said. She showed Hannah her vase. 'Isn't it horrible? But so well meant. I love fairs.'

Giles slipped his hand into his mother's. It occurred to him then that he might tell her after all, that he might simply say, I have got a friend. But she still remained linked with his father, and he did not.

'I love them too,' Gavin said. 'But I am rather too old now to go on roundabouts.'

'Oh, do,' said Melissa, 'it would be such fun.' She turned to Hannah. 'Wouldn't it?'

Giles knew that he was supposed to be unobservant; but he was not. He had noticed, during the past two days, that his mother had not seemed to care much for Melissa, and he wondered why. Not that he cared greatly for her himself, though he quite liked her; she made no appeal to his imagination, and he did not care if they never saw her again when they were back in London.

Hannah said unexpectedly, 'Yes, it would be fun. Let's all have one ride.'

She got on to the roundabout and on to one of the horses, handling her skirts neatly as she did so. She looked down at them, queenly, back straight, head held high. 'Come on, then!'

Gavin jumped up, then Melissa. Giles chose to ride on a white unicorn with a golden horn. As they whirled off, he was happy; it was good to be all together, good to do extraordinary things. 'I feel like Joan of Arc,' Hannah called out.

'Melissa felt like that,' said Giles.

All was joyful; they were swept away on the tide of music.

They rode on, all time forgotten, till at last Gavin said, 'Isn't this thing ever going to stop?'

They all realised that it had been a very long ride. Looking in at the driver's cab, they saw that it was empty. Giles began to panic.

'Don't,' called Hannah, 'he's only gone off for a drink or something. We can't come to any harm.'

'Or to the loo,' shouted Gavin. 'Hang on.'

The roundabout's strange behaviour was attracting the attention of the circling crowd. There were whistles, cat-calls. The machine was going at full speed, causing them to hang on with unnecessary fervour. People don't really fall off, Giles said to himself, They never do. There's no reason why they should. But he had begun to feel giddy. Hannah, who was riding beside him, put an arm about his waist.

'This damned thing's got to stop,' said Gavin, and tried to get from his horse on to the platform, but it was moving too steeply up and down.

The people began to clap and cheer.

Then they saw the driver pushing his way through. He wore a blue cap on the back of his head and was smoking a cigarette. He swung himself up without difficulty and entered the cab. In a leisurely fashion, he pulled a switch. The horses and the music began to slow down. Giles was determined not to show that he had been frightened.

'Well, we had a lot for our money, didn't we, Mummy?' he said, when they were all safely back on the cobbles.

'We certainly did. Far too much.'

'Were you scared? I wasn't. I thought it was fun. Were you, Melissa?'

'A bit,' she replied, 'it was making me feel sick.'

'What we need is something for our nerves,' said Gavin, pushing a way for them through the people. 'It ought to be Armand's medicinal brandy, but we can't ask for that. We'll go over here.' He took them to a *patisserie* beyond the market place, the one selling Giles's favourite meringues.

Giles's legs were trembling. He was glad to sit with them quietly and drink cokes. He had no desire to go to the beach, knowing that no one would be there. When they asked him what he would like to do next, he said, to play golf; they all agreed to play with him, Gavin and Hannah against himself and Melissa; a strong player on each side. In his absorption, he soon forgot about the roundabout.

But that night he had a dream. He was on the green horse, flying through darkness in pursuit of someone he could not see. He could not stop. He tried to call out, but his voice made no sound. He knew there was music, but he could not hear it. Afraid of falling, he gripped first at the reins, then clung around the golden pole with sweating hands. For all the speed of his riding he could get no nearer the pursued, could not even catch a glimpse of him. For he knew who it was, but knew also that he must not tell. A great white charger rose suddenly in front of him, a real horse; it turned its head and he saw its scarlet nostrils, its foaming mouth. He knew it would kick out at him with its immense hind legs, but he could not escape. His own horse began to shrink and shrink, till it was no larger than a baby's bicycle. He clung on desperately, gripping it between his legs. The charger reared, and seemed as if it would topple right back on to him.

He awoke, and heard himself screaming. The maid came running in, and she went to fetch his mother.

26

Melissa had tea with them that day, but afterwards returned to the *pension*. She might see them that evening, or not; she did not know, and she did not want to push her luck too far. It seemed to her that all had been smoothed over, and that they had been united by the adventure on the roundabout. It was hard for her to behave normally to Gavin, yet she knew that she must if she were to be allowed to see him at all. Hannah, she thought, was of course behaving beautifully; she was the kind of woman who would. Melissa had come to believe that Gavin had kept nothing from her, and at the thought her face burned. But I can carry it off now, can carry it through. Hannah can't harm me.

It had been a great act of courage to speak to them that day, her passion for Gavin unabated. She went up to lie on her bed and give herself up to the luxury of fantasy. Some of her fantasies were childish, and she knew it; for instance, she dreamed of saving Giles from drowning (though who could drown in that shallow sea?) and thereby putting them under a lifelong obligation to her. She thought of her letter. It had been a horror and a delight to compose, another way of talking to him. When they were back in London she would find more ways. They would not be confined within this coastal strip, they would all be more free. She could telephone him: she would do so, after a decent interval. If she stayed away for a while, he might miss her. She still could not believe that she had occupied no part in his life.

Love breeds love, she thought, it must.

She got off the bed to look at herself in the glass. No make-up today; she thought it was like this that he had liked her best. For he had liked her, she knew it.

She remembered him as he had appeared at his lectures, elegant, lean, his long forelock, his bright broad tie making some small concession to the age he lived in. He spoke evenly, with the slightest of gestures, conveying his enthusiasms only by his phraseology. He was much admired, she was not the only one to admire him.

She tried to fight off her fierce jealousy of Hannah and Giles. She could not expect him easily to forget them. They had been so much part of his life, as she had not. Hannah had spoken regretfully of the fact that they had only had one child. If he came to me, Melissa said to herself, I would give him children. She saw herself pregnant, refusing abortion. Somehow I would keep them; I don't know how, but I would.

The heat of her thoughts was too intense for endurance. She sprang up and walked about the room. It was too hot in there. She would go out before dinner, to the café hidden at the end of the lane, where nobody would know her. Only a few days left. She must see him tonight.

She did meet someone she knew, the young man who had spoken to her that night at the golf-course. He asked if he might sit at her table.

'I don't own the chairs,' she said ungraciously.

Not deterred by this, he took the seat opposite. He was, he said, a student at the university of Brussels; he was on holiday. His name was Jean, and he was lonely. 'Tell me about yourself,' he urged her. He had very bright eyes, which admired her.

She answered him, but would not accept a drink.

'I hoped I'd see you again,' he said. 'There's a dance on here tonight. Will you come?'

220

'I don't dance.'

'I'll teach you. Please let me!'

She refused. She did not want his admiration, though a few months ago it might have pleased her. The thought of Gavin pervaded her, leaving room for nothing else.

'If you won't, you won't,' he said. He was very disappointed, but he chattered on. What did she like to do? Music? The cinema? He went to a film three times a week. How long was she here for?

In his persistence he reminded her of Bob, though he had not the latter's puppy-like appeal. She gave him short answers, her mind straying to the evening ahead. It might be better, perhaps, to stay away from them; but then, there was so little time! It was still very warm, it would be a warm night. It would be only natural if she walked up towards the town.

She told the young man she must go. He said he would walk back with her, she couldn't deny him that; just as far as her door.

'It's only a step,' she said, 'but come if you like.'

There were a good many people in the lane, taking the short cut back from the beach, children with spades and pails, and bathing suits rolled in damp towels. They came to the *pension*. 'Here I am,' she said.

As if they were alone on a desert island, he put his arm around her waist and kissed her wetly. She recoiled with the shock of it, and raised her hand as if to strike him, but he pulled it down. 'Be a bitch if you like,' he said, and walked off.

Melissa went indoors, trembling. He had violated her dream of Gavin, it was as though he had put a finger on the very wire of her strung nerves. She scrubbed her face, lit a cigarette and sat down to wait until calm returned. Though it was past the dinner-hour, she did not come down till the meal was half over; she had little appetite. After that she went back to her room and lay in the gathering dusk, waiting until it was time to go. As before, the minutes crept, and she wondered whether her watch had stopped.

27

As they sat outdoors in the afterglow, it seemed both to Hannah and to Gavin that the halcyon days had returned. All had been well that day, and they were peaceful together. There was nothing either liked so much as the company of the other; even Giles, whom they loved so much, interrupted that. Hannah was reminded of *Little Eyolf*, of the Allmers's dreams of gold and green forests, and her comfort momentarily fled; for the sake of their passion, Rita and her husband had let the little boy be lamed for life. We are not like that to Giles, though, he comes first. She said nothing of this to Gavin, and in a moment the recollection was swept away in the delight of the evening.

It was the beautiful hour when the sun was not quite faded from the sky but the lamps are lit. 'We're lucky with the weather,' she said, 'if it lasts.'

'Very lucky.'

They saw Melissa coming very slowly up the road. 'Oh, dear,' Gavin said, 'here she is. Pretend you don't see her.'

But Melissa would not permit them to pretend. She raised her hand, smiled, and waved as if to pass on. Then she stopped.

'Where are you going to?' asked Hannah. She knew the girl had made a great effort that day, and she could not help but be kind to her.

'Just as far as the square.'

'Drop in here on your way back.'

'You don't want me again today,' Melissa said.

Gavin said, in his hearty-seeming voice, that of course they did. She walked on.

'If she behaves herself as well as she did this afternoon, it will be bearable,' Gavin said. The worst of his fears were now dispersed. The distant sound of the music from the market-place was mingled with the piped music from the bar. An old song, *J'attendrai*.

Armand came to them. 'Marie says the little boy is crying.'

Hannah and Gavin jumped to their feet, leaving full glasses behind them on the table. They rushed upstairs. 'Now what do you suppose?' he said.

Giles had stopped screaming and was sitting bolt upright in bed, his arms held out to them. Hannah turned on the light and came to him. She could feel his heart thudding beneath the thin pyjama jacket. He was in a heavy sweat, his hair was dank with it.

'Oh, what is it, my pet? Tell Mummy. Have you been having another nightmare?'

'It was the roundabout,' he said, 'the roundabout.'

She held him tightly, to subdue his trembling. 'I don't wonder it gave you bad dreams,' she said briskly, 'it would me, I expect. But you were never in any danger.'

'I couldn't get off, and my horse got smaller and smaller.'

'All gone now. Quiet.'

Gavin fetched a towel and wiped his head and face. Giles burrowed into Hannah's shoulder, clinging to her.

'That better?' Gavin asked him.

'You're quite awake now, aren't you, darling? It's all gone?'

'I can still hear the organ.'

'As a matter of fact, you can. It's just audible from here.'

'So that's real?'

'Yes.'

'I wish it would stop.'

'It will soon,' said Hannah, 'it will pack in for the night. Would you like a glass of water? 'She gave it him, and he seemed a little soothed. She laid him gently back on the pillows.

'You'll be all right now?' said Gavin. He kissed him; he seldom did so now.

'Are you coming to bed?'

'Not for half an hour. Come on, go to sleep again. I'll leave the bedside lamp on, and switch off the top light.

'Yes, do,' said Giles. His eyelids drooped. He said, 'The music's stopped.'

'I told you it would,' said Hannah. 'Shall I leave the door open? Marie's just along the passage.'

'Please.' He turned up his face to be kissed, and put his arms round her neck. 'Good night.'

'Good night, old boy,' said Gavin.

They left him and returned to the terrace. Melissa was sitting anxiously at their table. 'I hope you don't mind. I saw you'd left your books here, and your handbag.'

'Thank you for guarding them,' said Hannah. 'We had to go up to Giles, he had another nightmare. About that damned roundabout.'

The beer was flat in their glasses. Gavin offered Melissa a drink, but she was obdurate; she really didn't want one, she wasn't thirsty, she had only looked in for a moment. 'Poor Giles,' she said, 'he's very sensitive, isn't he?'

'Yes,' said Gavin, 'but I shouldn't as a rule call him high-strung. He usually goes his own placid way.'

'You're both of you very good with him,' she said. 'I don't know that I should be, I wouldn't know what to do.'

'That,' said Hannah, 'comes from pure experience. There's no mystique about it.' She smiled at the girl, to whom she could now talk in an ordinary way, even though she continued to dislike her. 'You'll have a family one of these days, and

225

then you'll find out.' She realised even as she spoke that there had been a touch of cruelty in her words, and she regretted them. It would, of course, be impossible for Melissa to imagine any kind of life that did not hold Gavin.

But Melissa answered calmly enough. 'I suppose I may, though I can't envisage it yet.'

They were on dangerous ground here, and Hannah was not sure of her next step. Changing the subject, she said that Giles sometimes worried them; he was not particularly good at school, did not seem to care for it or to have had his interest aroused. She would not ordinarily have wished to confide this to Melissa, but had been unable to think of anything else to say. 'Gavin thinks he's just a slow starter.' They were always saying this; it helped to reassure them.

Gavin asked Melissa whether she would not like to spend a day in Bruges before going back, but she shook her head. It was too late, she said, and she was lazy.

'A pity. You'd like the Musée Communale. Giles's favourite horror-picture is there.' He told her about the museum, what she ought to see, what she need not bother with. 'It's really the first five rooms. One day I went in there, and found all my favourites missing. I was so upset that I failed to notice at first what *was* all around me – a superb loan exhibition from Spain.'

'Just a moment,' said Hannah, 'listen! Is that Giles again?'

'I don't think so,' Gavin said, 'we couldn't hear him from the terrace.'

They were silent, straining their ears.

'Ought I to go up?' she said.

Melissa said quickly, 'Let me. I can run up so quickly.'

'Implying that we are somewhat stiff in the joints,' said Gavin, trying to joke with her. But he was still listening.

'Let me go,' she said. 'Where is he?'

'On the second floor, room fifteen. Yes,' said Hannah, 'do that. It would be kind of you.' When we permit her to do us a

226

favour, we do her a favour, she thought. She is brought by this means back into the family. Yet if the thought were ungenerous, it was succeeded by another. Gavin would have some kind of responsibility to this girl, he might save her from herself. Already he had done much.

'I don't believe you heard anything,' said Gavin.

Feeling the need for him, she took his hand across the table. She dropped it as Melissa came back.

'It's all right, Mrs Eastwood, he's sleeping like a log. Did you want him to have the light on?'

Hannah said she did, and thanked her. She noticed that the girl still did not use her Christian name. 'Sometimes we do let him have it on all night, if he seems at all disturbed. It certainly doesn't keep him awake.'

'I must go,' Melissa said. She listened. 'Was that thunder? I believe it was.'

'Can't be,' said Gavin, 'it's so serene.'

'Perhaps it wasn't, then. But I'll say good night.'

When she had gone, they watched her down the road as far as the lamps would let them.

'I don't want to go in yet,' Hannah said, 'do you?' They, like the night, could be serene, Little Eyolf unharmed. She wondered how she had let this thought, with its token threat, intrude. She was not Rita, nor Gavin Allmers; Giles was wrapped around in their care, too much so, maybe, but safely.

So they sat out until past eleven.

'Bed now?' asked Gavin, his voice a little thick.

She looked at him. 'Plans?'

'Perhaps plans,' he said. 'The sea air has this effect on me.' They had never taken sex other than jocosely; there had been no solemnity in it.

Gavin was thinking, guiltily, that it was strange how any contact with Melissa moved him towards Hannah. His aversion to the girl had lessened somewhat since she had begun

227

to behave herself reasonably again; all the same, no fantasy of touching her could enter his mind. Even to kiss her, as he would a child or one of Hannah's closer friends, would now be impossible. Yet it had been a pleasure, on the day of the swim, to feel her body for a moment alongside his own.

And now the thought of her thinness made Hannah seem all the more bountiful. 'Come on,' he said, raising her from her chair.

'That was thunder,' she said, 'very far off.'

'Never mind.'

The storm did not develop. Nevertheless, the weather next day had changed. It was still fairly warm, but the clouds hung blackly and there were no shadows. An unattractive morning, though the rain did not fall. Only the yellow pane in the bedroom window deceived them with its impression of sun.

'I don't think we'll get much of the beach,' he called to Hannah as he dressed, 'and it's hardly worth going far afield.'

It was Sunday; the church bells were ringing.

'I like the sound,' she said, lying on her back in the bed, her hair dark on the pillows. She never had to pin it up at night, or to make herself unsightly in any other way. He came out to her, in an uxorious mood. 'Was it good last night?'

'You know.' She put her arms about his neck. She smelled warm and pleasant, flowery.

Giles knocked and asked if he might come in. They moved apart.

He was ready, dressed for breakfast. He looked quite himself again, as if he had had no dreams in the night.

'I'll be with you in a minute,' said Gavin.

'What are we going to do today? Three more days, that's all we've got.'

'The weather looks a bit doubtful. We'd better stay inland, for this morning, at any rate.'

'I don't mind. We can go to the beach this afternoon.'

'Not if it's still like this,' said Hannah.

'Oh, yes,' said Giles, 'do let's.' He frowned. 'I wish this was a place like the South of France, where the sun was always shining.'

'And that can be damned chilly, at times,' Gavin said. 'But we might see about it next year.'

'I think I like it best here, all the same.'

Hannah's tray came up, coffee steaming. 'Pass me my jacket, darling,' she said.

Giles did so, and she shrugged herself into it. 'You didn't have any more nightmares,' she said.

He smiled at her. 'That one was enough. It was awful.'

'And you practically roused the whole hotel. Go on, both of you, downstairs and get your breakfast.'

When they had gone, she ate slowly. She was wondering about the coming day, and how Melissa would behave; because of course she would seek them out. Even subdued, even repentant, she was stubborn. I shall be glad now to get away from here, Hannah thought, even though I have now begun to enjoy it again. I shall have Gavin to myself. It occurred to her that he and she were very self-sufficient. They had many friends, they liked to entertain, but they permitted few over the real borders of intimacy. We are ingrown, people would say: as if we should care.

28

Melissa, searching for them on the darkling Sunday morning, found the beach almost deserted, except for a few intrepid children. There were not many people in the café. She went back down the road towards the town. Glancing at the golf course, she saw Giles nearby, concentrating upon the third hole. She called to him over the hedge.

'Hullo, you all alone?'

He came up to her, swaggering with his club. Neither his father or mother had wanted to go out, he said, they had let him come to the Golf by himself. He was obviously delighted by this. He liked playing alone, it was better practice; he didn't have to score, and if he made a mistake he could just go back and try a hole again.

'So you don't want a game with me?'

'Thank you very much,' he said, 'but I'm all right. Really.'

Small, fair-haired, intent on the game, he went on. She thought, He is a pretty child. Yes, the back of his head is just like Gavin's. He likes me all right, but not that much.

It seemed to her that she was liked by most people; but not very much. What was there lacking in her, that called for a tame response? Yet she was not much given to self-pity. She had tenacity, she knew; she would get what she wanted in the end.

She went directly to the hotel. At least she could tell them that she had seen Giles, that he was all right.

She found Gavin in the bar, alone. At first she thought he looked put out; but he greeted her cheerfully enough and told her to sit down. 'Hannah's gone to see if she can get any papers. She won't be long.'

She flushed hot and cold. She was grateful for this bonus; that for a few minutes, at least, she had him to herself. She must make the most of it. She said quickly, 'You got my letter.'

'Yes,' he said, frowning, 'but there's no need to talk about it.'

'I wanted to know that you'd forgiven me.' Her voice seemed to her to come from a long way off. 'I must have been intolerable.'

'Look,' he said, 'have some beer and for the Lord's sake drop the subject. Are you taking the Wednesday boat back?'

She told him she would go on Tuesday. 'They couldn't keep me any longer.' On the table was his empty cigarette packet. She would steal it, if she could; just to have something of him. Her hand edged towards it. 'I've had a wonderful time,' she said. 'You must believe that.'

'Pity you're not going home with us. Are you a good sailor? It's always choppy on that crossing.'

She told him she was.

He rose and went to the bar. Quickly she swept the packet into her bag. What she would have given for a photograph! If she had brought a camera, he could not have stopped her from snapping him. She was wearing make-up that day; it had been agony for her to decide whether or not she would do so, to guess how he found her most attractive.

He came back to the table with three glasses, one of them for Hannah. 'When do you have your finals?' he asked her.

She told him. 'I'll have to work hard.'

'People inform me that you do. Dr Grown says so.'

'Oh, do you know him?' She was delighted. Gavin had been interested enough to talk about her. 'He's very kind.'

She felt surreptitiously in her bag, held the packet in her hand.

Hannah came back. 'Hullo, Melissa,' she said cheerfully. 'Not a nice day.' She said to Gavin, 'That shop's very good. I've got all the papers.' To Melissa, 'Would you like one?'

She accepted it, but could not keep her mind on the print. The headlines were meaningless; just trouble everywhere. Ulster, Rhodesia, Pakistan. My love for Gavin has shut the world out, she thought, I am enclosed in its shell. She turned a page, making the pretence of reading.

I shall not come here much more, not to this dark little bar where the fairy-lights glow and the smoke wreaths hang below the ceiling. The piped music insinuated itself.

J'attendrai
Le jour et la nuit
J'attendrai toujours
Ton retour.

She would never, for the rest of her life, hear it without thinking of him. Tears prickled behind her lids.

'What a bloody mess it all is,' said Gavin to Hannah, 'what one would give for a bit of good news. Some peaceful headline, such as "England all out for a hundred and four." Don't you think so, Melissa?'

She rallied sufficiently to make a joke. 'Or, "Minor Earthquake in Chile, No One Killed." '

They laughed with her. 'Never mind,' said Hannah, 'one can but live from day to day. One can't think of trouble all the time.'

'I feel I ought to,' Melissa-said, 'but this place—' she indicated the bar – 'is a long way out of the world. Don't you think so?'

232

'That's why we came here,' said Hannah. 'Isn't it time Giles was back?'

'Shall I go along and fetch him?' Melissa asked, always eager to be of help to Gavin, if not to Hannah.

'No, don't,' Gavin said, 'he can't have finished his round yet and he'll think we're babying him. Give the poor chap some self-respect.' He turned back to his newspaper.

'We are trying so hard not to coddle Giles,' said Hannah, 'and I think we're at last succeeding. But old habits die hard.' She passed Melissa a cigarette.

'I had a packet somewhere,' said Gavin, 'I think there was one left in it, I'm not sure.' He looked around him. 'Where's it gone to?'

Melissa was frightened. She knew that she had coloured in the unbecoming way, about neck and jawline. 'One of the waiters picked it up,' she lied.

'Oh. Well, perhaps it was empty. I'll get some more.' He left them for a moment, and as he did so Giles came in. Hannah greeted him lightly, artificially. 'Have a good game, darling?'

'Super. I went round in forty-eight. Michel says there's a tournament for under-fifteens next week. I wish we could stay for it. Couldn't we?'

'No, we couldn't,' said Hannah. 'We shall just about make our money last out as it is, and we can't keep your Aunt Katey holding the fort any longer.'

'It was only a thought,' he said, but regretfully. 'I might have won.'

'I'm afraid I haven't helped your money to last out,' Melissa said boldly. 'You've been so generous.'

'Oh, I didn't mean for odds and ends,' Hannah said quickly. 'That's nothing. But a week's bed and board would be more than we could manage. Besides, I must release my poor sister.'

233

Gavin came back with cigarettes. He asked Giles how the game had been, and received the same reply. 'Do you want anything? Coke? Orangeade?'

Melissa said she must be going.

'We'll see you on the beach this afternoon, I expect,' said Giles.

'No, we don't,' said Hannah, 'not under a sky as threatening as this one.'

'Oh, Mummy! I want to. Please let's go. If it rains we can shelter in the café. It's warm as anything, too. Please!'

'We'll see. We're not going to take any firm decisions.'

Melissa left them. On her way down the road, she met the young man, Jean. She swerved to avoid him, but he sprang nimbly in front of her.

'All forgiven and forgotten?' he asked, in his American-English.

'I don't want to talk to you.'

'Oh, come, don't be cruel. It was your fault for being so attractive. We start again, yes?'

'No,' said Melissa. It was detestable to be admired, and not to admire. Could Gavin feel like that about her? She shuddered the thought away, unable to bear it.

'Now I will tell you,' he said, 'what we will do. We will meet for coffee this afternoon, isn't that right? In that little place where we first met. And you won't be angry with me any more.'

'I am not going to meet you,' she said. 'Please go away.'

'You are a virgin,' he said accusingly, 'I know. But I won't do you any harm.'

'Will you let me pass?'

She made a move; again he dodged in front of her.

'Don't be so unkind. You are very cold-hearted. I tell you what, we will just have a chat, the two of us, nothing more. I think you are a beautiful girl. You like me a little bit, don't you? I will teach you to like me a little bit.'

'If you don't let me go, I shall tell people that you are pestering me.'

He opened his eyes comically wide. 'What people? Police? I don't see any. Oh, come on, come on, I am only having my fun. And I expect you like fun, too, don't you? There, I have said I am sorry. What more can I do?'

This time she took a determined sidestep, and got away from him. He followed her for a moment or so, pleading with her, but at last fell back. She hurried on to the *pension*, troubled in mind. She did not want him to dog her steps everywhere she went, to have Gavin see him with her. For I am utterly faithful to Gavin, she thought, whether he likes it or not, I always shall be. He shall not even imagine that I could look at another man – it might give him a way of escape, she added to herself, and then was ashamed. But he is free, as I am not. So what should he escape from? The image of the succubus came to her. But he would not think of me like that, he is too kind, and his thoughts are not ugly. He is all sweetness. He has more sweetness than anyone I ever knew. She felt as pure as a nun, a bride of Christ.

Despite the heavy clouds, the beach was crowded that afternoon; on Sundays, failing a downpour, it always was. Hannah and Gavin were of course down there, persuaded by Giles. The sea was leaden and still, the sands grey. They were sitting against the wind-break, looking rather chilled, though in reality it was not cold.

'So you came after all,' Melissa said.

'No option,' said Gavin, 'it didn't rain, or it hasn't rained yet, and Giles would take no denying.'

She dropped to the sand, feeling graceful. She noticed for the first time that Hannah's wrists and ankles were rather thick.

'Only one more day,' she said, 'at any rate, for me.'

'Do you get on well with your flat-mates?' Hannah asked.

'All right. But they're so hideously untidy. I can't bear that.'

'I'm afraid I am, rather.'

'I can't believe it,' said Melissa, wanting to sound generous, 'you always look perfect.'

'Our flat looks tidy. But the drawers are all in a terrible state.'

Jean came by, and he stopped. 'Hullo.'

She barely nodded. He did not move on. He said impudently, 'You are with friends. Won't you introduce me?'

She was at a loss. Gavin and Hannah were staring at them with interest. 'This is Jean,' she muttered, and that was all.

'Hullo, Jean,' said Hannah.

'I am interrupting? You will tell me if I am.'

'We've got things to talk about,' said Melissa. 'I might see you later.'

'There, you see?' he said to Gavin. 'She makes me a concession. She is a very cold lady. You should bring her up to be more friendly.' Plainly he had reached the conclusion that they were her parents.

'Where's Giles?' Melissa asked Hannah. She ignored Jean.

'Off on his usual scramble,' Hannah answered. 'He'll be down soon.'

'So I am not wanted,' Jean said, unbudging. She did not reply, but Gavin did, and rather sharply. 'You'll see her later. She said so.'

'O.K., O.K., I can take a hint.' Bending down, he squeezed Melissa's shoulder, and she flinched away from him. 'Goodbye now.' At last he went away.

'Who on earth is that?' Gavin asked. 'I could see he wasn't popular.'

'Just someone I met,' said Melissa, 'and no, he isn't popular. He's been pestering me. I don't want him.'

Hannah said there was little, at Les Roseaux, that one could do about that. 'There's no escape when they're persistent, is there?' She turned her head away.

Melissa took this to herself, and hated Hannah again. 'He's harmless, I suppose, but I just don't like him.'

'Apparently you can't stop him liking you,' Gavin said, laughing, but he had made a mistake. 'I tell you what,' he added quickly, 'come and have dinner with us tonight, as it's for the last time.' The bluff note had returned to his voice.

'Not quite the last time,' she said, 'I've got one more day.'

'Well,' said Hannah, 'I expect you'll be packing tomorrow. If you come to us, I expect you can dodge your admirer.'

'Thank you, then. I should like to.'

Gavin told her that the menu had been put up before they went out, and that he and Hannah, always greedy on holiday, had taken a look at it. They were to have steak. 'With those beautiful golden chips,' he said, 'I never eat chips at home.'

'They're always sodden at home, or else they're hard,' Hannah said, 'that's why.'

Melissa felt that the moments of awkwardness had passed. She was at one with them again, or so she believed; almost a daughter of the house, only she could not think of herself as their daughter.

Giles came back from the direction of the dunes, looking pleased with himself, clicking the jacks together. 'Enjoy yourself?' Hannah asked.

'Super, thanks.'

'I don't know how you can spend hours playing with those things,' said Gavin.

'I was only up there an hour. There are plenty of people picnicking. Not up there, though, down here.'

'Why down here?' Hannah asked.

'The sand's all loose there. It would get in the food.'

'Well, I'm afraid packed lunches are the one thing M. Croisset wouldn't stand for. You'll have to make do with Mr Van Damm's.'

'I'm hungry. Are you coming too, Melissa?' asked Giles.

They all went up together.

29

In the dining-room, the lights from the spoked chandelier and the small, red-covered lamps on the tables, shone upon brass and pewter. There was a comfortable glitter all about them. Gavin, feeling at ease and convivial, his mind at rest, smiled upon his guest. She was wearing the black frock, and her hair was bound about her head. He thought she looked pretty and harmless.

He called to Armand, asking him what wine he would recommend. Armand said he had some Clos du Tart, something of a rarity.

'We'll have two bottles,' Gavin said expansively, and Hannah slightly frowned at him. 'After all, there are four of us.'

'Come,' she said, 'Giles hardly takes his whack.'

'I will tonight,' Giles said. 'With water.'

It seemed to Gavin that Melissa was without tension, that the difficult days were over. They ate *hors d'œuvre*, and she praised them. She seemed very hungry. Even Hannah, watching her, believed that she was cured. It had only been, as she had once said, a brain-storm. The steaks came next, *à point*, tender, and the silvery dishes piled high with fried potatoes, crisp and golden.

'Goody,' said Giles.

'Well,' said Hannah, 'it's a shame we're going home.' Though she was not sure that she really thought so.

'It's been lovely for me,' said Melissa, in a natural voice. She gulped first at her wine, as if she were thirsty, then began to sip it in a genteel manner. 'You've all been very patient, putting up with so much of my company.'

Gavin told her they had been glad of it. And indeed, it seemed to him that he really had not minded her at all. As a private celebration, he drank two glasses one after the other.

'If you do that, darling, I'll have to keep up with you,' Hannah said, 'and I'm not sure I want to.' She was remembering another occasion on which he had drunk too much.

Madame came into the room; she rarely did, during meals, leaving the supervision to her son. She stopped by their table and Gavin rose, dropping his napkin as he did so.

'Please.' She laid a gentle hand on his shoulder, urging him down into his seat. 'Is everything well?'

'*Tout va tès bien,*' he said; he had little French, though he knew German and some Italian.

'It is all delicious as usual,' said Hannah, speaking fluently.

'The little boy is happy?'

'*Très heureux,*' said Giles proudly.

Hannah said, 'Will you sit down and have a glass of wine with us?'

But this Madame would not do. She never drank wine these days, she explained, it did not suit her stomach. A little cognac sometimes, at night; that was all.

'And how is mademoiselle?' she asked Melissa, who responded warmly, as if she had not a care in the world.

'I don't suppose we shall be here next year,' said Hannah, surprising Gavin who did not know a decision had been taken, 'but perhaps the year after that. We shall always come back.'

'We shall be delighted to welcome you at all times,' said Madame. Imperially, she passed on.

Armand came to ask if they liked the wine. He seemed indefatigable; Gavin did not know when he managed to have a meal himself.

'It's splendid,' he said, 'everything is.'

'We are only a small place, but we like to keep up our standards. We try our best.'

'And succeed triumphantly,' said Gavin, who was already feeling faintly the effect of the wine. He told himself to go steady.

'Oh, why can't we come next year?' said Giles, with the hint of a wail in his voice. Armand went away.

'Because it's about time you had a change,' said Hannah. 'Wouldn't you like to see France or Italy? I think we could just about budget for it.'

'I like it here,' he said. He took another large helping of potatoes from the dish which had been left on a side-table. 'Please let's come here again.'

'Well, a year ahead is a long way to see,' said Hannah pacifically. 'Anything may happen. But I don't think you ought to get set in your ways.'

'I don't know why not, when they're nice ways.'

She smiled at him. 'And if you're going to eat such an awful lot, I advise you to take it slowly. I don't want you with a bad tummy, my pet.'

She determined to drink glass for glass with Gavin. Melissa would not allow hers to be refilled yet, and Giles was only drinking a token amount, watered to the colour of *rosé*.

Nevertheless, the feeling of celebration was beginning to stir even in her. What were they celebrating? Escape from Melissa? But this did not seem so important as it had been. Gavin was not acting at all now, was being neither bluff nor avuncular. She smiled at him with open affection, and he responded.

'What will you do when you get back?' Melissa asked, 'The vacation is very long.'

'Do you know,' said Gavin, 'I am seriously meaning to write a book, that is, if I have the stamina.'

'You didn't tell me that,' Hannah said. Then she thought Melissa seemed rather pleased that he had not told her something.

'To tell you the truth, it's only just entered my head. Let's drink to it, even if that's a bit premature.'

Melissa asked him what it would be about, and he said, the Sienese school. There was a good deal written about it, but probably room for something more. 'It will be quite a small book, with as many plates as I can get them to use. Though of course, they send the price rocketing up.'

'I can never afford art books,' said Melissa.

'I will send you a copy,' he told her largely; he was not sure whether he would ever set pen to paper.

'No, you mustn't. I shall save up for it. I know authors don't get many free copies. They don't, do they?'

'A mean allowance. Still, you shall have one.'

It seemed to him now that the book was already written; he could see it in his mind's eye, handsomely bound, a fine colour reproduction on the jacket. They drank to it.

The waiter brought chocolate *éclairs*. Hannah and Gavin had cheese.

'And what will you do?' he asked Melissa.

She replied that she thought she must do some work. Time was getting short, she did not want to fall behind. It was easy for her to get the peace for it, since her flat-mates were out most evenings.

'And you?' he said. 'Don't you get out?'

'Sometimes. But I can keep at it if I want to.'

'Such determination,' said Hannah, and he was for a moment afraid lest she should sound sharp. She kept an eye on Giles's plate. 'No, my pet, you cannot have three.'

'Oh, let him for once,' said Gavin, 'they won't hurt him.' He was anxious for everyone to be happy. Giles beamed.

Gavin cut himself another piece of brie. It was soft and runny.

'I like Simone Martini,' said Melissa, and he knew she wanted him to realise that she had given her attention to his lectures, as well as to himself. He made an appreciative comment, and she smiled into her lap. On her best behaviour, nothing allusive.

'Can I go into the bar?' asked Giles.

'Go into the parlour at the back,' Hannah answered, 'we shan't be long.'

'And I won't be hurried,' said Gavin. 'I'm enjoying this.' Again he saw the edge of a frown, but he took no notice. To Melissa he said, 'Drink up. You can't leave us to finish this all by ourselves.' But she would take no more than half a glass. 'How we bore our children when we sit over meals! But they must learn to be bored. It's a most important part of life, and they can't learn it too soon.'

'He is a *nice* boy,' said Melissa emphatically, bringing a look of pleasure to Hannah's face.

'I'm glad you think so. We do.'

'I envy you Giles.' (Was that a bit too much, Gavin thought? But such thoughts did not stay with him long that night.)

Hannah smiled, gave no reply. This time she did not make the mistake of telling the girl that she, too, some day, would have children, and Gavin was glad of it. For some reason that was not clear to him, this was a golden evening.

'It's damned hot,' Hannah said.

'The wine,' he suggested.

'No, this weather is going to break.' They looked through the window at the people still sitting out on the terrace, through the strip of green glass at the geraniums, steady, unstirred by the wind.

'We've had some beautiful days,' said Gavin. He looked with surprise at the empty bottles. Somehow, they had got through them, and he had drunk the most. But he was perfectly clear-headed. 'Shall we join the gentleman? Gentleman, singular.' They rose. 'Good Lord,' he said in surprise, 'it's past nine!'

They went into the bar. Hannah called Giles, and told him to get undressed.

'But it's early, Mummy!',

'You can read for a while. Go on, do as I tell you.'

Melissa said, 'I don't suppose I shall see you tomorrow, Giles, so I'll say good-bye. It's been nice.' She held out her hand.

'Why shan't we see you?' asked Gavin.

'I thought I might go to Bruges.'

'Well,' he said, 'you'll enjoy it. Good-night, old boy,' he added to Giles.

They did not go on to the outer terrace, even though it was still warm. The sky had the inky-black opacity of a felt-tipped pen. Gavin settled happily to beer, which both Hannah and Melissa refused. He was feeling peaceful, confident, and content. It occurred to him that he and Hannah had behaved to the girl very well indeed, with calm and with good judgement. He was glad that they were unlikely to see her tomorrow, though what had motivated her he could not guess. The music went round in his head, *J'Attendrai, People Will Say We're in Love*. He caught himself humming beneath his breath. Then, *Gymnopédies*; which he quickly dismissed.

'Don't drone, darling,' said Hannah.

No, few people could have done so well. He felt more united than ever with his wife in good behaviour.

244

The room was full. Local people elbowed one another along the length of the bar, and Armand greeted them all. Across the way, the trees were brilliant in the lights from the terrace.

'I shall never forget all this,' Melissa said. One of her plaits began to uncoil, and she quickly pinned it up again; she blushed, as if she had been caught doing something ridiculous. She began to talk again, her speech a little blurred, but coherently. Gavin noticed that she spoke of the future as if it now existed for her, and was more pleased still. He had only that morning destroyed her note, and in Hannah's sight flushing it down the bathroom lavatory.

Then the skies cracked open and the rain come storming down. The streets were loud with the sound of running feet.

'There! What did I say?' said Hannah.

'I must go,' said Melissa, 'I have to get back.'

'You can't, not in this,' Gavin told her, 'you'll have to wait for it to stop.'

'I'll tuck Giles down,' said Hannah, 'I won't be a moment.'

'Do have a beer, Melissa,' he said, 'I'm going to. And you can't move for the moment. Go on, indulge yourself.'

Now he was not so sure that the wine hadn't taken effect; but it was a pleasant feeling and he was content to repose in it. He caught the waiter's eye and ordered for them both.

'I shouldn't,' she said.

Very harmless now. The lights glittered on the fine hairs along her thin arms. She applied more lipstick; he had never seen her do so before.

In a few minutes Hannah came down. 'All well. It's not showing any signs of letting up, is it?'

It was not. The rain was striking down in rods of silver. People were racing home from the golf course with coats over their heads.

'I've got a scarf,' said Melissa. 'It's sure to stop soon.'

'Cloud-burst,' Gavin said.

The first fury of the rain abated, but it still slashed strongly onto the roadway.

'I think it's slackening off,' said Melissa, 'I really must go.'

'Finish your beer first.'

He thought, if this doesn't stop I shall have to see her home; there's no option. We can take my umbrella. Hannah won't mind.

They waited, and this time conversation drifted into slackness.

Melissa stood up firmly. 'Thank you both for everything. You've been so good to me. Perhaps we'll meet in London.'

'Look here, I'll walk back with you. I can give you some shelter.'

She looked at him in a startled way. 'There's really no need. I've got a coat, and I've nothing to spoil.'

'Of course Gavin will go,' Hannah said lightly. 'You'll be drenched to the skin otherwise.' She smiled at them both. She is really a most remarkable woman, Gavin thought. Melissa shook hands with her, thanking her again.

We don't want more of his indiscretions tonight, Hannah thought, but of course there won't be, not now everything is comparatively smooth. A doubt stirred in her, but she dismissed it. So far as she could see, he was sober. He would not be tricked. 'Till London,' she said.

Under the big umbrella Gavin took Melissa's arm. The lights were garish in the rainy dark; puddles glittered under their feet. 'It won't take five minutes,' he said. He felt a faint tremor run through her, but this he disregarded. He was on top of things now. They did not talk much as they walked along. He wished he could drop her arm, but he had to keep her near him so she should not get drenched.

'It's lucky I didn't wait,' she said, 'this is going on for hours.'

It was like the night they had walked before through the sandy slush of Byronlaan, but now it was different. Their relationship had changed.

They came to her door, and stopped. They were held in the dark of the umbrella, the rain battering down on it.

'Well,' she said, 'good night and good-bye.'

'Good night, my dear,' he said, feeling he could spare her this much.

Then, unexpectedly, she raised her face in a manner so childish yet so natural, that he stooped and kissed her on the mouth. It was a light kiss, and he moved quickly away; but she clung to him now.

'My darling, oh my darling, oh my darling.'

With his free hand, he tried to unclasp her fingers from his lapels. 'Now what did we say?'

'Oh, I know, I know. But I can't help it.'

'I'm afraid you must help it,' he said briskly, 'because this is the end. Come on, you know it is. Be good.'

She smelled of some scent, cheap but not unpleasant. He gave her a fatherly hug, determinedly put her away from him. 'Be good, now,' he said again. 'It's all over.'

He could not see her face, but her blurred voice came to him through the dark. 'I will be good. I know it is all over.' But she spoke with excitement.

He took her up on the porch, and only when she was in its shelter took the umbrella away. In the light from the hallway, he saw to his surprise that she was smiling. She rang the bell, and in a moment was admitted. She did not turn her head.

To his surprise, he felt neither remorse nor apprehension. The wine had betrayed him again, but not too far. Peace, he determined, should continue; he would tell Hannah nothing this time. On his way back he thought of Melissa, skin and bone in the white bathing-suit, the tail of hair down her protruding shoulder-blades. She would be a good girl.

247

Anyway, they would not see her in Les Roseaux again; she had said so.

He got back to the Albert and stuck the sopping umbrella in the hallstand.

'Well?' asked Hannah, when he rejoined her.

She was looking determinedly cheerful.

'Nothing to report.'

'No more scenes?'

'No, that's the back of her.'

He was not even perturbed by the thought of his lie. Nothing, really, had happened, nothing of importance; there had been no need to make her angry. Besides, I don't want her angry with Melissa. 'I'm going to have a nightcap,' he said.

'You're not. You've had enough for one evening.'

'Xanthippe. I'm not in the least drunk.'

'Not particularly, but you will be.'

'Not in the least drunk,' he repeated, and went to the bar. When he returned he said, 'Drink to our untrammelled future.'

'That was a difficult word, wasn't it?'

'Un-tram-melled. That O.K.?' He took her hand. 'I've been feeling very close to you this evening.'

'And I have to you,' she said, but he could not be sure that it was true. Still, he was content to sit at her side in his new-found peace. Tomorrow was to be a wonderful day, they would have it all to themselves.

'And did you kiss her good night?' said Hannah without expression.

He replied boldly, 'A peck. Can't be cruel to dumb animals.' He had been caught out, but he did not mean to be caught out very far. 'She made nothing of it.'

'One can't trust you, can one? But I suppose you are like that.'

'No harm done.'

'You swear?'

'No harm. All's well.'

She relaxed. 'Get a beer for me, too. I'll indulge you that far.'

He stopped thinking about Melissa.

30

Melissa was happy. 'Such sober certainty of waking bliss I never' – what, knew, dreamed, what was it? 'till now.' All had gone as she had planned. She unpinned her hair before the mirror, giving it fifty strokes. She had prayed that he would see her back to the *pension*, though the rainstorm was an unexpected bonus. He had kissed her; and she knew that it was not an end but a beginning. In London, it should all begin again. She was not drunk tonight; the room did not swim round. Cool, sure of herself, Undine, she followed the movement of the brush as it went through her hair.

She had fully intended not to see them again next day, although she knew that she might be making a sacrifice. But she had meant to carry everything to a conclusion, or a semi-conclusion, and she had done so. For Hannah, she could not bring herself to care at all. Let what must happen, happen. She was quite sure he would not sleep with his wife that night.

The rain was a delightful pouring in her ears. She did not draw the curtains, for she was not overlooked; it pleased her to see the drops running together into deltas down the windowpane. History repeats itself, she thought. Before, it was like this. She had no intention of going to Bruges; she had enough to think about, even if she confined herself to her own room. And Gavin would think of her, she would be in the forefront of all this thoughts. She listened to the slight stirring of the trees; when the wind rose the rain would stop, and she wished it to rain for ever. She would always associate him with rain, and with the sheltering from it. She recalled them passing the golf course, it had been deserted and dark, for Michel, seeing the hopelessness of the weather, had closed it down for the night. In her mind she saw Giles playing his solitary round, and she loved him, because he was Gavin's.

She lay down to sleep. It was wonderful how peaceful she was, how free from inner tumult. The very feel of her body on the mattress was delicious, as thought it had no weight. She slept and dreamed beautifully, but not about Gavin.

When she awoke next morning, delight was still with her. She asked for her breakfast to be brought up; she had about enough money for that.

It was still raining, or perhaps it had passed in the night and was raining again. The patter of it was audible in the trees, and on the road-ways. There was nothing for her to do but lie there, and think about him. Eyes wide, she stared at the shadowless ceiling. I will have you, she thought, I shall have you yet. She could still feel his mouth upon her own.

Coffee, strong and steaming, hot rolls, butter, no jam. How long is it since I had breakfast in bed? She remembered her mother, who on Sundays would give her this as a treat. A crumb fell down the front of her nightdress and she raked it out again.

Hail, Bishop Valentine, whose day this is. The Seventh Heaven, she thought. But what are the first, second, third, fourth, fifth, sixth? I am in the Sixth Heaven. The seventh is yet to come.

Pushing the tray to the end of the bed, she counted her money. She had her last travellers' cheques to cash; she had been very prudent. Nevertheless, she would be unable to afford a porter (assuming that there were any) or lunch on the boat. When she was dressed, she tied a scarf tightly around her head and went out in the rain, which was gentler now. She made her way by back lanes to the town, and cashed the remaining cheques at the bank. Then she returned to her room, and for the rest of the morning read a favourite book, Aldous Huxley's *Texts and Pretexts*, which she had found in a battered condition in a second-hand shop. The binding had once been jade green, but the spine had faded to a seaweed brown. The bed had been made, so she was left blessedly alone.

Here she found much to match her mood.

'When her loose gown did from her shoulders fall,
And she me caught in her arms long and small,
And there withal so sweetly did me kiss,
    And softly said, "Dear heart, how like you this?"'

Her arms, long and small, would some day hold him. What the sensible voice had once dismissed as fantasy, now seemed to her quite real.

She ate her lunch, but, though the rain had stopped, did not at first go out. She was determined to avoid them: what could she be to him if she did not keep promises? For him she would be all things, made perfect.

She slept for an hour that afternoon, and in her dreams saw the crimson mast. But she was not climbing it, she was watching herself climb. The small figure, flood-lit, was almost at the top.

When she awoke, the thought that she had had a recurrent dream, or nearly so, excited her. There seemed to be great importance in it. She had heard of an old play called *Peter Ibbetson*, in which someone 'dreamed true', and she wondered what it had been like. Where had she heard of it, anyway? It seemed abstruse enough. She knew. In a lecture on late nineteenth-century drama; it had caught her fancy.

She looked out of the window. The rain had ceased, though no sun shone. Though all things looked sodden and dull, they had no power to affect her mood. But the room was stuffy and she had been smoking in it. She looked at her watch. Four o'clock. She would walk a little way into the town, crossing over when she came to the Albert, so that they might not notice her on the far side of the street.

She had just reached the golf course, when she met Gavin and Hannah. They called to her.

Their faces were white.

31

Hannah and Gavin were reading peaceably. A great sense of relief filled them both. In a corner of the parlour Giles, who had been found another jig-saw puzzle, was fitting the pieces in contentment.

'I'm afraid it's going to pour all day,' Hannah said, 'but I don't much care. I'm rather tired of the beach and the Golf; that is, for the moment.' She was not quite sure that Melissa would not come that day, but was nearly so. After all, they had made their formal good-byes.

Gavin was quite sure. He had not taken Hannah last night, but had fondled her for a long while before they slept, letting her head lie sweetly but rather uncomfortably upon his shoulder. He felt guiltless and purified, which was a pleasant feeling for him. Also, he was experiencing the rather agreeable sensation of a hangover passing off.

He thought quite seriously about the book. It would be useful to publish something, it would help in his career. What career he had ahead of him was uncertain, but he was hopeful. To be a lecturer was good enough at the moment, but he could do with a step up. He and Hannah, though they behaved generously to all their friends, had certain money worries; Giles's school fees, for instance. A year or so ago Gavin had inherited three thousand pounds from his mother, and had invested it carefully, without *panache*; but it did not go far. Luckily, Hannah was quite good at making her own clothes.

Giles came up and asked if it was coke-time.

'Your drinking,' said Gavin facetiously, 'will be the ruin of us. But go ahead. It's the last day.' He put an arm around him, and hugged him to his side. 'You're my boy,' he said.

'Mine too,' said Hannah, not looking up from her book, 'don't forget me.'

Gavin began to dream about Giles's future. How would he look when he was a man? His features, even now, were set in no adult mould. But he was growing a little, perhaps; it was unreasonable that, with such parents, he should not be tall. Gavin brooded on the destroyed report, which had apparently been so good, or comparatively good; he did not know quite what standards the headmaster applied to Giles. Did he excel in anything? His French was very fair, he liked the subject. His Latin was poor, he might need coaching. And in maths, too. But then, thought Gavin, I was never any good at that, and though Hannah ought to be, because she is generally efficient, she isn't. A crammer might be needed for Common Entrance; another expense.

He skipped the years. Giles was a young man, slender, still feathery of hair, they were walking together shoulder to shoulder. They went into a pub for a drink, and talked of men's affairs. There should be something special between them, different from the specialness between Giles and Hannah, something as strong, but more astringent.

After lunch it stopped raining. 'Like a turn?' Gavin said to Hannah, but she said no. It was soggy outside, and she was too comfortable. 'Don't let's feel we have to do anything.'

He asked her what she thought lotus had tasted like, and she replied, somewhat like sugared rose-petals. 'A monotonous diet,' said Gavin.

At three o'clock, Giles put the pieces of his jig-saw back in the box and announced that he was going to play golf.

'By yourself?' Hannah answered mechanically.

'I did yesterday.'

'You know what it's like when that ground's waterlogged. And we're not coming with you.'

'I don't want you to. I like it on my own.'

'Can he go?' Hannah asked Gavin, who looked doubtfully at the sky.

'I suppose so, if he takes his mac.' He gave the boy some money.

'Oh, fantastic.'

'Don't be too long, darling,' Hannah said, 'have a good time.'

When Giles had gone, Gavin stirred in his chair. 'Ought I to go after him?'

'Leave him alone,' Hannah answered, 'it makes him feel grown-up. And he can't come to any harm there.'

They saw the fair head bobbing past the window.

They relaxed in their chairs.

'Do you remember,' said Hannah rather shyly (she was always shy when she recalled their past together), 'how it rained all through our honeymoon?'

'Do I ever forget these things? Yes, cats and dogs. I can't remember us minding.'

'That hotel lounge, with the china elephants on the mantelpiece.'

'And the pampas grasses in a huge red vase. And the foxed print of the Raphael Madonna. We sat there hour after hour. I always wish I'd been rich enough to take you somewhere more enticing.'

Hannah said nothing could have seemed more so. 'But I wonder why we had to get married in a register office? Such an in-and-out sort of business.'

'Didn't we have some sort of principle about it then? That is, not being noticeably religious, we had no right to the forms. I shouldn't have such scruples if we were beginning again.'

256

'It was a lovely wedding. I shall always say so.'

He took her hand and swung it slackly. 'A sentimental couple. What would the young think of us?'

'Damn the young.'

They laid aside their books and went into a long spell of reminiscence. Hannah thought how little she regretted the coming of middle-age, and how comfortable she was about the future. She had never been greedy for more than he could give her. They had been better off while she was teaching, but she knew she could never go back to it. A good cook, otherwise not specially domesticated, she made the most of her days.

Time went by.

Gavin said, 'Surely that boy ought to be back by now?' He looked at his watch. 'Come on, let's go and find him.'

They walked to the golf course, taking their time. A few drops of rain were falling, making black stars on the pavement.

'I don't see him,' said Hannah sharply. They searched the course with their eyes, hole by hole.

'Yes, there he is, just coming up to the eighteenth.'

'No, that's not Giles.' Panic, still distant, stirred in her. 'It's too tall for him.'

'I wonder if he doubled back to the hotel the back way?' said Gavin. 'If so, he'll get in before us.'

'I'm going to ask Michel when he left,' said Hannah. They went towards the hut, where Michel was reading a newspaper. He greeted them cordially; he knew them well. 'Going to have a game?' Rising, he moved towards the rack of clubs.

'No, thank you,' Hannah said. 'I just wondered whether you knew what time our little boy left here.'

He turned to them his brown, creased face. 'Little boy?'

'You must know him,' Gavin said, panic rising in him now. 'He came down about three.'

257

Michel spread his hands. 'He hasn't been here today, monsieur.'

Hannah felt a lurch of terror in her whole body. 'He must have been. Couldn't you just not have noticed him?'

'Impossible. I see everyone who comes here.'

'Oh, God,' said Hannah. She gripped Gavin's arm, as if she would fall.

'Don't worry,' he said, but his voice had risen, 'he'll be all right.'

They left the hut. Michel called to them, 'If I do see him, I'll tell him you want him, quick-sharp.'

'He must have gone to the beach,' said Hannah. 'Oh, I thought I could trust him! I'll give him such a dressing-down when he gets back.'

Neither of them felt capable of moving. They stood looking wildly along the road, hoping to see the green mackintosh.

'Oh, dear God,' she said again.

'Don't get in a state,' said Gavin, 'we must look for him, that's all. Come on.'

It was then that they saw Melissa. They shouted to her, both at once, and she came quickly up to them.

'What's the matter?'

'We can't find Giles,' said Hannah, with an attempt at steadiness, 'he said he was going to the Golf, but he didn't go. He's been gone over an hour. You haven't passed him, have you?'

Melissa caught the infection of their fear. 'No. Shall I go and look on the beach? I can run.'

'Yes, run,' Hannah said, 'we'll come as quickly as we can.'

Without a word, Melissa turned and ran; she was very fleet.

They attempted to run with her, but could not keep up. 'Stop,' said Hannah, panting, 'I must go more slowly.'

'She'll come back with him, don't worry. He's just playing the fool somewhere. He knows it's tea-time, he must come back soon.'

'Could he have gone to the hills behind the town?'

'If I go there, and you go down to the beach—' Gavin began.

'No,' she said, shivering, 'don't leave me.'

They were walking fast now. The road seemed interminable. Ahead of them they saw Melissa sprinting across the motorway, disappearing up the hill past the Disney shops and cafés.

'Oh, I will have something to say to him,' Hannah said, tears in her voice, 'frightening us like that, the little devil.'

'So shall I, this time.'

It was raining quite hard now. In the sky was a dense band of charcoal-coloured cloud, and below that a belt of oyster-white, satiny, but having no glow in it. They came at last to the promenade.

32

Gasping with her exertion, Melissa looked over the rail.

The beach was deserted, not a soul in sight. Nothing but a few sandpipers, hopping along the margin of the sea, and the sullen sound of the surf. The tide was in, so far as it ever came, so she did not have to look over great distances. The chairs and the wind-breaks had been taken in, and were stacked under canvas against the sea-wall. Pushing the wet hair back from her face, she ran down the steps, hoping he might be hiding from the weather where she could not at once see him.

Nobody. She remembered his fancy for playing on the dunes, so she raced up there, her feet heavy in the wet sand. A wind was just springing up, the spiny grasses whistled in it. Nobody. For miles and miles, the dunes lay in their loneliness, white as bone-dust. It might have been November.

She began to search hollow after hollow.

Then, crying with relief, she saw him. He was lying on his face, as if asleep, the mackintosh thrown over his shoulders. She called to him, 'Giles! Giles!' But he did not stir.

Kneeling down beside him, she shook him. 'Giles, you must get up. Your father and mother are looking for you.'

There were small pieces of metal littered around him, some half buried in the sand.

The terror began. Had he fainted? Been taken ill? Gavin and Hannah would be upon them soon.

Then she saw that there was something around his neck; tied tightly; a long piece of material, patterned in green. She heard herself scream, a thin, pale sound carrying nowhere.

They were coming up to the dunes now. She ran to stop them.

'You've found him?' Hannah cried. 'Why doesn't he come?'

'Oh, God,' said Melissa, 'he can't come. He can't come.'

They were up there with her.

'Don't look, don't look.'

'Don't be a fool,' said Gavin, 'we must look.'

It was Hannah who seemed like fainting. Melissa caught her arm, but she threw it off.

And then they were kneeling beside the body, crying and praying, oblivious of her. Gavin was busy with the knot, trying to loosen it. His face was grey.

Hannah said, 'My darling, my darling. Giles. Wake up, speak to me.'

She must know, Melissa thought, she must know. But she cannot bear it to be yet.

Gavin turned the boy over on his back, and he saw.

He turned to Melissa, his face terrible. Hannah was covering her eyes.

'Go up to Van Damm, tell him to send a doctor, ambulance, police.'

He was not seeing her. Such was the force of her passion, that she was enraged that in this hour he did not know her; he might have been looking right through her.

Hannah was cradling the body in her arms. The rain streamed off her hair and down her cheeks.

'Gavin, my love—' said Melissa.

He saw her then. He gave her a look in which anguish was mingled with hatred for herself; she had never seen such hate.

Blind with shock, she ran from the dunes, through the long desolation, the future that held nothing for her.

She stumbled along the beach, up the steps of the café, which was glowing sharply golden in the ponderous light. M. Van Damm came to the door to welcome her, his face beaming.

'Why, mademoiselle, what brings you here on such a day?' And then he saw her face.

I made up my mind that I would not see Iris Allbright again,
not after so many years. I do not like looking back down the
chasm of the past and seeing, in a moment of vertigo, some
terror that looks like a joy, some joy crouched like a terror.
It is better to keep one's eyes on the rock-face of the present,
for that is real; what is under your nose is actual, but the
past is full of lies, and the only accurate memories are those
we refuse to admit to our consciousness. I did not want to
see Iris; we had grown out of each other twenty years ago
and could have nothing more to say. It might be interesting
to see if she had kept her looks, if she had worn as well as I
had; but not so interesting that I was prepared to endure an
afternoon of reminiscence for the possible satisfaction of a
vanity.

Also, she had had only one brief moment of real importance in my life, which was now shrivelled by memory almost
to silliness. I doubted whether she herself would remember it
at all. I would not see her; I had made up my mind.

But it was not so easy. Iris was determined that I should
visit her, now she had returned to Clapham, and to this end
kept up a campaign of letters and telephone calls. Didn't I
want to talk over old times? If not, why not? She was longing
to tell me all about her life in South America, all about her
marriage, her children, her widowhood – didn't I *want* to
hear? She was longing to hear all about me. ('How you've got
on! Little Christie!') I couldn't be so busy as to be unable to
spare just half an hour. Why not this Wednesday? Or

Wednesday week? Or any day the following week? She was always at home.

I began to feel like the unfortunate solicitor badgered with tea invitations by Armstrong, the poisoner of Hay. Knowing that if he accepted he would be murdered with a meat-paste sandwich, in constant touch with the police who had warned him what his fate was likely to be, he was nevertheless tortured by his social sense into feeling that if Armstrong were not soon arrested he would have to go to tea, to accept the sandwich, and to die. It was a hideous position for a man naturally polite and of good feeling.

My own position was in a sense more difficult, for no one was likely to arrest Iris Allbright, and I felt the time approaching when I must either bitterly offend her or go to Clapham.

In the end I went to Clapham.

In a London precariously balanced between two wars, how is a young woman supposed to make her way in the world? This is the question which Christine faces. Dissatisfied with her life spent working in a bank and living in the shadow of her more beautiful and beguiling best friend, Iris, Christine is quick to fall under the smooth, heady charm of Ned, an older man who seems to hold the key to the future she wants.

But appearances are fickle, and soon, Christine finds herself isolated inside an increasingly sinister marriage. As time begins to tick, Christine must find her way out, at the risk of becoming trapped forever. . .

An Impossible Marriage | 9781473679801 | £8.99 | Hodder

Pamela Hansford Johnson

Pamela Hansford Johnson was born in Clapham in 1912 to an actress and a colonial civil servant, who died when she was 11, leaving the family in debt. Pamela excelled in school, particularly in English and Drama, and became Dylan Thomas' first love after writing to him when they had poems in the same magazine. She went on to write her daring first novel, *This Bed Thy Centre*, aged 23, marking the beginning of a prolific literary career which would span her lifetime.

In 1936 she married journalist Neil Stewart, who left her for another woman; in 1950, she married novelist C.P. Snow, and for thirty years they formed an ambitious and infamous couple.

Johnson remained a productive and acclaimed writer her whole life, and was the recipient of several honorary degrees as well as a CBE in 1975. She was also made a Fellow of the Royal Society of Literature. By her death in 1981, she was one of Britain's best-known and best-selling authors, having written twenty-seven novels, alongside several plays, critical studies of writers such as Thomas Wolfe and Marcel Proust, poetry, translation and a memoir.

Praise for Pamela Hansford Johnson

'Very funny' *Independent*

'Witty, satirical and deftly malicious' Anthony Burgess

'Sharply observed, artfully constructed and always enlivened by the freshness of an imagery that derives from [Johnson's] poetic beginnings' *TLS*

'Miss Johnson is one of the most accomplished of the English women writers' *Kirkus*